Enoch Arnold Bennett, the son of a solicitor, was born in 1867 in Hanley, Staffordshire. At twenty-one, he moved to London, initially to work as a solicitor's clerk, but he soon turned to writing popular serial fiction and editing a women's magazine. After the publication of his first novel, *A Man From the North* in 1898, he became a professional writer. He moved to Paris and became a man of cosmopolitan and discerning tastes.

Bennett's great reputation is built upon the success of his novels and short stories set in the Potteries, an area of north Staffordshire that he recreated as the 'Five Towns'. *Anna of the Five Towns* and *The Old Wives' Tale* show the influence of Flaubert, Maupassant and Balzac as Bennett describes provincial life in great detail. Arnold Bennett is an important link between the English novel and European realism. He wrote several plays and lighter works such as *The Grand Babylon Hotel* and *The Card*.

Arnold Bennett died in 1931.

GW00467558

The Pretty Lady

Arnold Bennett

HOUSE OF
STRATUS

This edition published in 2008 by House of Stratus, an imprint of Stratus Books Ltd., 21 Beeching Park, Kelly Bray, Cornwall, PL17 8QS, UK.

www.houseofstratus.com

Typeset, printed and bound by House of Stratus.

A catalogue record for this book is available from the British Library and the Library of Congress.

ISBN 07551-159-8-8

"Virtue has never yet been adequately represented by any who have had any claim to be considered virtuous. It is the sub-vicious who best understand virtue. Let the virtuous people stick to describing vice – which they can do well enough."

SAMUEL BUTLER

INTRODUCTION

The majority of readers, coming afresh to the work of Arnold Bennett, have a clear picture of him in their minds. It is the picture of a short, fat vulgarian with vast projecting teeth and a monstrous coif, who worshipped sumptuous hotels and stank of brass. To such readers every word he wrote, apart from the four or five hundred thousand contained in *The Old Wives' Tale, Clay-hanger,* and *Riceyman Steps,* is tainted with the love of money and the craving for social success. Without in the least meaning to do so, they seek confirmation of the picture as they read. What, in another writer, would pass unnoticed, is caught up, put slightly out of proportion, and used thereafter against Bennett.

I think this is a pity; for the real Bennett, whom I knew with ever-increasing familiarity, trust, and affection from *1914* until his death, was not at all a gaping provincial. He was a quiet, modest, extraordinary sensitive, and much-loved man whose only interest in money was that of a self-respecting citizen. Though very highly paid by English newspapers and American magazines at a period when rates to celebrities were high, his earnings from books were never excessive; he gave away (privately) a good deal of his income; and his estate consisted, at his death, almost solely of a valuation of his copyrights. So far from gaping at Imperial Palaces, he thought a good hotel was one in which – he slept little and read much in the night – one could switch a bedside lamp on and off without exertion. He was not short, or fat. His teeth were irregular but did not noticeably project. His coif was no more than the flourish that many men wear. He had a very bad stammer, to which he refused to yield; and his voice was harsh. He pronounced such words as "bath" and "dance," as many Englishmen and most Americans do, with a flat "a," and the word "room" as if it were "rheum." Otherwise you would not have known, from his speech, that he was anything but a Londoner. You certainly would not have known, from his demeanour, that he was a celebrity, or that he saw any social difference between a waiter and a duchess. Nor do I think he saw any difference. His interest in people was exclusively humane, and his earnest wish as a man was the achievement of what, early in life, he described as the essential characteristic of a great novelist, "a Christ-like, all-embracing compassion."

Compassion is at present out of the mode. Scorn, irony, righteous wrath, and a new form of nihilism are all more to the taste of a younger generation exasperated by wars, politics, and the discovery that idealism is everywhere exploited. Both scorn and self-righteousness were foreign to Arnold Bennett, whose fiction belonged in spirit to the world in which he grew up; a Victorian world in which a tolerant man could hope to live and die at peace with his neighbours. For this reason, his best work always deals with the life of the Potteries, where he was born, and where he spent his first twenty-one years. None of his London books can compare with *Whom God Hath Joined*, *The Old Wives' Tale*, *Clayhanger*, *These Twain*, or, in its different genre, *The Card*. But whereas the London books were written from observation, the Five Towns books came from the timeless wisdom of the heart; and in the Potteries, long ago, the crimes of even sinners were no more than hard avarice or an instinct to dominate and domineer. The novelist could still, without being charged with betraying reality, be amused by his characters and his craft.

When Bennett, at the age of twenty-one, came to London, and when, sixteen years later, he went to live in or near Paris

ii

until the hour of his great fame, he entered strange new worlds. He also became a professional writer and a work addict. His production, like Balzac's, was tremendous, and it varied greatly in quality. He saw, felt, and thought; but he no longer absorbed with the unconscious avidity of childhood. Two of his books, *Sacred and Profane Love* and *The Dream*, were written deliberately in the French manner, and have never satisfied English critics, who find them (I think rightly) both distasteful and incredible. *The Pretty Lady*, which also would not have been written but for Bennett's sojourn in Paris, is sometimes set beside these early failures. It is one of the three most seriously under-valued novels Bennett ever wrote, and, like *Lord Raingo*, has been completely misunderstood and misinterpreted by those who try to fit it into the accepted caricature of a provincial vulgarian.

As far as the character of Christine is concerned, it is a tragic tale of two incompatible attitudes to life, the censoriousness of a man who, while loving, has the Englishman's deep-seated hatred of being "done" and fear of being betrayed by his chosen woman; and the singular scrupulousness of a French girl who, also loving, has in an extreme degree the unmoral realism and (to English male eyes) extravagant irrationalism of her sex. Though G.J. feels genuine attachment to Christine, he never forgets what she is; her very tact, which, although professional, arises from fundamental simplicity, becomes deception as soon as he loves. And great insight is shown when G.J. makes his instinctive and destructive comparison between Queenie and Christine. In that comparison we see why the English regard marriage outside their own class as a disaster. G.J. is a respectable, a conventional man. Christine, able by a feminine juggle to consider herself a respectable woman, and by equally feminine sophistry to combine mysticism with practicality and evasion of the confessional, is essentially a cocotte. She was not drawn, as some imagined, directly from life; she was drawn from generalised observation of French types. Her irrationality is of a similar order to Hilda Clayhanger's irrationality.

But the character of Christine is not the only interest of *The Pretty Lady*. Prior to the first World War Bennett's social acquaintance, once he had left the Five Towns, had been among writers, painters, and musicians. With the coming of the War, and especially after he had met Lord Beaverbrook and through Lord Beaverbrook had become involved in the work of Allied propaganda, the acquaintance had extended to what used to be called the Governing Classes and the Smart Set. Both in *Lord Raingo* (which is a self-portrait of Bennett in fear of death as well as the picture of a Cabinet Minister) and in *The Pretty Lady*, Bennett expressed his sensitive detestation of those classes and that set. He did not pretend to understand either; he merely found the first brimming with chicane and the second abandoned to triviality. The Methodism of his early years was reawakened; it fought a great battle with his compassion. Hence *The Pretty Lady* is an exposure, perhaps timid, perhaps only partial, of worthlessness. Where G.J. makes a conventional comparision between Queenie and Christine, the author of *The Pretty Lady* makes quite another comparison.

This helps the differentiation between G. J. and Arnold Bennett. There are one or two similarities between them. They both spoke fluent French and played the piano; they both attended the meetings of wartime committees; they both impressed others by their firmness of demeanour and marvelled at such impressiveness. But this book does not contain a self-portrait. G. J., indeed, is under-emphasized, is largely a negative personality, simply because Bennett was trying to draw a man with whom, in spite of these similar traits, he was not fully in sympathy. G. J. was not a man of humour; and A. B., who in some respects was rather like Mr Prohack, was decidedly a man of humour, a man of idiosyncrasy. G. J., therefore, is a subdued, unmagnetic creature. His use in the book is as a foil to Christine.

For the rest, *The Pretty Lady*, although the writing is unequal, is almost entirely free from mannerism. It yields a vivid impression of wartime. It is rich in contrasts of class and character. It does perhaps, technically waver towards the end, when Christine leaves the picture for too long (that is because the passage of time must be indicated, as well as the contrasts in feminine mysticism and feminine social behaviour); but until that wavering, as to which others may disagree with me, it does, I think, maintain its inevitably dual narrative with the greatest possible skill. If not in the very highest flight of Bennett's work, it is life presented with great sincerity and much brilliance. It ought not to be forgotten or disregarded; and I am delighted that Mr Martin Secker is assuring its continued popularity by means of this new and attractive edition.

FRANK SWINNERTON

CONTENTS

1

THE PROMENADE

The peice was a West-end success so brilliant that even if you belonged to the intellectual despisers of the British theatre you could not hold up your head in the world unless you had seen it; even for such as you it was undeniably a success of curiosity at least.

The stage scene flamed extravagantly with crude orange and viridian light, a rectangle of bedazzling illumination; on the boards, in the midst of great width, with great depth behind them and arching height above, tiny squeaking figures ogled the primeval passion in gesture and innuendo. From the arc of the upper circle convergent beams of light pierced through gloom and broke violently on this group of the half-clad lovely and the swathed grotesque. The group did not quail. In fullest publicity it was licensed to say that which in private could not be said where men and women meet, and that which could not be printed. It gave a voice to the silent appeal of pictures and posters and illustrated weeklies all over the town; it disturbed the silence of the most secret groves in the vast, undiscovered hearts of men and women young and old. The half-clad lovely were protected from the satyrs in the audience by an impalpable screen made of light and of ascending music in which strings, brass, and concussion exemplified the naïve sensuality of lyrical niggers. The guffaw which, occasionally leaping sharply out of the dim, mysterious auditorium, surged round the silhouetted conductor and drove like a cyclone between the barriers of plush and gilt and fat cupids on to the stage – this huge guffaw seemed to indicate what might have happened if the magic protection of the impalpable screen had not been there.

Behind the audience came the restless Promenade, where was the reality which the stage reflected. There it was, multitudinous, obtainable, seizable, dumbly imploring to be carried off. The stage, very daring, yet dared no more than hint at the existence of the bright and joyous reality. But there it was, under the same roof.

Christine entered with Madame Larivaudière. Between shoulders and broad hats, as through a telescope, she glimpsed in the far distance the illusive, glowing oblong of the stage; then the silhouetted conductor and the tops of instruments; then the dark, curved concentric rows of spectators. Lastly she took in the Promenade, in which she stood. She surveyed the Promenade with a professional eye. It instantly shocked her, not as it might have shocked one ignorant of human nature and history, but by reason of its frigidity, its constraint, its solemnity, its pretence. In one glance she embraced all the figures, moving or stationary, against the hedge of shoulders in front and against the mirrors behind – all of them: the programme girls, the cigarette girls, the chocolate girls, the cloak-room girls, the waiters, the overseers, as well as the vivid courtesans and their clientèle in black, tweed, or khaki. With scarcely an exception they all had the same strange look, the same absence of gesture. They were northern, blond, self-contained, terribly impassive. Christine impulsively exclaimed – and the faint cry was dragged out of her, out of the bottom of her heart, by what she saw:

"My god! How mournful it is!"

Lise Larivaudière, a stout and benevolent Bruxelloise, agreed with uncomprehending indulgence. The two chatted together for a few moments, each ceremoniously addressing the other as

"Madame," "Madame," and then they parted, insinuating themselves separately into the slow, confused traffic of the Promenade.

2

THE POWER

Christine knew Piccadilly, Leicester Square, Regent Street, a bit of Oxford Street, the Green Park, Hyde Park, Victoria Station, Charing Cross. Beyond these, London, measureless as the future and the past, surrounded her with the unknown. But she had not been afraid, because of her conviction that men were much the same everywhere, and that she had power over them. She did not exercise this power consciously; she had merely to exist and it exercised itself. For her this power was the mystical central fact of the universe. Now, however, as she stood in the Promenade, it seemed to her that something uncanny had happened to the universe. Surely it had shifted from its pivot! Her basic conviction trembled. Men were not the same everywhere, and her power over them was a delusion. Englishmen were incomprehensible; they were not human; they were apart. The memory of the hundreds of Englishmen who had yielded to her power in Paris (for she had specialised in travelling Englishmen) could not re-establish her conviction as to the sameness of men. The presence of her professed rivals of various nationalities in the Promenade could not restore it either. The Promenade in its cold, prim languor was the very negation of desire. She was afraid. She foresaw ruin for herself in this London, inclement, misty and inscrutable.

And then she noticed a man looking at her, and she was herself again and the universe was itself again. She had a sensation of warmth and heavenly reassurance, just as though she had drunk an anisette or a crème de menthe. Her features took on an innocent expression; the characteristic puckering of the brows denoted not discontent, but a gentle concern for the whole world and also virginal curiosity. The man passed her. She did not stir. Presently he emerged afresh out of the moving knots of promenaders and discreetly approached her. She did not smile, but her eyes lighted with a faint amiable benevolence – scarcely perceptible, doubtful, deniable even, but enough. The man stopped. She at once gave a frank, kind smile, which changed all her face. He raised his hat an inch or so. She liked men to raise their hats. Clearly he was a gentleman of means, though in morning dress. His cigar had a very fine aroma. She classed him in half a second and was happy. He spoke to her in French, with a slight, unmistakable English accent, but very good, easy, conversational French – French French. She responded almost ecstatically:

"Ah, you speak French!"

She was too excited to play the usual comedy, so flattering to most Englishmen, of pretending that she thought from his speech that he was a Frenchman. The French so well spoken from a man's mouth in London most marvellously enheartened her and encouraged her in the perilous enterprise of her career. She was candidly grateful to him for speaking French.

He said after a moment:

"You have not at all a fatigued air, but would it not be preferable to sit down?"

A man of the world! He could phrase his politeness. Ah! There were none like an Englishman of the world. Frenchmen, delightfully courteous up to a point, were unsatisfactory past that point. Frenchmen of the south were detestable, and she hated them.

"You have not been in London long?" said the man, leading her away to the lounge.

She observed then that, despite his national phlegm, he was in a state of rather intense excitation. Luck! Enormous luck! And also an augury for the future! She was professing in London for the first time in her life; she had not been in the Promenade for five minutes; and lo! the ideal admirer. For he was not young. What a fine omen for her profound mysticism and superstitiousness!

3

THE FLAT

Her flat was in Cork Street. Aa soon as they entered it the man remarked on its warmth and its cosiness, so agreeable after the November streets. Christine only smiled. It was a long, narrow flat – a small sitting-room with a piano and a sideboard, opening into a larger bedroom shaped like a thick L. The short top of the L, not cut off from the rest of the room, was installed as a *cabinet de toilette*, but it had a divan. From the divan, behind which was a heavily curtained window, you could see right through the flat to the curtained window of the sitting-room. All the lights were softened by paper shades of a peculiar hot tint between Indian red and carmine, giving a rich, romantic effect to the gleaming pale enamelled furniture, and to the voluptuous engravings after Sir Frederick Leighton, and the sweet, sentimental engravings after Marcus Stone, and to the assorted knicknacks. The flat had homogeneity, for everything in it, except the stove, had been bought at one shop in Tottenham Court Road by a landlord who knew his business. The stove, which was large, stood in the bedroom fireplace, and thence radiated celestial comfort and security throughout the home; the stove was the divinity of the home and Christine the priestess; she had herself bought the stove, and she understood its personality – it was one of your finite gods.

"Will you take something?" she asked, the hostess.

Whisky and a siphon and glasses were on the sideboard.

"Oh no, thanks!"

"Not even a cigarette?" Holding out the box and looking up at him, she appealed with a long, anxious glance that he should honour her cigarettes.

"Thank you!" he said. "I should like a cigarette very much."

She lit a match for him.

"But you – do you not smoke?"

"Yes. Sometimes."

"Try one of mine – for a change."

He produced a long, thin gold cigarette-case, stuffed with cigarettes.

She lit a cigarette from his.

"Oh!" she cried after a few violent puffs. "I like enormously your cigarettes. Where are they to be found?"

"Look!" said he. "I will put these few in your box." And he poured twenty cigarettes into an empty compartment of the box, which was divided into two.

"Not all!" she protested.

"Yes."

"But I say No!" she insisted with a gesture suddenly firm, and put a single cigarette back into his case and shut the case with a snap, and herself returned it to his pocket. "One ought never to be without a cigarette."

He said:

"You understand life… How nice it is here!" He looked about and then sighed.

"But why do you sigh?"

"Sigh of content! I was just thinking this place would be something else if an English girl had it. It is curious, lamentable, that English girls understand nothing – certainly not love."

"As for that, I've always heard so."

"They understand nothing. Not even warmth. One is cold in their rooms."

"As for that – I mean warmth – one may say that I understand it; I do."

"You understand more than warmth. What is your name?"

"Christine."

She was the accidental daughter of a daughter of joy. The mother, as frequently happens in these cases, dreamed of perfect respectability for her child and kept Christine in the country far away in Paris, meaning to provide a good dowry in due course. At forty-two she had not got the dowry together, nor even begun to get it together, and she was ill. Feckless, dilatory and extravagant, she saw as in a vision her own shortcomings and how they might involve disaster for Christine. Christine, she perceived, was a girl imperfectly educated – for in the affair of Christine's education the mother had not aimed high enough – indolent, but economical, affectionate, and with a very great deal of temperament. Actuated by deep maternal solicitude, she brought her daughter back to Paris, and had her inducted into the profession under the most decent auspices. At nineteen Christine's second education was complete. Most of it the mother had left to others, from a sense of propriety. But she herself had instructed Christine concerning the five great plagues of the profession. And also she had adjured her never to drink alcohol save professionally, never to invest in anything save bonds of the City of Paris, never to seek celebrity, which according to the mother meant ultimate ruin, never to mix intimately with other women. She had expounded the great theory that generosity towards men in small things is always repaid by generosity in big things – and if it is not the loss is so slight! And she taught her the fundamental differences between nationalities. With a Russian you had to eat, drink and listen. With a German you had to flatter, and yet adroitly insert, "Do not imagine that I am here for the fun of the thing." With an Italian you must begin with finance. With a Frenchman you must discuss finance before it is too late. With an Englishman you must talk, for he will not, but in no circumstances touch finance until he has mentioned it. In each case there was a risk, but the risk should be faced. The course of instruction finished, Christine's mother had died with a clear conscience and a mind consoled.

Said Christine, conversational, putting the question that lips seemed then to articulate of themselves in obedience to its imperious demand for utterance:

"How long do you think the war will last?"

The man answered with serenity:

"The war has not begun yet."

"How English you are! But all the same, I ask myself whether you would say that if you had seen Belgium. I came here from Ostend last month." The man gazed at her with new vivacious interest.

"So it is like that that you are here!"

"But do not let us talk about it," she added quickly with a mournful smile.

"No, no!" he agreed… "I see you have a piano. I expect you are fond of music."

"Ah!" she exclaimed in a fresh, relieved tone. "Am I fond of it! I adore it, quite simply. Do play for me. Play a boston – a two-step."

"I can't," he said.

"But you play. I am sure of it."

"And you?" he parried.

She made a sad negative sign.

"Well, I'll play something out of *The Rosenkavalier.*"

"Ah! But you are a *musician!*" She amiably scrutinised him. "And yet – no."

Smiling, he, too, made a sad negative sign.

"The waltz out of *The Rosenkavalier*, eh?"

"Oh, yes! A waltz. I prefer waltzes to anything."

As soon as he had played a few bars she passed demurely out of the sitting-room, through the main part of the bedroom into the *cabinet de toilette*. She moved about in the *cabinet de toilette* thinking that the waltz out of *The Rosenkavalier* was divinely exciting. The delicate sound of her movements and the plash of water came to him across the bedroom. As he played he threw a glance at her now and then; he could see well enough, but not very well because the smoke of the shortening cigarette was in his eyes.

She returned at length into the sitting-room, carrying a small silk bag about five inches by three. The waltz finished.

"But you'll take cold!" he murmured.

"No. At home I never take cold. Besides – "

Smiling at him as he swung round on the music-stool, she undid the bag, and drew from it some folded stuff which she slowly shook out, rather in the manner of a conjurer, until it was revealed as a full-sized kimono. She laughed.

"Is it not marvellous?"

"It is."

"That is what I wear. In the way of chiffons it is the only fantasy I have bought up to the present in London. Of course, clothes – I have been forced to buy clothes. It matches exquisitely the stockings, eh?"

She slid her arms into the sleeves of the transparency. She was a pretty and highly developed girl of twenty-six, short, still lissom, but with the fear of corpulence in her heart. She had beautiful hair and beautiful eyes, and she had that pucker of the forehead denoting, according to circumstances, either some kindly, grave preoccupation or a benevolent perplexity about something or other.

She went near him and clasped hands round his neck, and whispered:

"Your waltz was adorable. You are an artist."

And with her shoulders she seemed to sketch the movements of dancing.

4

CONFIDENCE

After putting on his thick overcoat and one glove he had suddenly darted to the dressing-table for his watch, which he was forgetting. Christine's face showed sympathetic satisfaction that he had remembered in time, simultaneously implying that even if he had not remembered, the watch would have been perfectly safe till he called for it. The hour was five minutes to midnight. He was just going. Christine had dropped a little batch of black and red Treasury notes on to the dressing-table with an indifferent if not perhaps an impatient air, as though she held these financial sequels to be a stain on the ideal, a tedious necessary, a nuisance, or simply negligible.

She kissed him goodbye, and felt agreeably fragile and soft within the embrace of his huge, rough overcoat. And she breathed winningly, delicately, apologetically into his ear:

"Thou wilt give something to the servant?" Her soft eyes seemed to say, "It is not for myself that I am asking, is it?"

He made an easy philanthropic gesture to indicate that the servant would have no reason to regret his passage.

He opened the door into the little hall, where the fat Italian maid was yawning in an atmosphere comparatively cold, and then, in a change of purpose, he shut the door again.

"You do not know how I knew you could not have been in London very long," he said confidentially.

"No."

"Because I saw you in Paris one night in July – at the Marigny Theatre."

"Not at the Marigny."

"Yes. The Marigny."

"It is true. I recall it. I wore white and a yellow stole."

"Yes. You stood on the seat at the back of the Promenade to see a contortionist girl better, and then you jumped down. I thought you were delicious – quite delicious."

"Thou flatterest me. Thou sayest that to flatter me."

"No, no. I assure you I went to the Marigny every night for five nights afterwards in order to find you."

"But the Marigny is not my regular music-hall. Olympia is my regular music-hall."

"I went to Olympia and all the other halls, too, each night."

"Ah, yes! Then I must have left Paris. But why, my poor friend, why didst thou not speak to me at the Marigny? I was alone."

"I don't know. I hesitated. I suppose I was afraid."

"Thou!"

"So to-night I was terribly content to meet you. When I saw that it was really you I could not believe my eyes."

She understood now his agitation on first accosting her in the Promenade. The affair very pleasantly grew more serious for her. She liked him. He had nice eyes. He was fairly tall and broadly built, but not a bit stout. Neither dark nor blond. Not handsome, and yet…beneath a certain superficial freedom, he was reserved. He had beautiful manners. He was refined, and he was refined in love; and yet he knew something. She very highly esteemed refinement in a man. She had never met a refined woman, and was convinced that few such existed. Of course he was rich. She could be quite sure, from his way of handling money, that he was accustomed to handling money. She would

swear he was a bachelor merely on the evidence of his eyes…
Yes, the affair had lovely possibilities. Afraid to speak to her, and
then ran round Paris after her for five nights! Had he, then, had
the lightning-stroke from her? It appeared so. And why not?
She was not like other girls, and this she had always known. She
did precisely the same things as other girls did. True. But
somehow, subtly, inexplicably, when she did them they were
not the same things. The proof: he, so refined and distinguished
himself, had felt the difference. She became very tender.

"To think," she murmured, "that only on that one night in all
my life did I go to the Marigny! And you saw me!"

The coincidence frightened her – she might have missed this
nice, dependable, admiring creature for ever. But the coincidence
also delighted her, strengthening her superstition. The hand of
destiny was obviously in this affair. Was it not astounding that
on one night of all nights he should have been at the Marigny?
Was it not still more astounding that on one night of all nights
he should have been in the Promenade in Leicester Square?…
The affair was ordained since before the beginning of time.
Therefore it was serious.

"Ah, my friend!" she said. "If only you had spoken to me that
night at the Marigny, you might have saved me from troubles
frightful – fantastic."

"How?"

He had confided in her – and at the right moment. With her
human lore she could not have respected a man who had begun
by admitting to a strange and unproved woman that for five
days and nights he had gone mad about her. To do so would
have been folly on his part. But having withheld his wild secret,
he had charmingly showed, by the gesture of opening and then
shutting the door, that at last it was too strong for his control.
Such candour deserved candour in return. Despite his age, he
looked just then attractively, sympathetically boyish. He was a
benevolent creature. The responsive kindliness of his enquiring
"How?" was beyond question genuine. Once more, in the warm

and dark-glowing comfort of her home, the contrast between the masculine, thick rough overcoat and the feminine, diaphanous, useless kimono appealed to her soul. It seemed to justify, even to call for, confidence from her to him.

The Italian woman behind the door coughed impatiently and was not heard.

5

OSTEND

In July she had gone to Ostend with an American. A gentleman,
but mad. One of those men with a fixed idea that everything
would always be all right and that nothing really and permanently
uncomfortable could possibly happen. A very fair man, with red
hair, and radiating wrinkles all round his eyes – phenomenon
due to his humorous outlook on the world. He laughed at her
because she travelled with all her bonds of the City of Paris on
her person. He had met her one night, and the next morning
suggested the Ostend excursion. Too sudden, too capricious, of
course; but she had always desired to see the cosmopolitanism
of Ostend. Trouville she did not like, as you had sand with every
meal if you lived near the front. Hotel Astoria at Ostend.
Complete flat in the hotel. Very chic. The red-haired one, the
rouquin, had broad ideas, very broad ideas, of what was due to
a woman. In fact, one might say that he carried generosity in
details to excess. But naturally with Americans it was necessary
to be surprised at nothing. The *rouquin* said steadily that war
would not break out. He said so until the day on which it broke
out. He then became a Turk. Yes, a Turk. He assumed rights over
her, the rights of protection, but very strange rights. He would
not let her try to return to Paris. He said the Germans might get
to Paris, but to Ostend, never – because of the English! Difficult

to believe, but he had locked her up in the complete flat. The Ostend season had collapsed – pluff – like that. The hotel staff vanished almost entirely. One or two old fat Belgian women on the bedroom floors – that seemed to be all. The *rouquin* was exquisitely polite, but very firm. In fine, he was a master. It was astonishing what he did. They were the sole remaining guests in the Astoria. And they remained because he refused to permit the management to turn him out. Weeks passed. Yes, weeks. English forces came to Ostend. Marvellous. Among nations there was none like the English. She did not see them herself. She was ill. The *rouquin* had told her that she was ill when she was not ill, but lo! the next day she was ill – oh, a long time. The *rouquin* told her the news – battle of the Marne and all species of glorious deeds. An old fat Belgian told her a different kind of news. The stories of the fall of Liége, Namur, Brussels, Antwerp. The massacres at Aerschot, at Louvain. Terrible stories that travelled from mouth to mouth among women. There was always rape and blood and filth mingled. Stories of a frightful fascination…unrepeatable! Ah!

The *rouquin* had informed her one day that the Belgian Government had come to Ostend. Proof enough, according to him, that Ostend could not be captured by the Germans! After that he had said nothing about the Belgian Government for many days. And then one day he had informed her casually that the Belgian Government was about to leave Ostend by steamer. But days earlier the old fat woman had told her that the German staff had ordered seventy-five rooms at the Hôtel des Postes at Ghent. Seventy-five rooms. And that in the space of a few hours Ghent had become a city of the dead… Thousands of refugees in Ostend. Thousands of escaped virgins. Thousands of wounded soldiers. Often, the sound of guns all day and all night. And in the daytime occasionally, a sharp sound, very loud; that meant that a German aeroplane was over the town – killing… Plenty to kill. Ostend was always full, behind the Digue, and yet people were always leaving – by steamer.

Steamers taken by assault. At first there had been formalities, permits, passports. But when one steamer had been taken by assault – no more formalities! In trying to board the steamers people were drowned. They fell into the water and nobody troubled – so said the old woman. Christine was better; desired to rise. The *rouquin* said No, not yet. He would believe naught. And now he believed one thing, and it filled his mind – that German submarines sank all refugee ships in the North Sea. Proof of the folly of leaving Ostend. Yet immediately afterwards he came and told her to get up. That is to say, she had been up for several days, but not outside. He told her to come away, come away. She had only summer clothes, and it was mid-October. What a climate, Ostend in October! The old woman said that thousands of parcels of clothes for refugees had been sent by generous England. She got a parcel; she had means of getting it. She opened it with pride in the bedroom of the flat. It contained eight corsets and a ball-dress. A droll race, all the same, the English. Had they no imagination? But, no doubt, society women were the same everywhere. It was notorious that in France…

Christine went forth in her summer clothes. The *rouquin* had got an old horse-carriage. He gave her much American money – or, rather, cheques – which, true enough, she had since cashed with no difficulty in London. They had to leave the carriage. The station square was full of guns and women and children and bundles. Yes, together with a few men. She spent the whole night in the station square with the *rouquin*, in her summer clothes and his overcoat. At six o'clock in the evening it was already dark. A night interminable. Babies crying. One heard that at the other end of the square a baby had been born. She, Christine, sat next to a young mother with a baby. Both mother and baby had the right arm bandaged. They had both been shot through the arm with the same bullet. It was near Aerschot. The young woman also told her… No, she could not relate that to an Englishman. Happily it did not rain. But the wind and the cold! In the morning the *rouquin* put her on to a fishing-vessel. She had nothing but her bonds of the City of Paris and her American cheques. The crush was frightful. The captain of the fishing-vessel, however, comprehended what discipline was. He made much money. The *rouquin* would not come. He said he was an American citizen and had all his papers. For the rest, the captain would not let him come, though doubtless the captain could have been bribed. As they left the harbour, with other trawlers, they could see the quays all covered with the disappointed, waiting. Somebody in the boat said that the Germans had that morning reached – She forgot the name of the place, but it was the next village to Ostend on the Bruges road. Thus Christine parted from the *rouquin*. Mad! Always wrong, even about the German submarines. But *chic*. Truly *chic*.

What a voyage! What adventures with the charitable people in England! People who resembled nothing else on earth! People who did not understand what life was… No understanding of that which it is – life! In fine…! However, she should stay in England. It was the only country in which one could have confidence. She was trying to sell the furniture of her flat in Paris. Complications! Under the emergency law she was not obliged to pay her rent to the landlord; but if she removed her furniture then she would have to pay the rent. What did it matter, though? Besides, she might not be able to sell her furniture after all. Remarkably few women in Paris at that moment were in a financial state to buy furniture. Ah no!

"But I have not told you the tenth part!" said Christine.

"Terrible! Terrible!" murmured the man.

All the heavy sorrow of the world lay on her puckered brow, and floated in her dark glistening eyes. Then she smiled, sadly but with courage.

"I will come to see you again," said the man comfortingly. "Are you here in the afternoons?"

"Every afternoon, naturally."

"Well, I will come – not to-morrow – the day after to-morrow."

Already, long before, interrupting the buttoning of his collar, she had whispered softly, persuasively, clingingly, in the classic manner:

"Thou art content, *chéri*? Thou wilt return?"

And he had said: "That goes without saying."

But not with quite the same conviction as he now used in speaking definitely of the afternoon of the day after to-morrow. The fact was, he was moved; she too. She had been right not to tell the story earlier, and equally right to tell it before he departed. Some men, most men, hated to hear any tale of real misfortune, at any moment, from a woman, because, of course, it diverted their thoughts.

In thus departing at once the man showed characteristic tact. Her recital left nothing to be said. They kissed again, rather like comrades. Christine was still the vessel of the heavy sorrow of the world, but in the kiss and in their glances was an implication that the effective, triumphant antidote to sorrow might be found in a mutual trust. He opened the door. The Italian woman, yawning and with her hand open, was tenaciously waiting.

Alone, carefully refolding the kimono in its original creases, Christine wondered what the man's name was. She felt that the mysterious future might soon disclose a germ of happiness.

6

THE ALBANY

G. J. Hoape – He was unusually addressed AS "G. J." by his friends, and always referred to as "G. J." by both friends and acquaintances – woke up finally in the bedroom of his flat with the thought:

"To-day I shall see her."

He inhabited one of the three flats at the extreme northern end of the Albany, Piccadilly, W.I. The flat was strangely planned. Its shape as a whole was that of a cube. Imagine the cube to be divided perpendicularly into two very unequal parts. The larger part, occupying nearly two-thirds of the entire cubic space, was the drawing-room, a noble chamber, large and lofty. The smaller part was cut horizontally into two storeys. The lower storey comprised a very small hall, a fair bathroom, the tiniest staircase in London, and G. J.'s very small bedroom. The upper storey comprised a very small dining-room, the kitchen, and servants' quarters.

The door between the bedroom and the drawing room, left open in the night for ventilation, had been softly closed as usual during G. J.'s final sleep, and the bedroom was in absolute darkness save for a faint grey gleam over the valance of the window curtains. G. J. could think. He wondered whether he was in love. He hoped he was in love, and the fact that the

with the Reveille note-heading was written by the managing director (who represented G. J.'s interests on the Board), and it stated that the War Office had been to the Reveille Company, and implored it to enlarge itself, and given it vast orders at grand prices for all sorts of things that it had never made before. The profits of 1915 would be doubled, if not trebled – perhaps quadrupled. G. J. was relieved, uplifted; and he sniggered at his terrible forebodings of August and September. Ruin? He was actually going to make money out of the greatest war that the world, etc, etc. And why not? Somebody had to make money, and somebody had to pay for the war in income tax. For the first time the incubus of the war seemed lighter upon G. J. And also he need feel no slightest concern about the financial aspect of any possible developments of the Christine adventure. He had a very clear and undeniable sensation of positive happiness.

7

FOR THE EMPIRE

Mrs Braiding came into the drawing-room, and he wondered, paternally, why she was so fidgety and why her tranquillising mate had not appeared. To the careless observer she was a cheerful woman, but the temple of her brightness was reared over a dark and frightful crypt in which the demons of doubt, anxiety, and despair year after year dragged at their chains, intimidating hope. Slender, small, and neat, she passed her life in bravely fronting the shapes of disaster with an earnest, vivacious, upturned face. She was thirty-five, and her aspect recalled the pretty, respected lady's-maid which she had been before Braiding got her and knocked some nonsense out of her and turned her into a wife.

G. J., still paternally, but firmly, took her up at once.

"I say, Mrs Braiding, what about this dish-cover?"

He lifted the article, of which the copper was beginning to show through the Sheffield plating.

"Yes sir. It does look rather impoverished, doesn't it?"

"But I told Braiding to use the new toast-dish I bought last week but one."

"Did you, sir? I was very happy about the new one as soon as I saw it, but Braiding never gave me your instructions in regard to it." She glanced at the cabinet in which the new toast-dish reposed with other antique metal-work. "Braiding's been rather upset this last few days, sir."

"What about?"

"This recruiting, sir. Of course, you are aware he's decided on it."

"I'm not aware of anything of the sort," said G. J. rather roughly, perhaps to hide his sudden emotion, perhaps to express his irritation at Mrs Braiding's strange habit of pretending that the most startling pieces of news were matters of common knowledge.

"Well, sir, of course you were out most of yesterday, and you dined at the club. Braiding attended at a recruiting office yesterday, sir. He stood three hours in the crowd outside because there was no room inside, and then he stood over two hours in a passage inside before his turn came, and nothing to eat all day, or drink either. And when his turn came and they asked him his age, he said 'thirty-six,' and the person was very angry and said he hadn't any time to waste, and Braiding had better go outside again and consider whether he hadn't made a mistake about his age. So Braiding went outside and considered that his age was only thirty-three after all, but he couldn't get in again, not by any means, so he just came back here and I gave him a good tea, and he needed it, sir."

"But he saw me last night, and he never said anything!"

"Yes, sir," Mrs Braiding admitted with pain. "I asked him if he had told you, and he said he hadn't and that I must."

"Where is he now?"

"He went off early, sir, so as to get a good place. I shouldn't be a bit surprised if he's in the army by this time. I know it's not the right way of going about things, and Braiding's only excuse is it's for the Empire. When it's a question of the Empire, sir..."

At that instant the white man's burden was Mrs Braiding's, and the glance of her serious face showed what the crushing strain of it was.

"I think he might have told me."

"Well, sir. I'm very sorry. Very sorry… But you know what Braiding is."

G. J. felt that that was just what he did not know, or at any rate had not hitherto known. He was hurt by Braiding's conduct. He had always treated Braiding as a friend. They had daily discussed the progress of the war. On the previous night Braiding, in all the customary sedateness of black coat and faintly striped trousers, had behaved just as usual! It was astounding. G. J. began to incline towards the views of certain of his friends about the utter incomprehensibility of the servile classes – views which he had often annoyed them by traversing. Yes; it was astounding. All this martial imperialism seething in the depths of Braiding, and G. J. never suspecting the ferment! Exceedingly difficult to conceive Braiding as a soldier! He was the Albany valet, and Albany valets were Albany valets and naught else.

Mrs Braiding continued:

"It's very inconsiderate to you, sir. That's a point that is appreciated by both Braiding and I. But let us fervently hope it won't be for long, sir. The consensus of opinion seems to be we shall be in Berlin in the spring. And in the meantime, I think" – she smiled an appeal – "I can manage for you by myself, if you'll be so good as to let me."

"Oh! It's not that," said G. J. carelessly. "I expect you can manage all right."

"Oh!" cried she. "I know how you feel about it, sir, and I'm very sorry. And at best it's bound to be highly inconvenient for a gentleman like yourself, sir. I said to Braiding, 'You're taking advantage of Mr Hoape's good nature,' that's what I said to Braiding, and he couldn't deny it. However, sir, if you'll be so good as to let me try what I can do by myself – "

"I tell you that'll be all right," he stopped her.

Braiding, his mainstay, was irrevocably gone. He realised that, and it was a severe blow. He must accept it. As for Mrs Braiding managing, she would manage in a kind of way, but the risks to

Regency furniture and china would be grave. She did not understand Regency furniture and china as Braiding did; no woman could. Braiding had been as much a "find" as the dome bed or the unique bookcase which bore the names of "Homer" and "Virgil" in bronze characters on its outer wings. Also, G. J. had a hundred little ways about neckties and about trouser-stretching which he, G. J., would have to teach Mrs Braiding. Still the war…

When she was gone he stood up and brushed the crumbs from his dressing-gown, and emitted a short, harsh laugh. He was laughing at himself. Regency furniture and china! Neckties! Trouser-stretching! In the next room was a youngish woman whose minstrel boy to the war had gone – gone, though he might be only in the next street! And had she said a word about her feelings as a wife? Not a word! But dozens of words about the inconvenience to the god-like employer! She had apologised to him because Braiding had departed to save the Empire without first asking his permission. It was not merely astounding – it flabbergasted. He had always felt that there was something fundamentally wrong in the social fabric, and he had long had a preoccupation to the effect that it was his business, his, to take a share in finding out what was wrong and in discovering and applying a cure. This preoccupation had worried him, scarcely perceptibly, like the delicate oncoming of neuralgia. There must be something wrong when a member of one class would behave to a member of another class as Mrs Braiding behaved to him – without protest from him.

"Mrs Braiding!" he called out.

"Yes, sir." She almost ran back into the drawing-room.

"When shall you be seeing your husband?" At least he would remind her that she had a husband.

"I haven't an idea, sir."

"Well, when you do, tell him that I want to speak to him; and you can tell him I shall pay you half his wages in addition to your own."

Her gratitude filled him with secret fury.

He said to himself:

"Futile – these grand gestures about wages."

8

BOOTS

In the very small hall G. J. gazed at himself in the mirror that was nearly as large as the bathroom door, to which it was attached, and which it ingeniously masked.

Although Mrs Braiding was present, holding his ebony stick, he carefully examined his face and appearance without the slightest self-consciousness. Nor did Mrs Braiding's demeanour indicate that in her opinion G. J. was behaving in a manner eccentric or incorrect. He was dressed in mourning. Honestly he did not believe that he looked anywhere near fifty. His face was worn by the friction of the world, especially under the eyes, but his eyes were youthful, and his hair and moustache and short, fine beard scarcely tinged with grey. His features showed benevolence, with a certain firmness, and they had the refinement which comes of half a century's instinctive avoidance of excess. Still, he was beginning to feel his age. He moved more slowly; he sat down, instead of standing up, at the dressing-table. And he was beginning also to take a pride in mentioning these changes and in the fact that he would be fifty on his next birthday. And when talking to men under thirty, or even under forty, he would say in a tone mingling condescension and envy: "But, of course, you're young."

He departed, remarking that he should not be in for lunch and might not be in for dinner, and he walked down the covered way to the Albany Courtyard, and was approved by the Albany porters as a resident handsomely conforming to the traditional high standard set by the Albany for its residents. He crossed Piccadilly, and as he did so he saw a couple of jolly fine girls, handsome, stylish, independent of carriage, swinging freely along and intimately talking with that mien of experience and broad-mindedness which some girls manage to wear in the streets. One of them in particular appealed to him. He thought how different they were from Christine. He had dreamt of just such girls as they were, and yet now Christine filled the whole of his mind.

"You can't foresee," he thought.

He dipped down into the extraordinary rectangle of St. James's, where he was utterly at home. A strange architecture, parsimoniously plain on the outside, indeed carrying the Oriental scorn for merely external effect to a point only reachable by a race at once hypocritical and madly proud. The shabby plainness of Wren's church well typified all the parochial parsimony. The despairing architect had been so pinched by his employers in the matter of ornament that on the whole of the northern façade there was only one of his favourite cherub's heads! What a parish!

It was a parish of flat brick walls and brass door-knobs and brass plates. And the first commandment was to polish every brass door-knob and every brass plate every morning. What happened in the way of disfigurement by polishing paste to the surrounding brick or wood had no importance. The conventions of the parish had no eye save for brass door-knobs and brass plates, which were maintained daily in effulgence by a vast early-rising population. Recruiting offices, casualty lists, the rumour of peril and of glory, could do nothing to diminish the high urgency of the polishing of those brass door-knobs and those brass plates.

The shops and offices seemed to show that the wants of customers were few and simple. Grouse moors, fisheries, yachts, valuations, hosiery, neckties, motor-cars, insurance, assurance, antique china, antique pictures, boots, riding-whips, and, above all, Eastern cigarettes! The master-passion was evidently Eastern cigarettes. The few provision shops were marmoreal and majestic, catering as they did chiefly for the multifarious palatial male clubs which dominated the parish and protected and justified the innumerable "bachelor" suites that hung forth signs in every street. The parish, in effect, was first an immense monastery, where the monks, determined to do themselves extremely well in dignified peace, had made a prodigious and not entirely unsuccessful effort to keep out the excitable sex. And, second, it was an excusable conspiracy on the part of intensely respectable tradesmen and stewards to force the non-bargaining sex to pay the highest possible price for the privilege of doing the correct thing.

G. J. passed through the cardiac region of St. James's, the Square itself, where knights, baronets, barons, brewers, viscounts, marquesses, hereditary marshals and chief butlers, dukes, bishops, banks, librarians and Government departments gaze throughout the four seasons at the statue of a Dutchman; and then he found himself at his bootmaker's.

Now, his bootmaker was one of the three first bootmakers in the West End, bearing a name famous from Peru to Hong Kong. An untidy interior, full of old boots and the hides of various animals! A dirty girl was writing in a dirty tome, and a young man was knotting together two pieces of string in order to tie up a parcel. Such was the "note" of the "house". The girl smiled, the young man bowed. In an instant the manager appeared, and G. J. was invested with the attributes of God. He informed the manager with pain, and the manager heard with deep pain, that the left boot of the new pair he then wore was not quite comfortable in the toes. The manager simply could not understand it, just as he simply could not have understood a failure in the working of the law of gravity. And if God had not told him he would not have believed it. He knelt and felt. He would send for the boots. He would make the boots comfortable or he would make a new pair. Expense was nothing. Trouble was nothing. Incidentally he remarked with a sigh that the enormous demand for military boots was rendering it more and more difficult for him to give to old patrons that prompt and plenary attention which he would desire to give. However, God in any case should not suffer. He noticed that the boots were not quite well polished, and he ventured to charge God with hints for God's personal attendant. Then he went swiftly across to a speaking-tube and snapped:

"Polisher!"

A trap-door opened in the floor of the shop and a horrible, pallid, weak, cringing man came up out of the earth of St. James's, and knelt before God far more submissively than even the manager had knelt. He had brushes and blacking, and he blacked and he brushed and breathed alternately, undoing continually with his breath or his filthy hand what he had done with his brush. He never looked up, never spoke. When he had made the boots like mirrors he gathered together his implements and vanished, silent and dutifully bent, through the trap-door back into the earth of St. James's. And because the trap-door had not shut properly the manager stamped on it and stamped down the pale man definitely into the darkness underneath. And then G. J. was wafted out of the shop with smiles and bows.

9

THE CLUB

The vast "Morning-room" of the Monumental Club (pre-eminent among clubs for its architecture) was on the whole tonically chilly. But as one of the high windows stood open, and there were two fires fluttering beneath the lovely marble mantelpieces, between the fires and the window every gradation of temperature could be experienced by the curious. On each wall bookshelves rose to the carved and gilded ceiling. The furlongs of shelves were fitted with majestic volumes containing all the Statutes, all the Parliamentary Debates, and all the Reports of Royal Commissions ever printed to narcotise the conscience of a nation. These calf-bound works were not, in fact, read; but the magnificent pretence of their usefulness was completed by carpeted mahogany ladders which leaned here and there against the shelfing, in accord with the theory that some studious member some day might yearn and aspire to some upper shelf. On reading-stands and on huge mahogany tables were disposed the countless newspapers of Great Britain and Ireland, Europe and America, and also the files of such newspapers. The apparatus of information was complete.

G. J. entered the splendid apartment like a discoverer. It was empty. Not a member; not a servant! It waited, content to be inhabited, equally content with its own solitude. This apartment had made an adjunct even of the war; the function of the war in this apartment was to render it more impressive, to increase, if possible, its importance, for nowhere else could the war be studied so minutely day by day.

A strange thing! G. J.'s sense of duty to himself had been quickened by the defection of his valet. He felt that he had been failing to comprehend in detail the cause and the evolution of the war, and that even his general ideas as to it were inexcusably vague; and he had determined to go every morning to the club, at whatever inconvenience, for the especial purpose of studying and getting the true hang of the supreme topic. As he sat down he was aware of the solemnity of the great room, last fastness of the old strict decorum in the club. You might not smoke in it until after 10 p.m.

Two other members came in immediately, one after the other. The first, a little, very old and very natty man, began to read *The Times* at a stand. The second, old too, but of larger and firmer build, with a long, clean-shaven upper lip, such as is only developed at the Bar, on the Bench, and in provincial circles of Noncomformity, took an easy-chair and another copy of *The Times*. A few moments elapsed, and then the little old man glanced round, and, assuming surprise that he had not noticed G. J. earlier, nodded to him with a very bright and benevolent smile.

G. J. said:

"Well, Sir Francis, what's your opinion of this Ypres business. Seems pretty complicated, doesn't it?"

Sir Francis answered in a tone whose mild and bland benevolence matched his smile:

"I dare say the complications escape me. I see the affair quite simply. We are holding on, but we cannot continue to hold on. The Germans have more men, far more guns, and infinitely more ammunition. They certainly have not less genius for war. What can be the result? I am told by respectable people that the Germans lost the war at the Marne. I don't appreciate it. I am told that the Germans don't realise the Marne. I think they realise the Marne at least as well as we realise Tannenberg."

The slightly trembling, slightly mincing voice of Sir Francis denoted such detachment, such politeness, such kindliness, that the opinion it emitted seemed to impose itself on G. J. with extraordinary authority. There was a brief pause, and Sir Francis ejaculated:

"What's your view, Bob?"

The other old man now consisted of a newspaper, two seamy hands and a pair of grey legs. His grim voice came from behind the newspaper, which did not move:

"We've no adequate means of judging."

"True," said Sir Francis. "Now, another thing I'm told is that the War Office was perfectly ready for the war on the scale agreed upon for ourselves with France and Russia. I don't appreciate that either. No War Office can be said to be perfectly ready for any war until it has organised its relations with the public which it serves. My belief is that the War Office had never thought for one moment about the military importance of public opinion and the Press. At any rate, it has most carefully left nothing undone to alienate both the public and the Press. My son-in-law has the misfortune to own seven newspapers, and the tales he tells about the antics of the Press Bureau – " Sir Francis smiled the rest of the sentence. "Let me see, they offered the Press Bureau to you, didn't they, Bob?"

The Times fell, disclosing Bob, whose long upper lip grew longer.

"They did," he said. "I made a few inquiries, and found it was nothing but a shuttlecock of the departments. I should have had no real power, but unlimited quantities of responsibility. So I respectfully refused."

Sir Francis remarked:

"Your hearing's much better, Bob."

"It is," answered Bob. "The fact is, I got hold of a marvellous feller at Birmingham." He laughed sardonically. "I hope to go down to history as the first judge that ever voluntarily retired because of deafness. And now, thanks to this feller at Birmingham, I can hear better than seventy-five per cent of the Bench. The Lord Chancellor gave me a hint I might care to return, and so save a pension to the nation. I told him I'd begin to think about that when he'd persuaded the Board of Works to ventilate my old Court." He laughed again. "And now I see the Press Bureau is enunciating the principle that it won't permit criticism that might in any way weaken the confidence of the people in the administration of affairs."

Bob opened his mouth wide and kept it open.

Sir Francis, with no diminution of the mild and bland benevolence of his detachment, said:

"The voice is the Press Bureau's voice, but the hands are the hands of the War Office. Can we reasonably hope to win, or not to lose, with such a mentality at the head? I cannot admit that the War Office has changed in the slightest degree in a hundred years. From time to time a brainy civilian walks in, like Cardwell or Haldane, and saves it from becoming patently ridiculous. But it never really alters. When I was War Secretary in a transient government it was precisely the same as it had been in the reign of the Duke of Cambridge, and to-day it is still precisely the same. I am told that Haldane succeeded in teaching our generals the value of Staff work as distinguished from dashing cavalry charges. I don't appreciate that. The Staffs are still wide open to men with social influence and still closed to men without social influence. My grandson is full of great modern notions about tactics. He may have talent for all I know. He got a Staff appointment – because he came to me and I spoke ten words to an old friend of mine with oak leaves in the club next door but one. No questions asked. I mean no serious questions. It was done to oblige me – the very existence of the Empire being at stake, according to all accounts. So that I venture to doubt whether we're going to hold Ypres, or anything else."

Bob, unimpressed by the speech, burst out:

39

"You've got the perspective wrong. Obviously the centre of gravity is no longer in the West – it's in the East. In the West, roughly, equilibrium has been established. Hence Poland is the decisive field, and the measure of the Russian success or failure is the measure of the Allied success or failure."

Sir Francis inquired with gentle joy:

"Then we're all right? The Russians have admittedly recovered from Tannenberg. If there is any truth in a map they are doing excellently. They're more brilliant than Potsdam, and they can put two men into the field to the Germans' one – two and a half in fact."

Bob fiercely rumbled:

"I don't think we're all right. This habit of thinking in men is dangerous. What are men without munitions? And without a clean administration? Nothing but a rabble. It is notorious that the Russians are running short of munitions and that the administration from top to bottom consists of outrageous rascals. Moreover I see to-day a report that the Germans have won a big victory at Kutno. I've been expecting that. That's the beginning – mark me!"

"Yes," Sir Francis cheerfully agreed. "Yes. We're spending one million a day, and now income tax is doubled! The country cannot stand it indefinitely, and since our only hope lies in our being able to stand it indefinitely, there is no hope – at any rate for unbiased minds. Facts are facts, I fear."

Bob cried impatiently:

"Unbiased be damned! I don't want to be unbiased. I won't be. I had enough of being unbiased when I was on the Bench, and I don't care what any of you unbiased people say – I believe we shall win."

G. J. suddenly saw a boy in the old man, and suddenly he too became boyish, remembering what he had said to Christine about the war not having begun yet; and with fervour he concurred:

"So do I."

He rose, moved – relieved after a tension which he had not noticed until it was broken. It was time for him to go. The two old men were recalled to the fact of his presence. Bob raised the newspaper again.

Sir Francis asked:

"Are you going to the – er – affair in the City?"

"Yes," said G. J. with careful unconcern.

"I had thought of going. My granddaughter worried me till I consented to take her. I got two tickets; but no sooner had I arrayed myself this morning than she rang me up to say that her baby was teething and she couldn't leave it. In view of this important creature's indisposition I sent the tickets back to the Dean and changed my clothes. Great-grandfathers have to be philosophers. I say, Hoape, they tell me you play uncommonly good auction bridge."

"I play," said G. J. modestly. "But no better than I ought."

"You might care to make a fourth this afternoon, in the card-room."

"I should have been delighted to, but I've got one of these war-committees at six o'clock." Again he spoke with careful unconcern, masking a considerable self-satisfaction.

10

THE MISSION

The great dim place was full, but crowding had not been permitted. With a few exceptions in the outlying parts, everybody had a seat. G. J. was favourably placed for seeing the whole length of the interior. Accustomed to the restaurants of fashionable hotels, auction-rooms, theatrical first-nights, the haunts of sport, clubs, and courts of justice, he soon perceived, from the numerous samples which he himself was able to identify, that all the London worlds were fully represented in the multitude – the official world, the political, the clerical, the legal, the municipal, the military, the artistic, the literary, the dilettante, the financial, the sporting, and the world whose sole object in life apparently is to be observed and recorded at all gatherings to which admittance is gained by privilege and influence alone.

There were in particular women the names and countenances and family history of whom were familiar to hundreds of thousands of illustrated-newspaper readers, even in the most distant counties, and who never missed what was called a "function," whether "brilliant," "exclusive," or merely scandalous. At murder trials, at the sales of art collections, at the birth of musical comedies, at boxing matches, at historic debates, at receptions in honour of the renowned, at luscious divorce cases, they were surely present, and the entire Press surely noted that they were present. And if executions had been public, they would in the same religious spirit have attended executions, rousing their maids at milkmen's hours in order that they might assume the right cunning frock to fit the occasion. And they were here. And no one could divine why or how, or to what eternal end.

G. J. hated them, and he hated the solemn self-satisfaction that brooded over the haughty faces of the throng. He hated himself for having accepted a ticket from the friend in the War Office who was now sitting next to him. And yet he was pleased, too. A disturbed conscience could not defeat the instinct which bound him to the whole fashionable and powerful assemblage. For ever afterwards, to his dying hour, he could say – casually, modestly, as a matter of course, but he could still say – that he had been there. The Lord Mayor and Sheriffs, tradesmen glittering like Oriental potentates, passed slowly across his field of vision. He thought with contempt of the City, living ghoulish on the buried past, and obstinately and humanly refusing to make a pile of its putrefying interests, set fire to it, and perish thereon.

The music began. It was the Dead March in *Saul*. The long-rolling drums suddenly rent the soul, and destroyed every base and petty thought that was there. Clergy, headed by a bishop, were walking down the cathedral. At the huge doors, nearly lost in the heavy twilight of November noon, they stopped, turned and came back. The coffin swayed into view, covered with the sacred symbolic bunting, and borne on the shoulders of eight sergeants of the old regiments of the dead man. Then followed the pall-bearers – five field-marshals, five full generals, and two admirals; aged men, and some of them had reached the highest dignity without giving a single gesture that had impressed itself on the national mind; nonentities, apotheosised by seniority; and some showed traces of the bitter rain that was falling in the fog outside. Then the Primate. Then the King, who had supervened from nowhere, the magic production of chamberlains and comptrollers. The procession, headed by the clergy, moved slowly, amid the vistas ending in the dull burning of stained glass, through the congregation in mourning and in khaki, through the lines of yellow-glowing candelabra, towards the crowd of scarlet under the dome; the summit of the dome was hidden in soft mist. The music became insupportable in its sublimity.

G. J. was afraid, and he did not immediately know why he was afraid. The procession came nearer. It was upon him... He knew why he was afraid, and he averted sharply his gaze from the coffin. He was afraid for his composure. If he had continued to watch the coffin he would have burst into loud sobs. Only by an extraordinary effort did he master himself. Many other people lowered their faces in self-defence. The searchers after new and violent sensations were having the time of their lives.

The Dead March with its intolerable genius had ceased. The coffin, guarded by flickering candles, lay on the lofty catafalque; the eight sergeants were pretending that their strength had not been in the least degree taxed. Princes, the illustrious, the champions of Allied might, dark Indians, adventurers, even Germans, surrounded the catafalque in the gloom. G. J. sympathised with the man in the coffin, the simple little man whose non-political mission had in spite of him grown political. He regretted horribly that once he, G. J., who protested that he belonged to no party, had said of the dead man: "Roberts! Well-meaning of course, but senile!"... Yet a trifle! What did it matter? And how he loathed to think that the name of the dead man was now befouled by the calculating and impure praise of schemers. Another trifle!

As the service proceeded G. J. was overwhelmed and lost in the grandeur and terror of existence. There he sat, grizzled, dignified, with the great world, looking as though he belonged to the great world; and he felt like a boy, like a child, like a helpless infant before the enormities of destiny. He wanted help, because of his futility. He could do nothing, or so little. It was as if he had been training himself for twenty years in order to be futile at a crisis requiring crude action. And he could not undo twenty years. The war loomed about him, co-extensive with existence itself. He thought of the sergeant who, as recounted that morning in the papers, had led a victorious storming party, been decorated – and died of wounds. And similar deeds were being done at that moment. And the simple little man in the coffin was being tilted downwards from the catafalque into the grave close by. G. J. wanted surcease, were it but for an hour. He longed acutely, unbearably, to be for an hour with Christine in her warm, stuffy, exciting, languorous, enervating room hermetically sealed against the war. Then he remembered the tones of her voice as she had told her Belgian adventures... Was it love? Was it tenderness? Was it sensuality? The difference was indiscernible; it had no importance. Against the stark background of infinite existence all human beings were alike and all their passions were alike.

The gaunt, ruthless autocrat of the War Office and the frail crowned descendant of kings fronted each other across the open grave, and the coffin sank between them and was gone. From the choir there came the chanted and soothing words:

Steals on the ear the distant triumph-song.

G. J. just caught them clear among much that was incomprehensible. An intense patriotism filled him. He could do nothing; but he could keep his head, keep his balance, practise magnanimity, uphold the truth amid prejudice and superstitition, and be kind. Such at that moment seemed to be his mission... He looked round, and pitied, instead of hating, the searchers after sensations.

A being called the Garter King of Arms stepped forward and in a loud voice recited the earthly titles and honours of the simple little dead man; and, although few qualities are commoner than physical courage, the whole catalogue seemed ridiculous and tawdry until the being came to the two words, "Victoria

Cross". The being, having lived his glorious moments, withdrew. The Funeral March of Chopin tramped with its excruciating dragging tread across the ruins of the soul. And finally the cathedral was startled by the sudden trumpets of the Last Post, and the ceremony ended.

"Come and have lunch with me," said the young red-hatted officer next to G. J. "I haven't got to be back till two-thirty, and I want to talk music for a change. Do you know I'm putting in ninety hours a week at the W.O.?"

"Can't," G. J. replied, with an affectation of jauntiness. "I'm engaged for lunch. Sorry."

"Who you lunching with?"

"Mrs Smith."

The Staff officer exclaimed aghast:

"Concepcion?"

"Yes. Why, dear heart?"

"My dear chap. You don't know. Carlos Smith's been killed. *She* doesn't know yet. I only heard by chance. News came through just as I left. Nobody knows except a chap or two in Casualties. They won't be sending out to-day's wires until two or three o'clock."

G. J., terrified and at a loss, murmured:

"What am I to do, then?"

"You know her extremely well, don't you? You ought to go and prepare her."

"But how can I prepare her?"

"I don't know. How do people prepare people?... Poor thing!"

G. J. fought against the incredible fact of death.

"But he only went out six days ago! They haven't been married three weeks."

The central hardness of the other disclosed itself as he said:

"What's that got to do with it? What does it matter if he went out six days ago or six weeks ago? He's killed."

"Well – "

"Of course you must go. Indicate a rumour. Tell her it's probably false, but you thought you owed it to her to warn her. Only for God's sake don't mention me. We're not supposed to say anything, you know."

G. J. seemed to see his mission, and it challenged him.

11

THE TELEGRAM

As soon as G. J. had been let into the abode by Concepcion's venerable parlour-maid, the voice of Concepcion came down to him from above:

"G. J., who is your oldest and dearest friend?"

He replied, marvellously schooling his voice to a similar tone of cheerful abruptness:

"Difficult to say, off-hand."

"Not at all. It's your beard."

That was her greeting to him. He knew she was recalling an old declined suggestion of hers that he should part with his beard. The parlour-maid practised an admirable deafness, faithfully to confirm Concepcion, who always presumed deafness in all servants. G. J. looked up the narrow well of the staircase. He could vaguely see Concepcion on high, leaning over the banisters; he thought she was rather fluffily dressed, for her.

Concepcion inhabited an upper part in a street largely devoted to the sale of grand pianos. Her front door was immediately at the top of a long, straight, narrow stairway; so that whoever opened the door stood one step higher than the person desiring entrance. Within the abode, which was fairly spacious, more and more stairs went up and up. "My motto is," she would say, "'One room, one staircase.'" The life of the abode was on the busy stairs. She called it also her Alpine Club. She had made upper-parts in that street popular among the select, and had therefore caused rents to rise. In the drawing-room she had hung a horrible enlarged photographic portrait of herself, with a chocolate-coloured mount, the whole framed in German gilt, and under it she had inscribed, "Presented to Miss Concepcion Iquist by the grateful landlords of the neighbourhood as a slight token of esteem and regard."

She was the only daughter of Iquist's brother, who had had a business and a palace at Lima. At the age of eighteen, her last surviving parent being dead, she had come to London and started to keep house for the bachelor Iquist, who at that very moment, owing to a fortunate change in the Ministry, had humorously entered the Cabinet. These two had immediately become "the most talked-of pair in London," London in this phrase signifying the few thousand people who do talk about the doings of other people unknown to them and being neither kings, princes, statesmen, artistes, artists, jockeys, nor poisoners. The Iquists had led the semi-intelligent, conscious-of-its-audience set which had ousted the old, quite unintelligent stately-homes-of-England set from the first place in the curiosity of the everlasting public. Concepcion had wit. It was stated that she furnished her uncle with the finest of his *mots*. When Iquist died, of course poor Concepcion had retired to the upper part, whence, though her position was naturally weakened, she still took a hand in leading the set.

G. J. had grown friendly and appreciative of her, for the simple reason that she had singled him out and always tried to please him, even when taking liberties with him. He liked her because she was different from her set. She had a masculine mind, whereas many even of the males of her set had a feminine mind. She was exceedingly well educated; she had ideas on everything; and she never failed in catching an allusion. She would criticise her set very honestly; her attitude to it and to herself seemed to be that of an impartial and yet indulgent philosopher; withal she could be intensely loyal to fools and worse who were friends. As for the public, she was apparently convinced of the sincerity of her scorn for it, while admitting that she enjoyed publicity, which had become indispensable to her as a drug may become indispensable. Moreover, there was her wit and her candid, queer respect for G. J.

Yes, he had greatly admired her for her qualities. He did not, however, greatly admire her physique. She was tall, with a head scarcely large enough for her body. She had a nice snub nose which in another woman might have been irresistible. She possessed very little physical charm, and showed very little taste in her neat, prim frocks. Not merely had she a masculine mind, but she was somewhat hard, a self-confessed egoist. She swore like the set, using about one "damn" or one "bloody" to every four cigarettes, of which she smoked, perhaps, fifty a day – including some in taxis. She discussed the sexual vagaries of her friends and her enemies with a freedom and an apparent learning which were remarkable in a virgin.

In the end she had married Carlos Smith, and, characteristically, had received him into her own home instead of going to his; as a fact, he had none, having been a parent's close-kept darling. London had only just recovered from the excitations of the wedding. G. J. had regarded the marriage with benevolence, perhaps with relief.

"Anybody else coming to lunch?" he discreetly inquired of his familiar, the parlour-maid.

She breathed a negative.

He had guessed it. Concepcion had meant to be alone with him. Having married for love, and her husband being rapt away by the war, she intended to resume her old, honest, quasi-sentimental relations with G. J. A reliable and experienced bachelor is always useful to a young grass-widow, and, moreover, the attendant hopeless adorer nourishes her hungry egotism as nobody else can. G. J. thought these thoughts, clearly and callously, in the same moment as, mounting the next flight of stairs, he absolutely trembled with sympathetic anguish for Concepcion. His errand was an impossible one; he feared, or rather he hoped, that the very look on his face might betray the dreadful news to that undeceivable intuition which women were supposed to possess. He hesitated on the stairs; he recoiled from the top step – (she had coquettishly withdrawn herself into the room) – he hadn't the slightest idea how to begin. Yes, the errand was an impossible one, and yet such errands had to be performed by somebody, were daily being performed by somebodies. Then he had the idea of telephoning privily to fetch her cousin Sara. He would open by remarking casually to Concepcion:

"I say, can I use your telephone a minute?"

He found a strange Concepcion in the drawing-room. This was his first sight of Mrs Carlos Smith since the wedding. She wore a dress such as he had never seen on her: a tea-gown – and for lunch! It could be called neither neat nor prim, but it was voluptuous. Her complexion had bloomed; the curves of her face were softer, her gestures more abandoned, her gaze full of a bold and yet shamed self-consciousness, her dark hair looser. He stood close to her; he stood within the aura of her recently aroused temperament, and felt it. He thought, could not help thinking: "Perhaps she bears within her the legacy of new life." He could not help thinking of her name. He took her hot hand. She said nothing, but just looked at him. He then said jauntily:

"I say, can I use your telephone a minute?"

Fortunately, the telephone was in the bedroom. He went farther upstairs and shut himself in the bedroom, and saw naught but the telephone surrounded by the mysterious influences of inanimate things in the gay, crowded room.

"Is that you, Mrs Trevise? It's G. J. speaking. G. J... Hoape. Yes. Listen. I'm at Concepcion's for lunch, and I want you to come over as quickly as you can. I've got very bad news indeed – the worst possible. Carlos has been killed at the Front. What?

Yes, awful, isn't it? She doesn't know. I have the job of telling her."

Now that the words had been spoken in Concepcion's abode the reality of Carlos Smith's death seemed more horribly convincing than before. And G. J., speaker of the words, felt almost as guilty as though he himself were responsible for the death. When he had rung off he stood motionless in the room until the opening of the door startled him. Concepcion appeared.

"If you've done corrupting my innocent telephone…" she said, "lunch is cooling."

He felt a murderer.

At the lunch-table she might have been a genuine South American. Nobody could be less like Christine than she was; and yet in those instants she incomprehensibly reminded him of Christine. Then she started to talk in her old manner of a professional and renowned talker. G. J. listened attentively. They ate. It was astounding that he could eat. And it was rather surprising that she did not cry out: "G. J. What the devil's the matter with you to-day?" But she went on talking evenly, and she made him recount his doings. He related the conversation at the club, and especially what Bob, the retired judge, had said about equilibrium on the Western Front. She did not want to hear anything as to the funeral.

"We'll have champagne," she said suddenly to the parlourmaid, who was about to offer some red wine. And while the parlourmaid was out of the room she said to G. J., "There isn't a country in Europe where champagne is not a symbol, and we must conform."

"A symbol of what?"

"Ah! The unusual."

"And what is there unusual to-day?" he almost asked, but did not ask. It would, of course, have been utterly monstrous to put such a question, knowing what he knew. He thought: I'm not a bit nearer telling her than I was when I came.

After the parlour-maid had poured out the champagne Concepcion picked up her glass and absently glanced through it and said:

"You know, G. J., I shouldn't be in the least surprised to hear that Carly was killed out there. I shouldn't, really."

In amazement G. J. ceased to eat.

"You needn't look at me like that," she said. "I'm quite serious. One may as well face the risks. *He* does. Of course they're all heroes. There are millions of heroes. But I do honestly believe that my Carly would be braver than anyone. By the way, did I ever tell you he was considered the best shot in Cheshire?"

"No. But I knew," answered G. J. feebly. He would have expected her to be a little condescending towards Carlos, to whom in brains she was infinitely superior. But no! Carlos had mastered her, and she was grateful to him for mastering her. He had taught her in three weeks more than she had learnt on two continents in thirty years. She talked of him precisely as any wee wifie might have talked of the soldier-spouse. And she called him "Carly"!

Neither of them had touched the champagne. G. J. decided that he would postpone any attempt to tell her until her cousin arrived; her cousin might arrive at any moment now.

While the parlour-maid presented potatoes Concepcion deliberately ignored her and said dryly to G. J.:

"I can't eat any more. I think I ought to run along to Debenham and Freebody's at once. You might come too, and be sure to bring your good taste with you."

He was alarmed by her tone.

"Debenham and Freebody's! What for?"

"To order mourning, of course. To have it ready, you know. A precaution, you know." She laughed.

He saw that she was becoming hysterical: the special liability of the war-bride for whom the curtain has been lifted and falls exasperatingly, enragingly, too soon.

"You think I'm a bit hysterical?" she questioned, half menacingly, and stood up.

"I think you'd better sit down, to begin with," he said firmly.

The parlour-maid, blushing slightly, left the room.

"Oh, all right!" Concepcion agreed carelessly, and sat down. "But you may as well read that."

She drew a telegram from the low neck of her gown and carefully unfolded it and placed it in front of him. It was a War Office telegram announcing that Carlos had been killed.

"It came ten minutes before you," she said.

"Why didn't you tell me at once?" he murmured, frightfully shocked. He was actually reproaching her!

She stood up again. She lived; her breast rose and fell. Her gown had the same voluptuousness. Her temperament was still emanating the same aura. She was the same new Concepcion, strange and yet profoundly known to him. But ineffable tragedy had marked her down, and the sight of her parched the throat.

She said:

"Couldn't. Besides, I had to see if I could stand it. Because I've got to stand it, G. J... And, moreover, in our set it's a sacred duty to be original."

She snatched the telegram, tore it in two, and pushed the pieces back into her gown.

"'Poor wounded name!'" she murmured, "'my bosom as a bed shall lodge thee.'"

The next moment she fell to the floor, at full length on her back. G. J. sprang to her, kneeling on her rich, outspread gown, and tried to lift her.

"No, no!" she protested faintly, dreamily, with a feeble frown on her pale forehead. "Let me lie. Equilibrium has been established on the Western Front."

This was her greatest *mot*.

12

RENDEZVOUS

When the Italian woman, having recognised him with a discreet smile, introduced G. J. into the drawing-room of the Cork Street flat, he saw Christine lying on the sofa by the fire. She too was in a tea-gown.

She said:

"Do not be vexed. I have my migraine – am good for nothing. But I gave the order that thou shouldst be admitted."

She lifted her arms, and the long sleeves fell away. G. J. bent down and kissed her. She joined her hands on the nape of his neck, and with this leverage raised her whole body for an instant, like a child, smiling; then dropped back with a fatigued sigh, also like a child. He found satisfaction in the fact that she was laid aside. It was providential. It set him right with himself. For, to put the thing crudely, he had left the tragic Concepcion to come to Christine, a woman picked up in a Promenade.

True, Sara Trevise had agreed with him that he could accomplish no good by staying at Concepcion's; Concepcion had withdrawn from the vision of men. True, it could make no difference to Concepcion whether he retired to his flat for the rest of the day and saw no one, or whether, having changed his ceremonious clothes there, he went out again on his own affairs. True, he had promised Christine to see her that afternoon, and a promise was a promise, and Christine was a woman who had behaved well to him, and it would have been impossible for him to send her an excuse, since he did not know her surname. These apparently excellent arguments were specious and worthless. He would, anyhow, have gone to Christine. The call was imperious within him, and took no heed of grief, nor propriety, nor the secret decencies of sympathy. The primitive man in him would have gone to Christine.

He sat down with a profound and exquisite relief. The entrance to the house was nearly opposite the entrance to a prim but fashionable and expensive hotel. To ring (and ring the right bell) and wait at Christine's door almost under the eyes of the hotel was an ordeal... The fat and untidy Italian had opened the door, and shut it again – quick! He was in another world, saved, safe! On the dark staircase the image of Concepcion with her temperament roused and condemned to everlasting hunger, the unconquerable Concepcion blasted in an instant of destiny – this image faded. She would re-marry... And now he was in Christine's warm room, and Christine, temporary invalid, reclined before his eyes. The lights were turned on, the blinds drawn, the stove replenished, the fire replenished. He was enclosed with Christine in a little world with no law and no conventions except its own, and no shames nor pretences. He was, as it were, in the East. And the immanence of a third person, the Italian, accepting naturally and completely the code of the little world, only added to the charm. The Italian was like a slave, from whom it is necessary to hide nothing and never to blush.

A stuffy little world with a perceptible odour! Ordinarily he had the common insular appetite for ventilation, but now stuffiness appealed to him; he scented it almost voluptuously. The ugliness of the wallpaper, of the furniture, of everything in the room was naught. Christine's profession was naught. Who could positively say that her profession was on her face, in her gestures, in her talk? Admirable as was his knowledge of French, it was not enough to enable him to criticise her speech. Her gestures were delightful. Her face – her face was soft; her puckered brow was touching in its ingenuousness. She had a kind and a trustful eye; it was a lewd eye, indicative of her incomparable endowment; but had he not encountered the lewd eye in the very arcana of the respectability of the world outside? On the sofa, open and leaves downward, lay a book with a glistening coloured cover, entitled *Fantomas*. It was the seventh volume of an interminable romance which for years had had a tremendous vogue among the concierges, the workgirls, the clerks, and the *cocottes* of Paris. An unreadable affair, not even indecent, which nevertheless had enchanted a whole generation. To be able to enjoy it was an absolute demonstration of lack of taste; but did not some of his best friends enjoy books no better? And could he not any day in any drawing-room see martyred books dropped open and leaves downwards in a manner to raise the gorge of a person of any bookish sensibility?

"Thou wilt play for me?" she suggested.

"But the headache?"

"It will do me good. I adore music, such music as thou playest."

He was flattered. The draped piano was close to him. Stretching out his hand he took a little pile of music from the top of it.

"But you play, then!" he exclaimed, pleased.

"No, no! I tap – only. And very little."

He glanced through the pieces of music. They were all, without exception, waltzes, by the once popular waltz-kings of Paris and Vienna, including several by the king of kings, Berger. He seated himself at the piano and opened the first waltz that came.

"Oh! I adore the waltzes of Berger," she murmured. "There is only he. You don't think so?"

He said he had never heard any of this music. Then he played every piece for her. He tried to see what it was in this music that so pleased the simple; and he saw it, or he thought he saw it. He abandoned himself to the music, yielding to it, accepting its ideals, interpreting it as though it moved him, until in the end it did produce in him a sort of factitious emotion. After all, it was no worse than much of the music he was forced to hear in very refined circles.

She said, ravished:

"You decipher music like an angel."

And hummed a fragment of the waltz from *The Rosenkavalier* which he had played for her two evenings earlier. He glanced round sharply. Had she, then, real taste?

"It is like that, isn't it?" she questioned, and hummed it again, flattered by the look on his face.

While, at her invitation, he repeated the waltz on the piano, whose strings might have been made of zinc, he heard a ring at the outer door and then the muffled sound of a colloquy between a male voice and the voice of the Italian. "Of course," he admitted philosophically, "she has other clients already." Such a woman was bound to have other clients. He felt no jealousy, nor even discomfort, from the fact that she lent herself to any male with sufficient money and a respectable appearance. The colloquy expired.

"Ring, please," she requested, after thanking him. He hoped that she was not going to interrogate the Italian in his presence. Surely she would be incapable of such clumsiness! Still, women without imagination – and the majority of women were without imagination – did do the most astounding things.

There was no immediate answer to the bell; but in a few minutes the Italian entered with a tea-tray. Christine sat up.

"I will pour the tea," said she, and to the Italian: "Marthe, where is the evening paper?" And when Marthe returned with a newspaper damp from the press, Christine said: "To Monsieur…"

Not a word of curiosity as to the unknown visitor!

G. J. was amply confirmed in his original opinion of Christine. She was one in a hundred. To provide the evening paper... It was nothing, but it was enormous.

"Sit by my side," she said. She made just a little space for him on the sofa – barely enough so that he had to squeeze in. The afternoon tea was correct, save for the extraordinary thickness of the bread-and-butter. But G. J. said to himself that the French did not understand bread-and-butter, and the Italians still less. To compensate for the defects of the bread-and-butter there was a box of fine chocolates.

"I perfect my English," she said. Tea was finished; they were smoking, the *Evening News* spread between them over the tea-things. She articulated with a strong French accent the words of some of the headings. "Mistair Carlos Smith keeled at the front," she read out. "Who is it, that woman there? She must be celebrated."

There was a portrait of the illustrious Concepcion, together with some sympathetic remarks about her, remarks conceived very differently from the usual semi-ironic, semi-worshipping journalistic references to the stars of Concepcion's set. G. J. answered vaguely.

"I do not like too much these society women. They are worse than us, and they cost you more. Ah! If the truth were known – " Christine spoke with a queer, restrained, surprising bitterness. Then she added, softly relenting: "However, it is sad for her... Who was he, this monsieur?"

G. J. replied that he was nobody in particular, so far as his knowledge went.

"Ah! One of those who are husbands of their wives!" said Christine acidly.

The disturbing intuition of women!

A little later he said that he must depart.

"But why? I feel better."

"I have a committee."

"A committee?"

"It is a work of charity – for the French wounded."

"Ah! In that case… But, beloved!"

"Yes?"

She lowered her voice.

"How dost thou call thyself?"

"Gilbert."

"Thou knowest – I have a fancy for thee."

Her tone was delicious, its sincerity absolutely convincing.

"Too amiable."

"No, no. It is true. Say! Return. Return after thy committee. Take me out to dinner – some gentle little restaurant, discreet. There must be many of them in a city like London. It is a city so romantic. Oh! The little corners of London!"

"But – of course. I should be enchanted – "

"Well, then."

He was standing. She raised her smiling, seductive face. She was young – younger than Concepcion; less battered by the world's contacts than Concepcion. She had the inexpressible virtue and power of youth. He was nearing fifty. And she, perhaps half his age, had confessed his charm.

"And say! My Gilbert. Bring me a few flowers. I have not been able to go out to-day. Something very simple. I detest that one should squander money on flowers for me."

"Seven-thirty, then!" said he. "And you will be ready?"

"I shall be very exact. Thou wilt tell me all that concerns thy committee. That interests me. The English are extraordinary."

13

In Committee

Within the hotel the glowing Gold Hall, whose Lincrusta Walton panels dated it, was nearly empty. Of the hundred small round tables only one was occupied; a bald head and a large green hat were almost meeting over the top of this table, but there was nothing on it except an ashtray. A waiter wandered about amid the thick plushy silence and the stagnant pools of electric light, meditating upon the curse which had befallen the world of hotels. The red lips beneath the green hat discernibly moved, but no faintest murmur therefrom reached the entrance. The hot, still place seemed to be enchanted.

The sight of the hotel flower-stall recessed on the left reminded G. J. of Christine's desire. Forty thousand skilled women had been put out of work in England because luxury was scared by the sudden vista of war, but the black-garbed girl, entrenched in her mahogany bower, was still earning some sort of a livelihood. In a moment, wakened out of her terrible boredom into an alert smile, she had sold to G. J. a bunch of expensive chrysanthemums whose yellow petals were like long curly locks. Thoughtless, he had meant to have the flowers delivered at once to Christine's flat. It would not do; it would be indiscreet. And somehow, in the absence of Braiding, it would be equally indiscreet to have them delivered at his own flat.

"I shall be leaving the hotel in about an hour; I'll take them away myself then," he said, and inquired for the headquarters of the Lechford French Hospitals Committee.

"Committee?" repeated the girl vaguely. "I expect the Onyx Hall's what you want." She pointed up a corridor, and gave change.

G. J. discovered the Onyx Hall, which had its own entrance from the street, and which in other days had been a café lounge. The precious pavement was now half hidden by wooden trestles, wooden cubicles, and cheap chairs. Temporary flexes brought down electric light from a stained glass dome to illuminate card-indexes and pigeonholes and piles of letters. Notices in French and Flemish were suspended from the ornate onyx pilasters. Old countrywomen and children in rough foreign clothes, smart officers in strange uniforms, privates in shabby blue, gentlemen in morning coats and spats, and untidy Englishwomen with eyes romantic, hard, or wistful, were mixed together in the Onyx Hall, where there was no enchantment and little order, save that good French seemed to be regularly spoken on one side of the trestles and regularly assassinated on the other. G. J., mystified, caught the grey eye of a youngish woman with a tired and fretful expression.

"And you?" she inquired perfunctorily.

He demanded, with hesitation:

"Is this the Lechford Committee?"

"The what Committee?"

"The Lechford Committee headquarters." He thought she might be rather an attractive little thing at, say, an evening party.

She gave him a sardonic look and answered, not rudely, but with large tolerance:

"Can't you read?"

By means of gesture scarcely perceptible she directed his attention to an immense linen sign stretched across the back of the big room, and he saw that he was in the ant-heap of some Belgian Committee.

"So sorry to have troubled you!" he apologised. "I suppose you don't happen to know where the Lechford Committee sits?"

"Never heard of it," said she with cheerful disdain. Then she smiled and he smiled. "You know, the hotel simply hums with committees, but this is the biggest by a long way. They can't let their rooms, so it costs them nothing to lend them for patriotic purposes."

He liked the chit.

Presently, with a page-boy, he was ascending in a lift through storey after storey of silent carpeted desert. Light alternated with darkness, winking like a succession of days and nights as seen by a god. The infant showed him into a private parlour furnished and decorated in almost precisely the same taste as Christine's sittingroom, where a number of men and women sat close together at a long deal table, whose pale, classic simplicity clashed with the rest of the apartment. A thin, dark, middle-aged man of austere visage bowed to him from the head of the table. Somebody else indicated a chair, which, with a hideous, noisy scraping over the bare floor, he modestly insinuated between two occupied chairs. A third person offered a typewritten sheet containing the agenda of the meeting. A blonde girl was reading in earnest, timid tones the minutes of the previous meeting. The affair had just begun. As soon as the minutes had been passed the austere chairman turned and said evenly:

"I am sure I am expressing the feelings of the committee in welcoming among us Mr Hoape, who has so kindly consented to join us and give us the benefit of his help and advice in our labours."

Sympathetic murmurs converged upon G. J. from the four sides of the table, and G. J. nervously murmured a few incomprehensible words, feeling both foolish and pleased. He had never sat on a committee; and as his war-conscience troubled him more and more daily, he was extremely anxious to start work which might placate it. Indeed, he had seized upon the request to join the committee as a swimmer in difficulties clasps the gunwale of a dinghy.

A man who kept his gaze steadily on the table cleared his throat and said:

"The matter is not in order, Mr Chairman, but I am sure I am expressing the feelings of the committee in proposing a vote of condolence to yourself on the terrible loss which you have sustained in the death of your son at the Front."

"I beg to second that," said a lady quickly. "Our chairman has given his only son – " Tears came into her eyes; she seemed to appeal for help. There were "Hear, hears," and more sympathetic murmurs.

The proposer, with his gaze still steadily fixed on the table, said:

"I beg to put the resolution to the meeting."

"Yes," said the chairman with calm self-control in the course of his acknowledgment. "And if I had ten sons I would willingly give them all – for the cause." And his firm, hard glance appeared to challenge any member of the committee to assert that this profession of parental and patriotic generosity of heart was not utterly sincere. However, nobody had the air of doubting that if the chairman had had ten sons, or as many sons as Solomon, he would have sacrificed them all with the most admirable and eager heroism.

The agenda was opened. G. J. had little but newspaper knowledge of the enterprises of the committee, and it would not have been proper to waste the time of so numerous a company in enlightening him. The common-sense custom evidently was that new members should "pick up the threads as they went along." G. J. honestly tried to do so. But he was preoccupied with the personalities of the committee. He soon saw that the whole body was effectively divided into two classes – the chairmen of the various subcommittees, and the rest. Few members were interested in any particular subject. Those who were not interested either stared at the walls or at the agenda paper, or laboriously drew intricate and meaningless designs on the agenda paper, or folded up the agenda paper into fantastic shapes until, when someone in authority brought out the formula, "I think the view of the committee will be – " a resolution was put and the issue settled by the mechanical raising of hands on the fulcrum of the elbow. And at each raising of hands everybody felt that something positive had indeed been accomplished.

The new member was a little discouraged. He had the illusion that the two hospitals run in France for French soldiers by the Lechford Committee were an illusion, that they did not really exist, that the committee was discussing an abstraction. Nevertheless, each problem as it was presented – the drains (postponed), the repairs to the motor-ambulances, the ordering of a new X-ray apparatus, the dilatoriness of a French Minister in dealing with correspondence, the cost per day per patient, the relations with the French civil authorities and the French military authorities, the appointment of a new matron who could keep the peace with the senior doctor, and the great principle involved in deducting five francs fifty centimes for excess luggage from a nurse's account for travelling expenses – each problem helped to demonstrate that the hospitals did exist and that men and women were toiling therein, and that French soldiers in grave need were being magnificently cared for and even saved from death. And it was plain, too, that none of these excellent things could have come to pass or could continue to occur if the committee did not regularly sit round the table and at short intervals perform the rite of raising hands...

G. J.'s attention wandered. He could not keep his mind off the thought that he should soon be seeing Christine again. Sitting at the table with a mien of intelligent interest, he had a waking dream of Christine. He saw her just as she was – ingenuous, and ignorant if you like – except that she was pure. Her purity, though, had not cooled her temperament, and thus she combined in herself the characteristics of at least two different women, both of whom were necessary to his happiness. And she was his wife, and they lived in a roomy house in Hyde Park Gardens, and the war was over. And she adored him and he was passionately fond of her. And she was always having children; she enjoyed having children; she demanded children; she had a child every year and there was never any trouble. And he never admired her more poignantly than at the periods just before his children were born, when she had the vast, exquisitely swelling figure of the French Renaissance Virgin in marble that stood on a console in his drawing-room at the Albany... Such was G. J.'s dream as he assisted in the control of the Lechford Hospitals. Emerging from it he looked along the table. Quite half the members were dreaming too, and he wondered what thoughts were moving secretly within them. But the chairman was not dreaming. He never loosed his grasp of the matter in hand. Nor did the earnest young blonde by the chairman's side who took down in stenography the decisions of the committee.

14

QUEEN

Then Lady Queenie Paulle entered rather hurriedly, filling the room with a distinguished scent. All the men rose in haste, and there was a frightful scraping of chair-legs on the floor. Lady Queenie cheerfully apologised for being late, and, begging no one to disturb himself, took a modest place between the chairman and the secretary and a little behind them.

Lady Queenie obviously had what is called "race". The renown of her family went back far, far beyond its special Victorian vogue, which had transformed an earldom into a marquisate and which, incidentally, was responsible for the new family Christian name that Queenie herself bore. She was young, tall, slim and pale, and dressed with the utmost smartness in black – her half-brother having gloriously lost his life in September. She nodded to the secretary, who blushed with pleasure, and she nodded to several members, including G. J. Being accustomed to publicity and to seeing herself nearly every week in either *The Tatler* or *The Sketch*, she was perfectly at ease in the room, and the fact that nearly the whole company turned to her as plants to the sun did not in the least disturb her.

The attention which she received was her due, for she had few rivals as a war-worker. She was connected with the Queen's

Work for Women Fund, Queen Mary's Needlework Guild, the Three Arts Fund, the Women's Emergency Corps, and many minor organisations. She had joined a Women's Suffrage Society because such societies were being utilised by the Government. She had had ten lessons in First Aid in ten days, had donned the Red Cross, and gone to France with two motorcars and a staff and a French maid in order to help in the great national work of nursing wounded heroes; and she might still have been in France had not an unsympathetic and audacious colonel of the R.A.M.C. insisted on her being shipped back to England. She had done practically everything that a patriotic girl could do for the war, except, perhaps, join a Voluntary Aid Detachment and wash dishes and scrub floors for fifteen hours a day and thirteen and a half days a fortnight. It was from her mother that she had inherited the passion for public service. The Marchioness of Lechford had been the cause of more philanthropic work in others than any woman in the whole history of philanthropy. Lady Lechford had said, "Let there be Lechford Hospitals in France," and lo! there were Lechford Hospitals in France. When troublesome complications arose Lady Lechford had, with true self-effacement, surrendered the establishments to a thoroughly competent committee, and while retaining a seat on the committee for herself and another for Queenie, had curved tirelessly away to the inauguration of fresh and more exciting schemes.

"Mamma was very sorry she couldn't come this afternoon," said Lady Queenie, addressing the chairman.

The formula of those with authority in deciding now became:

"I don't know exactly what Lady Lechford's view is, but I venture to think – "

Then suddenly the demeanour of every member of the committee was quickened, everybody listened intently to everything that was said; a couple of members would speak together; pattern-designing and the manufacture of paper ships, chains, and flowers ceased; it was as though a tonic had been mysteriously administered to each individual in the enervating room. The cause of the change was a recommendation from the hospitals management sub-committee that it be an instruction to the new matron of the smaller hospital to forbid any nurse and any doctor to go out alone together in the evening. Scandal was insinuated; nothing really wrong, but a bad impression produced upon the civilians of the tiny town, who could not be expected to understand the holy innocence which underlies the superficial license of Anglo-Saxon manners. The personal characters and strange idiosyncrasies of every doctor and every nurse were discussed; broad principles of conduct were enunciated, together with the advantages and disadvantages of those opposite poles, discipline and freedom. The argument continually expanded, branching forth like the timber of a great oak-tree from the trunk, and the minds of the committee ran about the tree like monkeys. The interest was endless. A quiet delegate who had just returned from a visit to the tiny town completely blasted one part of the argument by asserting that the hospital bore a blameless reputation among the citizens; but new arguments were instantly constructed by the adherents of the idea of discipline. The committee had plainly split into two even parties. G. J. began to resent the harshness of the disciplinarians.

"I think we should remember," he said in his modest voice, "I think we should remember that we are dealing with adult men and women."

The libertarians at once took him for their own. The disciplinarians gave him to understand with their eyes that it might have been better if he, as a new member attending his first meeting, had kept silence. The discussion was inflamed. One or two people glanced surreptitiously at their watches. The hour had long passed six thirty. G. J. grew anxious about his rendezvous with Christine. He had enjoined exactitude upon Christine. But the main body of the excited and happy committee had no thought of the flight of time. The amusements of the tiny town came up for review. As a fact, there was only one amusement, the cinema. The whole town went to the cinema. Cinemas were always darkened; human nature was human nature... G. J. had an extraordinarily realistic vision of the hospital staff slaving through its long and heavy day and its everlasting week and preparing in sections to amuse itself on certain evenings, and thinking with pleasant anticipation of the ecstasies of the cinema, and pathetically unsuspicious that its fate was being decided by a council of omnipotent deities in the heaven of a London hotel.

"Mamma has never mentioned the subject to me," said Lady Queenie in response to a question, looking at her rich muff.

"This is a question of principle," said somebody sharply, implying that at last individual consciences were involved and that the opinions of the Marchioness of Lechford had ceased to weigh.

"I'm afraid it's getting late," said the impassive chairman. "We must come to some decision."

In the voting Lady Queenie, after hesitation, raised her hand with the disciplinarians. By one vote the libertarians were defeated, and the dalliance of the hospital staff in leisure hours received a severe check.

"She *would* – of course!" breathed a sharpnosed little woman in the chair next but one to G. J., gazing inimically at the lax mouth and cynical eyes of Lady Queenie, who for four years had been the subject of universal whispering, and some shouting, and one or two ferocious battles in London.

Chair-legs scraped. People rose here and there to go as they rise in a music hall after the Scottish comedian has retired, bowing, from his final encore. They protested urgent appointments elsewhere. The chairman remarked that other important decisions yet remained to be taken; but his voice had no insistence because he had already settled the decisions in his own mind. G. J. seized the occasion to depart.

"Mr Hoape," the chairman detained him a moment. "The committee hope you will allow yourself to be nominated to the accounts subcommittee. We understand that you are by way of being an expert. The sub-committee meets on Wednesday mornings at eleven – doesn't it, Sir Charles?"

"Half-past," said Sir Charles.

"Oh! Half-past."

G. J., somewhat surprised to learn of his expertise in accountancy, consented to the suggestion, which renewed his resolution, impaired somewhat by the experience of the meeting, to be of service in the world.

"You will receive the notice, of course," said the chairman.

Down below, just as G. J. was getting away with Christine's chrysanthemums in their tissue paper, Lady Queenie darted out of the lift opposite. It was she who, at Concepcion's instigation, had had him put in the committee.

"I say, Queen," he said with a casual air – on account of the flowers, "who's been telling 'em I know about accounts?"

"I did."

"Why?"

"Why?" she said maliciously. "Don't you keep an account of every penny you spend?" (It was true.)

Here was a fair example of her sardonic and unscrupulous humour – a humour not of words but of acts. G. J. simply tossed his head, aware of the futility of expostulation.

She went on in a different tone:

"You were the first to see Connie?"

"Yes," he said sadly.

"She has lain in my arms all afternoon," Lady Queenie burst out, her voice liquid. "And now I'm going straight back to her." She looked at him with the strangest triumphant expression. Then her large, equivocal blue eyes fell from his face to the flowers, and their expression simultaneously altered to disdainful

ARNOLD BENNETT

amusement full of mischievous implications. She ran off
without another word. The glazed entrance doors revolved, and
he saw her nip into an electric brougham, which, before he had
time to button his overcoat, vanished like an apparition in the
rainy mist.

15

EVENING OUT

He found Christine exactly has he had left her, in the same tea-gown and the same posture, and on the same sofa. But a small table had been put by the sofa; and on this table was a penny bottle of ink in a saucer, and a pen. She was studying some kind of official form. The pucker between the eyes was very marked.

"Already!" she exclaimed, as if amazed. "But there is not a clock that goes, and I had not the least idea of the hour. Besides, I was splitting my head to fill up this form."

Such was her notion of being exact! He had abandoned an important meeting of a committee which was doing untold mercies to her compatriots in order to keep his appointment with her; and she, whose professional business it was that evening to charm him and harmonise with him, had merely flouted the appointment. Nevertheless, her gestures and smile as she rose and came towards him were so utterly exquisite that immediately he also flouted the appointment. What, after all, could it matter whether they dined at eight, nine, or even ten o'clock?"

"Thou wilt pardon me, monster?" she murmured, kissing him.

No woman had ever put her chin up to his as she did, nor with a glance expressed so unreserved a surrender to his masculinity.

She went on, twining languishingly round him:

"I do not know whether I ought to go out. I am yet far from – It is perhaps imprudent."

"Absurd!" he protested – he could not bear the thought of her not dining with him. He knew too well the desolation of a solitary dinner. "Absurd! We go in a taxi. The restaurant is warm. We return in a taxi."

"To please thee, then."

"What is that form?"

"It is for the telephone. Thou understandest how it is necessary that I have the telephone – me! But I comprehend nothing of this form."

She passed him the form. She had written her name in the space allotted. "Christine Dubois." A fair calligraphy! But what a name! The French equivalent of "Smith". Nothing could be less distinguished. Suddenly it occurred to him that Concepcion's name also was Smith.

"I will fill it up for you. It is quite simple."

"It is possible that it is simple when one is English. But English – that is as if to say Chinese. Everything contrary. Here is a pen."

"No. I have my fountain-pen." He hated a cheap pen, and still more a penny bottle of ink, but somehow this particular penny bottle of ink seemed touching in its simple ugliness. She was eminently teachable. He would teach her his own attitude towards penny bottles of ink... Of course she would need the telephone – that could not be denied.

As Christine was signing the form Marthe entered with the chrysanthemums, which he had handed over to her; she had arranged them in a horrible blue glass vase cheaply gilded; and while Marthe was putting the vase on the small table there was a ring at the outer door. Marthe hurried off.

Christine said, kissing him again tenderly:

"Thou art a squanderer! Fine for me to tell thee not to buy costly flowers! Thou has spent at least ten shillings for these. With ten shillings – "

"No, no!" he interrupted her. "Five." It was a fib. He had paid half a guinea for the few flowers, but he could not confess it.

They could hear a powerful voice indistinctly booming at the top of the stairs. "Two callers on one afternoon!" G. J. reflected. And yet she had told him she went out for the first time only the day before yesterday! He scarcely liked it, but his reason rescued him from the puerility of a grievance against her on this account. "And why not? She is bound to be a marked success."

Marthe returned to the drawing-room and shut the door.

"Madame – " she began, slightly agitated.

"Speak, then!" Christine urged, catching her agitation.

"It is the police!"

G. J. had a shock. He knew many of the policemen who lurked in the dark doorways of Piccadilly at night, had little friendly talks with them, held them for excellent fellows. But a policeman invading the flat of a courtesan, and himself in the flat, seemed a different being from the honest stalwarts who threw the beams of lanterns on the key-holes of jewellers' shops.

Christine steeled herself to meet the crisis with self-reliance. She pointedly did not appeal to the male.

"Well, what is it that he wants?"

"He talks of the chimney. It appears this morning there was a chimney on fire. But since we burn only anthracite and gas – He knows madame's name."

There was a pause. Christine asked sharply and mysteriously:

"How much do you think?"

"If madame gave five pounds – having regard to the *chic* of the quarter."

Christine rushed into the bedroom and came back with a five-pound note.

"Here! Chuck that at him – politely. Tell him we are very sorry."

"Yes, madame."

"But he'll never take it. You can't treat the London police like that!" G. J. could not help expostulating as soon as Marthe had gone. He feared some trouble.

"My poor friend!" Christine replied patronisingly. "Thou art not up in these things. Marthe knows her affair – a woman very experienced in London. He will take it, thy policeman. And if I do not deceive myself no more chimneys will burn for about a year… Ah! The police do not wipe their noses with broken bottles!" (She meant that the police knew their way about.) "I no more than they, I do not wipe my nose with broken bottles."

She was moved, indignant, stoutly defensive. G. J. grew self-conscious. Moreover, her slang disturbed him. It was the first slang he had heard her use, and in using it her voice had roughened. But he remembered that Concepcion also used slang – and advanced slang – upon occasion.

The booming ceased; a door closed. Marthe returned once more.

"Well?"

"He is gone. He was very nice, madame. I told him about madame – that madame was very discreet." Marthe finished in a murmur.

"So much the better. Now, help me to dress. Quick, quick! Monsieur will be impatient."

G. J. was ashamed of the innocence he had displayed, and ashamed, too, of the whole Metropolitan Police Force, admirable though it was in stopping traffic for a perambulator to cross the road. Five pounds! These ladies were bled. Five pounds wanted earning… It was a good sign, though, that she had not so far asked him to contribute. And he felt sure that she would not.

"Come in, then, poltroon!" She cooed softly and encouragingly from the bedroom, where Marthe was busy with her.

The door between the bedroom and the drawing-room was open. G. J., humming, obeyed the invitation and sat down on the bed between two heaps of clothes. Christine was very gay; she was like a child. She had apparently quite forgotten her migraine and also the incident of the policeman. She snatched the cigarette from G. J.'s mouth, took a puff, and put it back again. Then she sat in front of the large mirror and did her hair while Marthe buttoned her boots. Her corset fitted beautifully, and as she raised her arms above her head under the shaded lamp G. J. could study the marvellous articulation of the arms at the bare shoulders. The close atmosphere was drenched with femininity. The two women, one so stylish and the other by contrast piquantly a heavy slattern, hid nothing whatever from him, bestowing on him with perfect tranquillity the right to be there and to watch at his ease every mysterious transaction... The most convincing proof that Christine was authentically young! And G. J. had the illusion again that he was in the Orient, and it was extraordinarily agreeable. The recollection of the scene of the Lechford Committee amused him like a pantomime witnessed afar off through a gauze curtain. It had no more reality than that. But he thought better of the committee now. He perceived the wonderful goodness of it and of its work. It really was running those real hospitals; it had a real interest in them. He meant to do his very best in the accounts department. After all, he had been a lawyer and knew the routine of an office and the minutest phenomena of a ledger. He was eager to begin.

"How findest thou me?"

She stood for inspection.

She was ready, except the gloves. The angle of her hat, the provocation of her veil – these things would have quickened the pulse of a Patagonian. Perfume pervaded the room.

He gave the classic response that nothing could render trite:

"*Tu es exquise.*"

She raised her veil just above her mouth...

In the drawing-room she hesitated, and then settled down on the piano-stool like a bird alighting and played a few bars from the *Rosenkavalier* waltz. He was thunderstruck, for she had got not only the air but some of the accompaniment right.

"Go on! Go on!" he urged her, marvelling.

She turned, smiling, and shook her head.

"That is all that I can recall to myself."

The obvious sincerity of his appreciation delighted her.

"She is really musical!" he thought, and was convinced that while looking for a bit of coloured glass he had picked up an emerald. Marthe produced his overcoat, and when he was ready for the street Christine gazed at him and said:

"For the true *chic*, there are only Englishmen!"

In the taxi she proved to him by delicate effronteries the genuineness of her confessed "fancy" for him. And she poured out slang. He began to be afraid, for this excursion was an experiment such as he had never tried before in London; in Paris, of course, the code was otherwise. But as soon as the commissionaire of the restaurant at Victoria approached the door of the taxi her manner changed. She walked up the long interior with the demureness of a stockbroker's young wife out for the evening from Putney Hill. He thought, relieved, "She is the embodiment of common sense." At the end of the vista of white tables the restaurant opened out to the left. In a far corner they were comfortably secure from observation. They sat down. A waiter beamed his flatteries upon them. G. J. was serenely aware of his own skilled faculty for ordering a dinner. He looked over the menu card at Christine. Nobody could possibly tell that she was a professed enemy of society. "These French women are astounding!" he thought. He intensely admired her. He was mad about her. His bliss was extreme. He could not keep it within bounds meet for the great world-catastrophe. He was happy as for quite ten years he had never hoped to be. Yes, he grieved for Concepcion; but somehow grief could not mingle with nor impair the happiness he felt. And was not Concepcion lying in the affectionate arms of Queenie Paulle?

Christine, glancing about her contentedly, reverted to one of her leading ideas:

"Truly, it is very romantic, thy London!"

16

THE VIRGIN

Christine went into the Oratory of St Philip at Brompton on a
Sunday morning in the following January, dipped her finger into
one of the Italian basins at the entrance, and signed herself with
the holy water. She was dressed in black; she had the face of a
pretty martyr; her brow was crumpled by the world's sorrow;
she looked and actually was at the moment intensely religious.
She had months earlier chosen the Brompton Oratory for her
devotions, partly because of the name of Philip, which had been
murmured in accents of affection by her dying mother, and
partly because it lay on a direct, comprehensible bus-route from
Piccadilly. You got into the motor-bus opposite the end of the
Burlington Arcade, and in about six minutes it dropped you in
front of the Oratory; and you could not possibly lose yourself in
the topographical intricacies of the unknown city. Christine
never took a taxi except when on business.

The interior was gloomy with the winter forenoon; the broad
Renaissance arches showed themselves only faintly above; on
every side there were little archipelagos of light made by groups
of candles in front of great pale images. The church was
comparatively empty, and most of the people present were
kneeling in the chapels; for Christine had purposely come, as
she always did, at the slack hour between the seventh and last

of the early morning Low Masses and the High Mass at eleven.

She went up the right aisle and stopped before the Miraculous Infant Jesus of Prague, a charming and naive little figure about eighteen inches high in a stiff embroidered cloak and a huge symbol upon his curly head. She had put herself under the protection of the Miraculous Infant Jesus of Prague. She liked him; he was a change from the Virgin; and he stood in the darkest corner of the whole interior, behind the black statue of St. Peter with protruding toe, and within the deep shadow made by the organ-loft overhead. Also he had a motto in French: "Plus vous m'honorerez plus je vous favoriserai."

Christine hesitated, and then left the Miraculous Infant Jesus of Prague without even a transient genuflexion. She was afraid to devote herself to him that morning.

Of course she had been brought up strictly in the Roman Catholic faith. And in her own esteem she was still an honest Catholic. For years she had not confessed and therefore had not communicated. For years she had had a desire to cast herself down at a confessional-box, but she had not done so because of one of the questions in the *Petit Paroissien* which she used: "Avezvous péché, par pensée, parole, ou action, contre la pureté ou la modestie?" And because also of the preliminary injunction: "Maintenant essayez de vous rappeler vos péchés, *et combien de fois vous les avez commis.*" She could not bring herself to do that. Once she had confessed a great deal to a priest at Sens, but he had treated her too lightly; his lightness with her had indeed been shameful. Since then she had never confessed. Further, she knew herself to be in a state of mortal sin by reason of her frequent wilful neglect of the holy offices; and occasionally, at the most inconvenient moments, the conviction that if she died she was damned would triumph over her complacency. But on the whole she had hopes for the future; though she had sinned, her sin was mysteriously not like other people's sin of exactly the same kind.

And finally there was the Virgin Mary, the sweet and dependable goddess. She had been neglecting the very clement Virgin Mary in favour of the Miraculous Infant Jesus of Prague. A whim, a thoughtless caprice, which she had paid for! The Virgin Mary had withdrawn her defending shield. At least that was the interpretation which Christine was bound to put upon the terrible incident of the previous night in the Promenade. She had quite innocently been involved in a drunken row in the lounge. Two military officers, one of whom, unnoticed by Christine, was intoxicated, and two women – Madame Larivaudière and Christine! The Belgian had been growing more and more jealous of Christine... The row had flamed up in the tenth of a second like an explosion. The two officers – then the two women. The bright silvery sound of glass shattered on marble! High voices, deep voices! Half the Promenade had rushed vulgarly into the lounge, panting with a gross appetite to witness a vulgar scene. And as the Belgian was jealous of the French girl, so were the English girls horribly jealous of all the foreign girls, and scornful too. Nothing but the overwhelming desire of the management to maintain the perfect respectability of its Promenade had prevented a rough-and-tumble between the officers. As for Madame Larivaudière, she had been ejected and told never to return. Christine had fled to the cloakroom, where she had remained for half an hour, and thence had vanished away, solitary, by the side entrance. It was precisely such an episode as Christine's mother would have deprecated in horror, and as Christine herself intensely loathed. And she could never assuage the moral wound of it by confiding the affair to Gilbert. She was mad about Gilbert; she thrilled to be his slave; she had what seemed an immeasurable confidence in him; and yet never, never could she mention another individual man to him, much less tell him of the public shame that had fallen upon her in the exercise of her profession. Why had fate been thus hard on her? The answer was surely to be found in the displeasure of the Virgin. And so she did not dare to stay with the Miraculous Infant Jesus of Prague, nor even to murmur the prayer beginning: "Adorable Jésus, divin modèle de la perfection..."

She glanced round the great church, considering what were to her the major and minor gods and goddesses on their ornate thrones: St. Antony, St. Joseph, St. Sebastian, St. Philip, the Sacred Heart, St. Cecilia, St. Peter, St. Wilfrid, St. Mary Magdelene (Ah! Not at that altar could she be seen!), St. Patrick, St. Veronica, St. Francis, St. John Baptist, St. Teresa, Our Lady, Our Lady of Good Counsel. No! There was only one goddess possible for her – Our Lady of VII Dolours. She crossed the wide nave to the severe black and white marble chapel of the VII Dolours. The aspect of the shrine suited her. On one side she read the English words: "Of your charity pray for the soul of Flora Duchess of Norfolk who put up this altar to the Mother of Sorrows that they who mourn may be comforted." And the very words were romantic to her, and she thought of Flora Duchess of Norfolk as a figure inexpressibly more romantic than the illustrious female figures of French history. The Virgin of the VII Dolours was enigmatically gazing at her, waiting no doubt to be placated. The Virgin was painted, gigantic, in oil on canvas, but on her breast stood out a heart made in three dimensions of real silver and pierced by the swords of the seven dolours, three to the left and four to the right; and in front was a tiny gold figure of Jesus crucified on a gold cross.

Christine cast herself down and prayed to the painted image and the hammered heart. She prayed to the goddess whom the Middle Ages had perfected and who in the minds of the simple and the savage has survived the Renaissance and still triumphantly flourishes; the Queen of heaven, the Tyrant of heaven, the Woman in heaven; who was so venerated that even her sweat is exhibited as a relic; who was softer than Christ as Christ was softer than the Father; who in becoming a goddess had increased her humanity; who put living roses for a sign into the mouths of fornicators when they died, if only they had been faithful to her; who told the amorous sacristan to kiss her face and not her feet; who questioned lovers about their mistresses: "Is she as pretty as I?"; who fell like a pestilence on the nuptial chambers of young men who, professing love for her, had taken another bride; who enjoyed being amused; who admitted a weakness for artists, tumblers, soldiers and the common herd; who had visibly led both opponents on every battlefield for centuries; who impersonated absent disreputable nuns and did their work for them until they returned, repentant, to be forgiven by her; who acted always on her instinct and never on her reason; who cared nothing for legal principles; who openly used her feminine influence with the Trinity; who filled heaven with riff-raff; and who had never on any pretext driven a soul out of heaven. Christine made peace with this jealous and divine creature. She felt unmistakably that she was forgiven for her infidelity due to the Infant in the darkness beyond the opposite aisle. The face of the Lady of VII Dolours miraculously smiled at her; the silver heart miraculously shed its tarnish and glittered beneficent lightnings. Doubtless she knew somewhere in her mind that no physical change had occurred in the picture or the heart; but her mind was a complex, and like nearly all minds could disbelieve and believe simultaneously.

Just as High Mass was beginning she rose and in grave solace left the Oratory; she would not endanger her new peace with the Virgin Mary by any devotion to other gods. She was solemn but happy. The conductor who took her penny in the motor-bus never suspected that on the pane before her, where some Agency had caused to be printed in colour the words "Seek ye the *Lord*," she saw, in addition to the amazing oddness of the Anglo-Saxon race, a dangerous incitement to unfaith. She kept her thoughts passionately on the Virgin; and by the time the bus had reached Hyde Park Corner she was utterly sure that the horrible adventure of the Promenade was purged of its evil potentialities.

In the house in Cork Street she took out her latch-key, placidly opened the door, and entered, smiling at the solitude. Marthe, who also had a soul in need of succour, would, in the ordinary course, have gone forth to a smaller church and a late mass. But on this particular morning fat Marthe, in déshabille, came running to her from the little kitchen.

"Oh! Madame!... There is someone! He is drunk."

Her voice was outraged. She pointed fearfully to the bedroom. Christine, courageous, walked straight in. An officer in khaki was lying on the bed; his muddy, spurred boots had soiled the white lace coverlet. He was asleep and snoring. She looked at him, and, recognising her acquaintance of the previous night, wondered what the very clement Virgin could be about.

17

SUNDAY AFTERNOON

"What is Madame going to do?" Whispered Marthe, still alarmed and shocked, when they had both stepped back out of the bedroom; and she added: "He has never been here before."

Marthe was a woman of immense experience but little brains, and when phenomena passed beyond her experience she became rather like a foolish, raw girl. She had often dealt with drunken men; she had often – especially in her younger days – satisfactorily explained a situation to visitors who happened to call when her mistress for the time being was out. But only on the very rarest occasions had she known a client commit the awful solecism of calling before lunch; and that a newcomer, even intoxicated, should commit this solecism staggered her and left her trembling.

"What am I going to do? Nothing!" answered Christine. "Let him sleep."

Christine, too, was dismayed. But Marthe's weakness gave her strength, and she would not show her fright. Moreover, Christine had some force of character, though it did not often show itself as sudden firmness. She condescended to Marthe. She also condescended to the officer, because he was unconscious, because he had put himself in a false position, because sooner or later he would look extremely silly. She regarded the officer's intrusion as tiresome, but she did not gravely resent it. After all, he was drunk; and before the row in the Promenade he had asked her for her card, saying that he was engaged that night but would like to know where she lived. Of course she had protested – as what woman in her place would not? – against the theory that he was engaged that night, and she had been in a fair way to convince him that he was not really engaged that night – except morally to her, since he had accosted her – when the quarrel had supervened and it had dawned on her that he had been in the taciturn and cautious stage of acute inebriety.

He had, it now seemed, probably been drinking through the night. There were men, as she knew, who simply had to have bouts, whose only method to peace was to drown the demon within them. She would never knowingly touch a drunken man, or even a partially intoxicated man. if she could help it. She was not a bit like the polite young lady above, who seemed to specialise in noisy tipplers. Her way with the top-heavy was to leave them to recover in tranquillity. No other way was safe. Nevertheless, in the present instance she did venture again into the bedroom. The plight of the lace coverlet troubled her and practically drove her into the bedroom. She got a little towel, gently lifted the sleeper's left foot, and tied the towel round his boot; then she did the same to his other foot. The man did not stir; but if, later, he should stir, neither his boots nor his spurs could do further harm to the lace coverlet. His cane and gloves were on the floor; she picked them up. His overcoat, apparently of excellent quality, was still on his back; and the cap had not quite departed from his head. Christine had learned enough about English military signs and symbols to enable her to perceive that he belonged to the artillery.

"But how will madame change her dress?" Marthe demanded in the sitting-room. Madame always changed her dress immediately on returning from church, for that which is suitable for mass may not be proper to other ends.

"I shall not change," said Christine.

"It is well, madame."

Christine was not deterred from changing by the fact that the bedroom was occupied. She retained her church dress because she foresaw the great advantage she would derive from it in the encounter which must ultimately occur with the visitor. She would not even take her hat off.

The two women lunched, mainly on macaroni, with some cheese and an apple. Christine had coffee. Ah, she must always have her coffee. As for a cigarette, she never smoked when alone, because she did not really care for smoking. Marthe, however, enjoyed smoking, and Christine gave her a cigarette, which she lighted while clearing the table. One was mistress, the other servant, but the two women were constantly meeting on the plane of equality. Neither of them could avoid it, or consistently tried to avoid it. Although Marthe did not eat with Christine, if a meal was in progress she generally came into the sitting-room with her mouth more or less full of food. Their repasts were trifles, passovers, unceremonious and irregular peckings, begun and finished in a few moments. And if Marthe was always untidy in her person, Christine, up till three in the afternoon, was also untidy. They went about the flat in a wonderful state of unkempt and insecure slovenliness. And sometimes Marthe might be lolling in the sitting-room over the illustrations in *La Vie Parisienne*, which was part of the apparatus of the flat, while Christine was in the tiny kitchen washing gloves as she alone could wash them.

The flat lapsed into at any rate a superficial calm. Marthe, seeing that fate had deprived her of the usual consolations of religion, determined to reward herself by remaining a perfect slattern for the rest of the day. She would not change at all. She would not wash up either the breakfast things or the lunch things. Leaving a small ring. of gas alight in the gas stove, she sat down all dirty on a hard chair in front of it and fell into a luxurious catalepsy. In the sitting-room Christine sat upright on the sofa and read lusciously a French translation of *East Lynne*.

She was in no hurry for the man to waken; her sense of time was very imperfect; she was never pricked by the thought that life is short and that many urgent things demand to be done before the grave opens. Nor was she apprehensive of unpleasant complications. The man was in the flat, but it was her flat; her law ran in the flat; and the door was fast against invasion. Still, the gentle snore of the man, rising and falling, dominated the flat, and the fact of his presence preoccupied the one woman in the kitchen and the other in the sitting-room...

Christine noticed that the thickness of the pages read had imperceptibly increased to three-quarters of an inch, while the thickness of the unread pages had diminished to a quarter of an inch. And she also noticed, on the open page, another phenomenon. It was the failing of the day – the faintest shadow on the page. With incredible transience another of those brief interruptions of darkness which in London in winter are called days was ending. She rose and went to the discreetly-curtained window, and, conscious of the extreme propriety of her appearance, boldly pulled aside the curtain and looked across, through naked glass, at the hotel nearly opposite. There was not a sound, not a movement, in Cork Street. Cork Street, the flat, the hotel, the city, the universe, lay entranced and stupefied beneath the grey vapours of the Sabbath. The sensation to Christine was melancholy, but it was exquisitely melancholy.

The solid hotel dissolved, and in its place Christine saw the interesting, pathetic phantom of her own existence. A stern, serious existence, full of disappointments, and not free from dangerous episodes, an existence which entailed much solitude and loss of liberty; but the verdict upon it was that in the main it might easily have been more unsatisfactory than it was. With her indolence and her unappeasable temperament what other vocation indeed, save that of marriage, could she have taken up? And her temperament would have rendered any marriage an impossible prison for her. She was a modest success – her mother had always counselled her against ambition – but she was a success. Her magic power was at its height. She continued to save money and had become a fairly regular frequenter of the West End branch of the Crédit Lyonnais. (Incidentally she had come to an arrangement with her Paris landlord.)

But, more important than money, she was saving her health, and especially her complexion – the source of money. Her complexion could still survive the minutest examination. She achieved this supreme end by plenty of sleep and by keeping to the minimum of alcohol. Of course she had to drink professionally; clients insisted; some of them were exhilarated by the spectacle of a girl tipsy; but she was very ingenious in avoiding alcohol. When invited to supper she would respond with an air of restrained eagerness: "Oh, yes, with pleasure!" And then carelessly add: "Unless you would prefer to come quietly home with me. My maid is an excellent cook and one is very comfortable *chez-moi*." And often the prospect thus sketched would piquantly allure a client. Nevertheless at intervals she could savour a fashionable restaurant as well as any harumscarum minx there. Her secret fear was still obesity. She was capable of imagining herself at fat as Marthe – and ruined; for, though a few peculiar amateurs appreciated solidity, the great majority of men did not. However, she was not getting stouter.

She had a secret sincere respect for certain of her own qualities; and if women of the world condemned certain other qualities in her, well, she despised women of the world – selfish idlers who did nothing, who contributed nothing, to the sum of life, whereas she was a useful and indispensable member of society, despite her admitted indolence. In this summary way she comforted herself in her loss of caste.

Without Gilbert, of course, her existence would have been fatally dull, and she might have been driven to terrible remedies against ennui and emptiness. The depth and violence of her feeling for Gilbert were indescribable – at any rate by her. She turned again from the darkening window to the sofa and sat down and tried to recall the figures of the dozens of men who had sat there, and she could recall at most six or eight, and Gilbert alone was real. What a paragon!... Her scorn for girls who succumbed to *souteneurs* was measureless; as a fact she had met few who did... She would have liked to beautify her flat for Gilbert, but in the first place she did not wish to spend money on it, in the second place she was too indolent to buckle to the enterprise, and in the third place if she beautified it she would be doing so not for Gilbert, but for the monotonous procession of her clients. Her flat was a public resort, and so she would do nothing to it. Besides, she did not care a fig about the look of furniture; the feel of furniture alone interested her; she wanted softness and warmth and no more.

She moved across to the piano, remembering that she had not practised that day, and that she had promised Gilbert to practise every day. He was teaching her. At the beginning she had dreamt of acquiring brilliance such as his on the piano, but she had soon seen the futility of the dream and had moderated her hopes accordingly. Even with terrific efforts she could not make her hands do the things that his did quite easily at the first attempt. She had, for example, abandoned the *Rosenkavalier* waltz, having never succeeded in struggling through more than about ten bars of it, and those the simplest. But her French dances she had notably improved in. She knew some of them by heart and could patter them off with a very tasteful vivacity. Instead of practising, she now played gently through a slow waltz from memory. If the snoring man was wakened, so much the worse – or so much the better! She went on playing, and evening continued to fall, until she could scarcely see the notes. Then she heard movements in the bedroom, a sigh, a bump, some English words that she did not comprehend. She still, by force of resolution, went on playing, to protect herself, to give herself countenance. At length she saw a dim male figure against the pale oblong of the doorway between the two rooms, and behind the figure a point of glowing red in the stove.

"I say – what time is it?"

She recognised the heavy, resonant, vibrating voice. She had stopped playing because she was making so many mistakes.

"Late – late!" she murmured timidly.

The next moment the figure was kneeling at her feet, and her left hand had been seized in a hot hand and kissed – respectfully.

"Forgive me, you beautiful creature!" begged the deep, imploring voice. "I know I don't deserve it. But forgive me! I worship women, honestly."

Assuredly she had not expected this development. She thought: "Is he not sober yet?" But the query had no conviction in it. She wanted to believe that he was sober. At any rate he had removed the absurd towels from his boots.

18

THE MYSTIC

"Say you forgive me!" The officer insisted.

"But there is nothing –"

"Say you forgive me!"

She had counted on a scene of triumph with him when he woke up, anticipating that he was bound to cut a ridiculous appearance. He knelt dimly there without a sign of self-consciousness or false shame. She forgave him.

"Great baby!"

Her hand was kissed again and loosed. She detected a faint, sad smile on his face.

"Ah!"

He rose, towering above her.

"I know I'm a drunken sot," he said. "It was only because I knew I was drunk that I didn't want to come with you last night. And I called this morning to apologise. I did really. I'd no other thought in my poor old head. I wanted you to understand why I tried to hit that chap. The other woman had spoken to me earlier, and I suppose she was jealous, seeing me with you. She said something to him about you, and he laughed, and I had to hit him for laughing. I couldn't hit her. If I'd caught him an upper cut with my left he'd have gone down, and he wouldn't have got up by himself – *I* warrant you –"

"What did she say?" Christine interrupted, not comprehending the technical idiom and not interested in it.

"I dunno; but he laughed – anyhow he smiled."

Christine turned on the light, and then went quickly to the window to draw the curtains.

"Take off your overcoat," she commanded him kindly.

He obeyed, blinking. She sat down on the sofa and, raising her arms, drew the pins from her hat and put it on the table. She motioned him to sit down too, and left him a narrow space between herself and the arm of the sofa, so that they were very close together. Then, with puckered brow, she examined him.

"I'd better tell you," he said. "It does me good to confess to you, you beautiful thing. I had a bottle of whisky upstairs in my room at the Grosvenor. Night before last, when I arrived there, I couldn't get to sleep in the bed. Hadn't been used to a bed for so long, you know. I had to turn out and roll myself up in a blanket on the floor. And last night I spent drinking by myself. Yes, by myself. Somehow, I don't mind telling *you*. This morning I must have been worse than I thought I was – "

He stopped and put his hand on her shoulder.

"There are tears in your eyes, little thing. Let me kiss your eyes... No! I'll respect you. I worship you. You're the nicest little woman I ever saw, and I'm a brute. But let me kiss your eyes."

She held her face seriously, even frowning somewhat. And he kissed her eyes gently, one after the other, and she smelt his contaminated breath.

He was a spare man, with a rather thin, ingenuous, mysterious, romantic, appealing face. It was true that her eyes had moistened. She was touched by his look and his tone as he told her that he had been obliged to lie on the floor of his bedroom in order to sleep. There seemed to be an infinite pathos in that trifle. He was one of the fighters. He had fought. He was come from the horrors of the battle. A man of power. He had killed. And he was probably ten or a dozen years her senior.

Nevertheless, she felt herself to be older than he was, wiser, more experienced. She almost wanted to nurse him. And for her he was, too, the protected of the very clement Virgin. Inquiries from Marthe showed that he must have entered the flat at the moment when she was kneeling at the altar and when the Lady of VII Dolours had miraculously granted to her pardon and peace. He was part of the miracle. She had a duty to him, and her duty was to brighten his destiny, to give him joy, not to let him go without a charming memory of her soft womanly acquiescences. At the same time her temperament was aroused by his personality; and she did not forget she had a living to earn; but still her chief concern was his satisfaction, not her own, and her overmastering sentiment one of dutiful, nay religious, surrender. French gratitude of the English fighter, and a mystic, fearful allegiance to the very clement Virgin – these things inspired her.

"Ah!" he sighed. "My throat's like leather." And seeing that she did not follow, he added: "Thirsty." He stretched his arms. She went to the sideboard and half filled a tumbler with soda water from the siphon.

"Drink!" she said, as if to a child.

"Just a dash! The tiniest dash!" he pleaded in his rich voice, with a glance at the whisky. "You don't know how it'll pull me together. You don't know how I need it."

But she did know, and she humoured him, shaking her head disapprovingly.

He drank and smacked his lips.

"Ah!" he breathed voluptuously, and then said in changed, playful accents: "Your French accent is exquisite. It makes English sound quite beautiful. And you're the daintiest little thing."

"Daintiest? What is that? I have much to learn in English. But it is something nice – daintiest; it is a compliment." She somehow understood then that, despite appearances, he was not really a devotee of her sex, that he was really a solitary, that he would never die of love, and that her *rôle* was a minor *rôle* in his existence. And she accepted the fact with humility, with enthusiasm, with ardour, quite ready to please and to be forgotten. In playing the slave to him she had the fierce French illusion of killing Germans.

Suddenly she noticed that he was wearing two wrist-watches, one close to the other, on his left arm, and she remarked on the strange fact.

The officer's face changed.

"Have you got a wrist-watch?" he demanded.

"No."

Silently he unfastened one of the watches and then said:

"Hold out your beautiful arm."

She did so. He fastened the watch on her arm. She was surprised to see that it was a lady's watch. The black strap was deeply scratched. She privately reconstructed the history of the watch, and decided that it must be a gift returned after a quarrel – and perhaps the scratches on the strap had something to do with the quarrel.

"I beg you to accept it," he said. "I particularly wish you to accept it."

"It's really a lovely watch," she exclaimed. "How kind you are!" She rewarded him with a warm kiss. "I have always wanted a wristwatch. And now they are so *chic*. In fact, one must have one." Moving her arm about, she admired the watch at different angles.

"It isn't going. And what's more, it won't go," he said.

"Ah!" she politely murmured.

"No! But do you know why I give you that watch?"

"Why?"

"Because it is a mascot."

"True?"

"Absolutely a mascot. It belonged to a friend of mine who is dead."

"Ah! A lady – "

"No! Not a lady. A man. He gave it me a few minutes before he died – and he was wearing it – and he told me to take it off his arm as soon as he was dead. I did so."

Christine was somewhat alarmed.

"But if he was wearing it when he died, how can it be a mascot?"

"That was what made it a mascot. Believe me, I know about these things. I wouldn't deceive you, and I wouldn't tell you it was a mascot unless I was quite certain." He spoke with a quiet, initiated authority that reassured her entirely and gave her the most perfect confidence.

"And why was your friend wearing a lady's watch?"

"I cannot tell you."

"You do not know?"

"I do not know. But I know that watch is a mascot."

"Was it at the Front – all this?"

The man nodded.

"He was wounded, killed, your friend?"

"No, no, not wounded! He was in my Battery. We were galloping some guns to a new position. He came off his horse – the horse was shot under him – he himself fell in front of a gun. Of course, the drivers dared not stop, and there was no room to swerve. Hence they had to drive right over him... Later, I came back to him. They had got him as far as the advanced dressing-station. He died in less than an hour..."

Solemnity fell between Christine and her client.

She said softly: "But if it is a mascot – do you not need it, you, at the Front? It is wrong for me to take it."

"I have my own mascot. Nothing can touch me – except my great enemy, and he is not German." With an austere gesture he indicated the glass. His deep voice was sad, but very firm. Christine felt that she was in the presence of an adept of mysticism. The Virgin had sent this man to her, and the man had given her the watch. Clearly the heavenly power had her in its holy charge.

97

"Ah, yes!" said the man in a new tone, as if realising the solemnity and its inappropriateness, and trying to dissipate it. "Ah, yes! Once we had the day of our lives together, he and I. We got a day off to go and see a new trench mortar, and we did have a time."

"Trench mortar – what is that?"

He explained.

"But tell me how it works," she insisted, not because she had the slightest genuine interest in the technical details of war – for she had not – but because she desired to help him to change the mood of the scene.

"Well, it's not so easy, you know. It was a four and a half pound shell, filled with gun-cotton slabs and shrapnel bullets packed in sawdust. The charge was black powder in a paper bag, and you stuck it at the bottom end of the pipe and put a bit of fuse into the touch-hole – but, of course, you must take care it penetrates the charge. The shell-fuse has a pinner with a detonator with the right length of fuse shoved into it; you wrap some clay round the end of the fuse to stop the flash of the charge from detonating the shell. Well, then you load the shell – "

She comprehended simply nothing, and the man, professionally absorbed, seemed to have no perception that she was comprehending nothing. She scarcely even listened. Her face was set in a courteous, formal smile; but all the time she was thinking that the man, in spite of his qualities, must be lacking in character to give a watch away to a woman to whom he had not been talking for ten minutes. His lack of character was shown also in his unshamed confession concerning his real enemy. Some men would bare their souls to a *cocotte* in a fashion that was flattering neither to themselves nor to the *cocotte*, and Christine never really respected such men. She did not really respect this man, but respectèd, and stood in awe of, his mysticism; and, further, her instinct to satisfy him, to make a spoiled boy of him, was not in the least weakened. Then, just as the man was in the middle of his description of the functioning of the trench mortar, the telephone-bell rang, and Christine excused herself.

The telephone was in the bedroom, not by the bedside – for such a situation had its inconveniences – but in the farthest corner, between the window and the washstand. As she went to the telephone she was preoccupied by one of the major worries of her vocation, the worry of keeping clients out of each other's sight. She wondered who could be telephoning to her on Sunday evening. Not Gilbert, for Gilbert never telephoned on Sunday except in the morning. She insisted, of course, on his telephoning to her daily, or almost daily. She did this to several of her more reliable friends, for there was no surer way of convincing them of the genuineness of her regard for them than to vituperate them when they failed to keep her informed of their health, their spirits, and their doings. In the case of Gilbert, however, her insistence had entirely ceased to be a professional device; she adored him violently.

The telephoner was Gilbert. He made an amazing suggestion; he asked her to come across to his flat, where she had never been and where he had never asked her to go. It had been tacitly and quite amiably understood between them that he was not one who invited young ladies to his own apartments.

Christine cautiously answered that she was not sure whether she could come.

"Are you alone?" he asked pleasantly.

"Yes, quite."

"Well, I will come and fetch you."

She decided exactly what she would do.

"No, no. I will come. I will come now. I shall be enchanted." Purposely she spoke without conviction, maintaining a mysterious reserve.

She returned to the sitting-room and the other man. Fortunately the conversation on the telephone had been in French.

99

"See!" she said, speaking and feeling as though they were intimates. "I have a lady friend who is ill. I am called to see her. I shall not be long. I swear to you I shall not be long. Wait. Will you wait?"

"Yes," he replied, gazing at her.

"Put yourself at your ease."

She was relieved to find that she could so easily reconcile her desire to please Gilbert with her pleasurable duty towards the protégé of the very clement Virgin.

19

THE VISIT

In the doorway of his flat Christine kissed G. J. vehemently, but
with a certain preoccupation; she was looking about her, very
curious. The way in which she raised her veil and raised her face,
mysteriously glanced at him, puckered her kind brow – these
things thrilled him.

She said:

"You are quite alone, of course."

She said it nicely, even benevolently; nevertheless he seemed
to hear her saying: "You are quite alone, or, of course, you
wouldn't have let me come."

"I suppose it's through here," she murmured; and without
waiting for an invitation she passed direct into the lighted
drawing-room and stood there, observant.

He followed her. They were both nervous in the midst of the
interior which he was showing her for the first time, and which
she was silently estimating. For him she made an exquisite
figure in the drawing-room. She was so correct in her church-
dress, so modest, prim and demure. And her appearance clashed
excitingly with his absolute knowledge of her secret
temperament. He had often hesitated in his judgment of her.
Was she good enough or was she not? But now he thought more
highly of her than ever. She was ideal, divine, the realisation of

a dream. And he felt extraordinarily pleased with himself because, after much cautious indecision, he had invited her to visit him. By heaven, she was young physically, and yet she knew everything! Her miraculous youthfulness rejuvenated him.

As a fact he was essentially younger than he had been for years. Not only she, but his war work, had re-vitalised him. He had developed into a considerable personage on the Lechford Committee; he was chairman of a sub-committee; he bore responsibilities and had worries. And for a climax the committee had sent him out to France to report on the accountancy of the hospitals; he had received a special passport; he had had glimpses of the immense and growing military organisation behind the Front; he had chatted in his fluent and idiomatic French with authorities military and civil; he had been ceremoniously complimented on behalf of his committee and country by high officials of the Service de Santé. A wondrous experience, from which he had returned to England with a greatly increased self-respect and a sharper apprehension of the significance of the war.

Life in London was proceeding much as usual. If on the one hand the Treasury had startlingly put an embargo upon capital issues, on the other hand the King had resumed his patronage of the theatre, and the town talked of a new Lady Teazle, and a British dye-industry had been inaugurated. But behind the thin gauze of social phenomena G. J. now more and more realistically perceived and conceived the dark shape of the war as a vast moving entity. He kept concurrently in his mind, each in its place, the most diverse factors and events: not merely the Flemish and the French battles, but the hoped-for intervention of Roumania, the defeat of the Austrians by Servia, the menace of a new Austrian attack on Servia, the rise in prices, the Russian move north of the Vistula, the raid on Yarmouth, the divulgence of the German axioms about frightfulness, the rumour of a definite German submarine policy, the terrible storm that had disorganised the entire English railway-system, and the dim distant Italian earthquake whose death-roll of thousands had produced no emotion whatever on a globe monopolised by one sole interest.

And to-night he had had private early telephonic information of a naval victory in the North Sea in which big German cruisers had been chased to their ignominious lairs and one sunk. Christine could not possibly know of this grand affair, for the Sunday night extras were not yet on the streets; he had it ready for her, eagerly waiting to pour it into her delicious lap along with the inexhaustible treasures of his heart. At that moment he envisaged the victory as a shining jewel specially created in order to give her a throb of joy.

"It seems they picked up a lot of survivors from the *Blucher*," he finished his narration, rather proudly.

She retorted, quietly but terribly scornful:

"*Zut*! You English are so naive. Why save them? Why not let them drown? Do they not deserve to drown? Look what they have done, those Boches! And you save them! Why did the German ships run away? They had set a trap – that sees itself – in addition to being cowards. You save them, and you think you have made a fine gesture; but you are nothing but simpletons." She shrugged her shoulders in inarticulate disdain.

Christine's attitude towards the war was uncomplicated by any subtleties. Disregarding all but the utmost spectacular military events, she devoted her whole soul to hatred of the Germans – and all the Germans. She believed them to be damnably cleverer than any other people on earth, and especially than the English. She believed them to be capable of all villainies whatsoever. She believed every charge brought against them, never troubling about evidence. She would have imprisoned on bread and water all Germans and all persons with German names in England. She was really shocked by the transparent idiocy of Britons who opposed the retirement of Prince Louis of Battenberg from the Navy. For weeks she had

ARNOLD BENNETT

remained happily in the delusion that Prince Louis had been shot in the Tower, and when the awakening came she had instantly decided that the sinister influence of Lord Haldane and naught else must have saved Prince Louis from a just retribution. She had a vision of England as overrun with innumerable German spies who moved freely at inexpressible speed about the country in high-powered grey automobiles with dazzling headlights, while the marvellously stupid and blind British police touched their hats to them. G. J. smiled at her in silence, aware by experience of the futility of argument. He knew quite a lot of women who had almost precisely Christine's attitude towards the war, and quite a lot of men too. But he could have wished the charming creature to be as desirable for her intelligence as for her physical and her strange spiritual charm: he could have wished her not to be providing yet another specimen of the phenomena of woman repeating herself so monotonously in the various worlds of London. The simpleton of fifty made in his soul an effort to be superior, and failed. "What is it that binds me to her?" he reflected, imagining himself to be on the edge of a divine mystery, and never expecting that he and Christine were the huge contrivances of certain active spermatozoa for producing other active spermatozoa.

Christine did not wonder what bound her to G. J. She knew, though she had never heard such a word as spermatozoa. She had a violent passion for him; it would, she feared, be eternal, whereas his passion for her could not last more than a few years. She knew what the passions of men were – so she said to herself superiorly. Her passion for him was in her smile as she smiled back at his silent smile; but in her smile there was also a convinced apostleship – for she alone was the repository of the truth concerning Germans, which truth she preached to an unheeding world. And there was something else in her baffling smile, namely, a quiet, good-natured, resigned resentment against the richness of his home. He had treated her always with generosity, and at any rate with rather more than fairness; he had not attempted to conceal that he was a man of means; she had nothing to reproach him with financially. And yet she did reproach him – for having been too modest. She had a pretty sure instinct for the price of things, and she knew that this Albany interior must have been very costly; further, it displayed what she deemed to be the taste of an exclusive aristocrat. She saw that she had been undervaluing her Gilbert. The proprietor of this flat would be entitled to seek relations of higher standing than herself in the ranks of *cocotterie*; he would be justified in spending far more money on a girl than he had spent on her. He was indeed something of a fraud with his exaggerated English horror of parade. And he lived by himself, save for servants; he was utterly free; and yet for two months he had kept her out of these splendours, prevented her from basking in the glow of these chandeliers and lounging on these extraordinary sofas and beholding herself in these terrific mirrors. Even now he was ashamed to let his servants see her. Was it altogether nice of him? Her verdict on him had not the slightest importance – even for herself. In kissing other men she generally kissed him – to cheat her appetite. She was at his mercy, whatever he was. He was useful to her and kind to her; he might be the fount of very important future advantages; but he was more than that, he was indispensable to her.

She walked exploringly into the little glittering bedroom. Beneath the fantastic dome of the bed the sheets were turned down and a suit of pyjamas laid out. On a Chinese tray on a lacquered table by the bed was a spirit-lamp and kettle, and a box of matches in an embroidered case with one match sticking out ready to be seized and struck. She gazed, and left the bedroom, saying nothing, and wandered elsewhere. The stairs were so infinitesimal and dear and delicious that they drew from her a sharp exclamation of delight. She ran up them like a child. G. J. turned switches. In the little glittering dining-room a little cold repast was laid for two on an inlaid table covered with a sheet of glass. Christine gazed, saying nothing, and wandered again to the drawing-room floor, while G. J. hovered attendant. She went to the vast Regency desk, idly fingering papers, and laid hold of a document. It was his report on the accoutancy of the Lechford Hospitals in France. She scrutinised it carefully, murmuring sentences from it aloud in her French accent. At length she dropped it; she did not put it down, she dropped it, and murmured:

"All that – what good does it do to wounded men?... True, I comprehend nothing of it – I!"

Then she sat to the piano, whose gorgeous and fantastic case might well have intimidated even a professional musician.

"Dare I?" She took off her gloves.

As she began to play her best waltz she looked round at G. J. and said:

"I adore thy staircase."

And that was all she did say about the flat. Still, her demeanour, mystifying as it might be, was benign, benevolent, with a remarkable appearance of genuine humility.

G. J., while she played, discreetly picked up the telephone and got the Marlborough Club. He spoke low, so as not to disturb the waltz, which Christine in her nervousness was stumbling over.

"I want to speak to Mr Montague Ryper. Yes, yes; he is in the club. I spoke to him about an hour ago, and he is waiting for me to ring him up... That you, Monty? Well, dear heart, I find I shan't be able to come to-night after all. I should like to awfully, but I've got these things I absolutely must finish... You understand... No, no... Is she, by Jove? By-bye, old thing."

When Christine had pettishly banged the last chord of the coda, he came close to her and said, with an appreciative smile, in English:

"Charming, my little girl."

She shook her head, gazing at the front of the piano.

He murmured – it was almost a whisper:

"Take your things off."

She looked round and up at him, and the light diffused from a thousand lustres fell on her mysterious and absorbed face.

"My little rabbit, I cannot stay with thee to-night."

The words, though he did not by any means take them as final, seriously shocked him. For five days he had known that Mrs Braiding, subject to his convenience, was going down to Bramshott to see the defender of the Empire. For four days he had hesitated whether or not he should tell her that she might stay away for the night. In the end he had told her to stay away; he had insisted that she should stay; he had protested that he was quite ready to look after himself for a night and a morning. She had gone, unwillingly, having first arranged a meal which he said he was to share with a friend – naturally, for Mrs Braiding, a male friend. She had wanted him to dine at the club, but he had explained to Mrs Braiding that he would be busy upon hospital work, and that another member of the committee would be coming to help him – the friend, of course. Even when he had contrived this elaborate and perfect plot he had still hesitated about the bold step of inviting Christine to the flat. The plan was extremely attractive, but it held dangers. Well, he had invited her. If she had not been at home, or if she had been unwilling to come, he would not have felt desolated; he would have accepted the fact as perhaps providential. But she was at home; she was willing; she had come. She was with him; she had put him into an ecstasy of satisfaction and anticipation. One evening alone with her in his own beautiful flat! What a frame for her and for love! And now she said that she would not stay. It was incredible; it could not be permitted.

"But why not? We are happy together. I have just refused a dinner because of – this. Didn't you hear me on the 'phone?"

"Thou wast wrong," she smiled. "I am not worth a dinner. It is essential that I should return home. I am tired – tired. It is Sunday night, and I have sworn to myself that I will pass this evening at home – alone."

Exasperating, maddening creature! He thought: "I fancied I knew her, and I don't know her. I'm only just beginning to know her." He stared steadily at her soft, serious, worried, enchanting face, and tried to see through it into the arcana of her queer little brain. He could not. The sweet face foiled him.

"Then why come?"

"Because I wished to be nice to thee, to prove to thee how nice I am."

She seized her gloves. He saw that she meant to go. His demeanour changed. He was aware of his power over her, and he would use it. She was being subtle; but he could be subtle too, far subtler than Christine. True, he had not penetrated her face. Nevertheless his instinct, and his male gift of ratiocination, informed him that beneath her gentle politeness she was vexed, hurt, because he had got rid of Mrs Braiding before receiving her. She had her feelings, and despite her softness she could resent. Still, her feelings must not be over-indulged; they must not be permitted to make a fool of her. He said, rather teasingly, but firmly:

"I know why she refuses to stay."

She cried, plaintive:

"It is not that I have another rendezvous. No! But naturally thou thinkest it is that."

He shook his head.

"Not at all. The little silly wants to go back home because she finds there is no servant here. She is insulted in her pride. I noticed it in her first words when she came in. And yet she ought to know – "

Christine gave a loud laugh that really disconcerted him.

"Au revoir, my old one. Embrace me." She dropped the veil.

"No!"

He could play a game of pretence longer than she could. She moved with dignity towards the door, but never would she depart like that. He knew that when it came to the point she was at the mercy of her passion for him. She had confessed the tyranny of her passion, as such victims foolishly will. Moreover he had perceived it for himself. He followed her to the door. At the door she would relent. And, sure enough, at the door she leapt at him and clasped his neck with fierceness and fiercely kissed him through her veil, and exclaimed bitterly:

"Ah! Thou dost not love me, but I love thee!"

But the next instant she had managed to open the door and she was gone.

He sprang out to the landing. She was running down the stone stairs.

"Christine!"

She did not stop. G. J. might be marvellously subtle; but he could not be subtle enough to divine that on that night Christine happened to be the devotee of the most clement Virgin, and that her demeanour throughout the visit had been contrived, half unconsciously, to enable her to perform a deed of superb self-denial and renunciation in the service of the dread goddess. He ate most miserably alone, facing an empty chair; the desolate solitude of the evening was terrible; he lacked the force to go seeking succour in clubs.

20

MASCOT

A single light burned in Christine's bedroom. It stood low on the pedestal by the wide bed and was heavily shaded, so that only one half of the bed, Christine's half, was exempt from the general gloom of the chamber. The officer had thus ordained things. The white, plump arm of Christine was imprisoned under his neck. He had ordered that too. He was asleep. Christine watched him. On her return from the Albany she had found him apparently just as she had left him, except that he was much less talkative. Indeed, though unswervingly polite – even punctilious with her – he had grown quite taciturn and very obstinate and finicking in self-assertion. There was no detail as to which he did not formulate a definite wish. Yet not until by chance her eye fell on the whisky decanter did she perceive that in her absence he had been copiously drinking again. He was not, however, drunk. Remorseful at her defection, she constituted herself his slave; she covered him with acquiescences; she drank his tippler's breath. And he was not particularly responsive. He had all his own ideas. He ought, for example, to have been hungry, but his idea was that he was not hungry; therefore he had refused her dishes.

She knew him better now. Save on one subject, discussed in the afternoon, he was a dull, narrow, direct man, especially in love. He had no fancy, no humour, no resilience. Possibly he worshipped women, as he had said, perhaps devoutly; but his worship of the individual girl tended more to ritualism than to ecstasy. The Parisian devotee was thrown away on him, and she felt it. But not with bitterness. On the contrary, she liked him to be as he was; she liked to be herself unappreciated, neglected, bored. She thought of the delights which she had renounced in the rich and voluptuous drawing-room of the Albany; she gazed under the reddish illumination at the tedious eternal market-place on which she exposed her wares, and which in Tottenham Court Road went by the name of bedstead; and she gathered nausea and painful longing to her breast as the Virgin gathered the swords of the Dolours at the Oratory, and was mystically happy in the ennui of serving the miraculous envoy of the Virgin. And when Marthe, uneasy, stole into the sitting-room, Christine, the door being ajar, most faintly transmitted to her a command in French to tranquillise herself and go away. And outside a boy broke the vast lull of the Sunday night with a shattering cry of victory in the North Sea.

Possibly it was this cry that roused the officer out of his doze. He sat up, looked unseeing at Christine's bright smile and at the black gauze that revealed the reality of her youth, and then reached for his tunic which hung at the foot of the bed.

"You asked about my mascot," he said, drawing from a pocket a small envelope of semitransparent oilskin. "Here it is. Now that is a mascot!"

He had wakened under the spell of his original theme, of his sole genuine subject. He spoke with assurance, as one inspired. His eyes, as they masterfully encountered Christine's eyes, had a strange, violent, religious expression. Christine's eyes yielded to his, and her smile vanished in seriousness. He undid the envelope and displayed an oval piece of red cloth with a picture of Christ, his bleeding heart surrounded by flames and thorns and a great cross in the background.

"That," said the officer, "will bring anybody safe home again." Christine was too awed even to touch the red cloth. The vision of the dishevelled, inspired man in khaki shirt, collar and tie, holding the magic saviour in his thin, veined, aristocratic hand, powerfully impressed her, and she neither moved nor spoke.

"Have you seen the 'Touchwood' mascot?" he asked. She signified a negative, and then nervously fingered her gauze. "No? It's a well-known mascot. Sort of tiny imp sort of thing, with a huge head, glittering eyes, a khaki cap of *oak*, and crossed legs in gold and silver. I hear that tens of thousands of them are sold. But there is nothing like my mascot."

"Where have you got it?" Christine asked in her queer but improving English.

"Where did I get it? Just after Mons, on the road, in a house."

"Have you been in the retreat?"

"I was."

"And the angels? Have you seen them?"

He paused, and then said with solemnity:

"Was it an angel I saw?... I was lying doggo by myself in a hole, and bullets whizzing over me all the time. It was nearly dark, and a figure in white came and stood by the hole; he stood quite still and the German bullets went on just the same. Suddenly I saw he was wounded in the hand; it was bleeding. I said to him: 'You're hit in the hand.' 'No,' he said – he had a most beautiful voice – 'that is an old wound. It has reopened lately. I have another wound in the other hand.' And he showed me the other hand, and that was bleeding too. Then the firing ceased, and he pointed, and although I'd eaten nothing at all that day and was dead-beat, I got up and ran the way he pointed, and in five minutes I ran into what remained of my unit."

The officer's sonorous tones ceased; he shut his lips tightly, as though clinching the testimony, and the life of the bedroom was suspended in absolute silence.

"That's what *I* saw… And with the lack of food my brain was absolutely clear."

Christine, on her back, trembled.

The officer replaced his mascot. Then he said, waving the little bag:

"Of course, there are fellows who don't need mascots. Fellows that if their name isn't written on a bullet or a piece of shrapnel it won't reach them any more than a letter not addressed to you would reach you. Now my Colonel, for instance – it was he who told me how good my mascot was – well, he can stop shells, turn 'em back. Yes. He's just got the D.S.O. And he said to me, 'Edgar,' he said, 'I don't deserve it. I got it by inspiration.' And so he did… What time's that?"

The gilded Swiss clock in the drawing-room was striking its tiny gong.

"Nine o'clock."

The officer looked dully at his wrist-watch which, not having been wound on the previous night, had inconsiderately stopped.

"Then I can't catch my train at Victoria." He spoke in a changed voice, lifeless, and sank back on the bed.

"Train? What train?"

"Nothing. Only the leave train. My leave is up to-night. To-morrow I ought to have been back in the trenches."

"But you have told me nothing of it! If you had told me – But not one word, my dear."

"When one is with a woman – !"

He seemed gloomily and hopelessly to reproach her.

21

THE LEAVE-TRAIN

"What o'clock – your train?"

"Nine-thirty."

"But you can catch it. You must catch it."

He shook his head. "It's fate," he muttered, bitterly resigned. "What is written is written."

Christine sprang to the floor, shuffled off the black gauze in almost a single movement, and seized some of her clothes.

"Quick! You shall catch your train. The clock is wrong – the clock is too soon."

She implored him with positive desperation. She shook him and dragged him, energised in an instant by the overwhelming idea that for him to miss his train would be fatal to him – and to her also. She could and did believe in the efficacy of mascots against bullets and shrapnel and bayonets. But the traditions of a country of conscripts were ingrained in her childhood and youth, and she had not the slightest faith in the efficacy of no matter what mascot to protect from the consequences of indiscipline. And already during her short career in London she had had good reason to learn the sacredness of the leave-train. Fantastic tales she had heard of capital executions for what seemed trifling laxities – tales whispered half proudly by the army in the rooms of horrified courtesans – tales in which the

114

remote and ruthless imagined figure of the Grand Provost-Marshal rivalled that of God himself. And, moreover, if this man fell into misfortune through her, she would eternally lose the grace of the most clement Virgin who had confided him to her and who was capable of terrible revenges. She secretly called on the Virgin. Nay, she became the Virgin. She found a miraculous strength, and furiously pulled the poor sot out of bed. The fibres of his character had been soaked away, and she mystically replaced them with her own. Intimidated and, as it were, mesmerised, he began to dress. She rushed as she was to the door.

"Marthe! Marthe!"

"Madame?" replied the fat woman in alarm.

"Run for a taxi."

"But, madame, it is raining terribly."

"*Fe m'en fous!* Run for a taxi."

Turning back into the room she repeated; "The clock is too soon." But she knew that it was not. Nearly nude, she put on a hat.

"What are you doing?" he asked.

"Do not worry. I come with you."

She took a skirt and a jersey and then threw a cloak over everything. He was very slow; he could find nothing; he could button nothing. She helped him. But when he began to finger his leggings with the endless laces and the innumerable eyelets she snatched them from him.

"Those – in the taxi," she said.

"But there is no taxi."

"There will be a taxi. I have sent the maid."

At the last moment, as she was hurrying him on to the staircase, she grasped her handbag. They stumbled one after the other down the dark stairs. He had now caught the infection of her tremendous anxiety. She opened the front door. The glistening street was absolutely empty; the rain pelted on the pavements and the roadway, each drop falling like a missile and raising a separate splash, so that it seemed as if the flood on the earth was leaping up to meet the flood from the sky.

"Come!" she said with hysterical impatience. "We cannot wait. There will be a taxi in Piccadilly, I know."

Simultaneously a taxi swerved round the corner of Burlington Street. Marthe stood on the step next to the driver. As the taxi halted she jumped down. Her drenched white apron was over her head and she was wet to the skin.

In the taxi, while the officer struck matches, Christine knelt and fastened his leggings; he could not have performed the nice operation for himself. And all the time she was doing something else – she was pushing forward the whole taxi, till her muscles ached with the effort. Then she sat back on the seat, smoothed her hair under the hat, unclasped the bag, and patted her features delicately with the powder-puff. Neither knew the exact time, and in vain they tried to discern the faces of clocks that flew past them in the heavy rain. Christine sighed and said:

"These tempests. This rain. They say it is because of the big cannons – which break the clouds."

The officer, who had the air of being in a dream, suddenly bent towards her and replied with a most strange solemnity:

"It is to wash away the blood!"

She had not thought of that. Of course it was! She sighed again.

As they neared Victoria the officer said: "My kit-bag! It's at the hotel. Shall I have time to pay my bill and get it? The Grosvenor's next to the station, you know."

She answered unhesitatingly: "You will go direct to the train. I will try the hotel."

"Drive round to the Grosvenor entrance like hell," he instructed the driver when the taxi stopped in the station yard.

In the hotel she would never have got the bag, owing to her difficulties in explaining the situation in English to a haughty reception-clerk, had not a French-Swiss waiter been standing by. She flung imploring French sentences at the waiter like a stream from a hydrant. The bill was produced in less than half a minute. She put down money of her own to pay for it, for she had refused to wait at the station while the officer fished in the obscurities of his purse. The bag, into which a menial had crammed a kit probably scattered about the bedroom, arrived unfastened. Once more at the station, she gave the cabman all the change which she had received at the hotel counter. By a miracle she made a porter understand what was needed and how urgently it was needed. He said the train was just going, and ran. She ran after him. The ticket-collector at the platform gate allowed the porter to pass, but raised an implacable arm to prevent her from following. She had no platform ticket, and she could not possibly be travelling by the train. Then she descried her officer standing at an open carriage door in conversation with another officer and tapping his leggings with his cane. How aristocratic and disdainful and self-absorbed the pair looked! They existed in a world utterly different from hers. They were the triumphant and negligent males. She endeavoured to direct the porter with her pointing hand, and then, hysterical again, she screamed out the one identifying word she knew: "Edgar!"

It was lost in the resounding echoes of the immense vault. Edgar certainly did not hear it. But he caught the great black initials, "E. W." on the kit-bag as the porter staggered along, and stopped the aimless man, and the kit-bag was thrown into the apartment. Doors were now banging. Christine saw Edgar take out his purse and fumble at it. But Edgar's companion pushed Edgar into the train and himself gave a tip which caused the porter to salute extravagantly. The porter, at any rate, had been rewarded. Christine began to cry, not from chagrin, but with relief. Women on the platform waved absurd little white handkerchiefs. Heads and khaki shoulders stuck out of the carriage windows of the shut train. A small green flag waved;

arms waved like semaphores. The train ought to have been gliding away, but something delayed it, and it was held as if spellbound under the high, dim semicircle of black glass, amid the noises of steam, the hissing of electric globes, the horrible rattle of luggage trucks, the patter of feet, and the vast, murmuring gloom. Christine saw Edgar leaning from a window and gazing anxiously about. The little handkerchiefs were still courageously waving, and she, too, waved a little wisp. But he did not see her; he was not looking in the right place for her.

She thought: Why did he not stay near the gate for me? But she thought again: Because he feared to miss the train. It was necessary that he should be close to his compartment. He knows he is not quite sober.

She wondered whether he had any relatives, or any relations with another woman. He seemed to be as solitary as she was.

On the same side of the platform-gate as herself a very tall, slim, dandy of an officer was bending over a smartly-dressed girl, smiling at her and whispering. Suddenly the girl turned from him with a disdainful toss of the head and said in a loud, clear Cockney voice:

"You can't tell the tale to me, young man. This is my second time on earth."

Christine heard the words, but was completely puzzled. The train moved, at first almost imperceptibly. The handkerchiefs showed extreme agitation. Then a raucous song floated from the train:

"John Brown's baby's got a pimple on his – *shoooo* –
John Brown's baby's got a pimple on his – *shoooo* –
John Brown's baby's got a pimple on his – *shoooo* –
and we all went marching home.
Glory, glory, Alleluia! Glory, glory..."

The rails showed empty where the train had been, and the sound of the song faded and died. Some of the women were crying. Christine felt she was in a land of which she understood nothing but the tears. She also felt very cold in the legs.

22

GETTING ON WITH THE WAR

The floors of the Renolds galleries were covered with some hundreds of very well-dressed and very expensively-dressed women and some scores of men. The walls were covered with a loan collection of oil-paintings, water-colour drawings, and etchings – English and French, but chiefly English. A very large proportion of the pictures were portraits of women done by a select group of very expensive painters in the highest vogue. These portraits were the main attraction of the elegant crowd, which included many of the sitters; as for the latter, they failed to hide under an unconvincing mask of indifference their curiosity as to their own effectiveness in a frame.

The portraits for the most part had every quality save that of sincerity. They were transcendantly adroit and they reeked of talent. They were luxurious, refined, sensual, titillating, exquisite, tender, compact, of striking poses and subtle new tones. And while the heads were well finished and instantly recognisable as likenesses, the impressionism of the hands and of the provocative draperies showed that the artists had fully realised the necessity of being modern. The mischief and the damnation were that the sitters liked them because they produced in the sitters the illusion that the sitters were really what the sitters wanted to be, and what indeed nearly every woman in the galleries wanted to be; and the ideal of the sitters was a low ideal. The portraits flattered; but only a few guessed that they flattered ignobly; scarcely any even of the artists guessed that.

The portraits were a success; the exhibition was a success; and all the people at the private view justly felt that they were part of and contributing to the success. And though seemingly the aim of everybody was to prove to everybody else that no war, not the greatest war, could disturb the appearances of social life in London, yet many were properly serious and proud in their seriousness. It was the autumn of 1915. British troops were triumphantly on the road to Kut, and British forces were approaching decisive victory in Gallipoli. The Russians had turned on their pursuers. The French had initiated in Champagne an offensive so dramatic that it was regarded as the beginning of the end. And the British on their left, in the taking of Loos and Hill 70, had achieved what might have been regarded as the greatest success on the Western Front, had it not been for the rumour, current among the informed personages at the Reynolds Galleries, that recent bulletins had been reticent to the point of deception and that, in fact, Hill 70 had ceased to be ours a week earlier. Further, Zeppelins had raided London and killed and wounded numerous Londoners, and all present in the Reynolds Galleries were aware, from positive statements in the newspapers, that whereas German morale was crumbling, all Londoners, including themselves, had behaved with the most marvellous stoic calm in the ordeal of the Zeppelins.

The assembly had a further and particular reason for serious pride. It was getting on with the war, and in a most novel way. Private views are customarily views gratis. But the entry to this private view cost a guinea, and there was absolutely no free list. The guineas were going to the support of the Lechford Hospitals in France. The happy idea was G. J.'s own, and Lady Queenie Paulle and her mother had taken the right influential measures to ensure its grandiose execution. A queen had visited the private view for half an hour. Thus all the very well-dressed and very expensively-dressed women, and all the men who admired and desired them as they moved, in voluptuous perfection, amid dazzling pictures with the soft illumination of screened skylights above and the reflections in polished parquet below – all of both sexes were comfortably conscious of virtue in the undoubted fact that they were helping to support two renowned hospitals where at that very moment dissevered legs and arms were being thrown into buckets.

In a little room at the end of the galleries was a small but choice collection of the etchings of Félicien Rops: a collection for connoisseurs, as the critics were to point out in the newspapers the next morning. For Rops, though he had an undeniable partiality for subjects in which ugly and prurient women displayed themselves in nothing but the inessentials of costume, was a classic before whom it was necessary to bow the head in homage.

G. J. was in this room in company with a young and handsome Staff officer, Lieutenant Molder, home on convalescent leave from Suvla Bay. Mr Molder had left Oxford in order to join the army; he had behaved admirably, and well earned the red shoulder-ornaments which pure accident had given him. He was a youth of artistic and literary tastes, with genuine ambitions quite other than military, and after a year of horrible existence in which he had hungered for the arts more than for anything, he was solacing and renewing himself in the contemplation of all the masterpieces that London could show. He greatly esteemed G. J.'s connoisseurship, and G. J. had taken him in hand. At the close of a conscientious and highly critical round of the galleries they had at length reached the Rops room, and they were discussing every aspect of Rops except his lubricity, when Lady Queenie Paulle approached them from behind. Molder was the first to notice her and turn. He blushed.

"Well, Queen," said G. J., who had already had several conversations with her in the galleries that day and on the previous days of preparation.

ARNOLD BENNETT

She replied:

"Well, I hope you're satisfied with the results of your beautiful idea."

The young woman, slim and pale, had long since gone out of mourning. She was most brilliantly attired, and no detail lacked to the perfection of her modish outfit. Indeed, just as she was, she would have made a marvellous mannequin, except for the fact that mannequins are not usually allowed to perfume themselves in business hours. Her thin, rather high voice, which somehow matched her complexion and carriage, had its customary tone of amiable insolence, and her tired, drooping eyes their equivocal glance, as she faced the bearded and grave middle-aged bachelor and the handsome, muscular boy; even the boy was older than Queen, yet she seemed to condescend to them as if she were an immortal from everlasting to everlasting and could teach both of them all sorts of useful things about life. Nobody could have guessed from that serene demeanour that her self-satisfaction was marred by any untoward detail whatever. Yet it was. All her frocks were designed to conceal a serious defect which seriously disturbed her: she was low-breasted.

G. J. said bluntly:

"May I present Mr Molder? – Lady Queenie Paulle."

And he said to himself, secretly annoyed:

"Dash the infernal chit. That's what she's come for. Now she's got it."

She gave the slightest, dubious nod to Molder, who, having faced fighting Turks with an equanimity equal to Queenie's own, was yet considerably flurried by the presence and the gaze of this legendary girl. Queenie, enjoying his agitation, but affecting to ignore him, began to talk quickly in the vein of exclusive gossip; she mentioned in a few seconds the topics of the imminent entry of Bulgaria into the war, the maturing Salonika expedition, the confidential terrible utterances of K. on recruiting, and, of course, the misfortune (due to causes which Queenie had at her finger-ends) round about Loos. Then in regard to the last she suddenly added, quite unjustifiably implying that the two phenomena were connected: 'You know, mother's hospitals are frightfully full just now... But, of course, you do know. That's why I'm so specially glad to-day's such a success."

Thus in a moment, and with no more than ten phrases, she had conveyed the suggestion that while mere soldiers, ageing men-about-town, and the ingenuous mass of the public might and did foolishly imagine the war to be a simple affair, she herself, by reason of her intelligence and her private sources of knowledge, had a full, unique apprehension of its extremely complex and various formidableness. G. J. resented the familiar attitude, and he resented Queenie's very appearance and the appearance of the entire opulent scene. In his head at that precise instant were not only the statistics of mortality and major operations at the Lechford Hospitals, but also the astounding desolating tales of the handsome boy about folly, ignorance, stupidity and martyrdoms at Suvla.

He said, with the peculiar polite restraint that in him masked emotion and acrimony:

"Yes, I'm glad it's a success. But the machinery of it is perhaps just slightly out of proportion to the results. If people had given to the hospitals what they have spent on clothes to come here and what they've paid painters so that they could see themselves on the walls, we should have made twenty times as much as we have made – a hundred times as much. Why, good god! Queen, the whole afternoon's takings wouldn't buy what you're wearing now, to say nothing of the five hundred other women here." His eye rested on the badge of her half-brother's regiment which she had had reproduced in diamonds.

At this juncture he heard himself addressed in a hearty, heavy voice as "G. J., old soul." An officer with the solitary crown on his sleeve, bald, stoutish, but probably not more than forty-five, touched him – much gentlier than he spoke – on the shoulder.

"Craive, my son! You back! Well, it's startling to see you at a picture-show, anyhow."

The Major, saluting Lady Queenie as a distant acquaintance, retorted:

"Morally, you owe me a guinea, my dear G. J. I called at the flat, and the young woman there told me you'd surely be here."

While they were talking G. J. could hear Queenie Paulle and Molder:

"Where are you back from?"

"Suvla, Lady Queenie."

"You must be oozing with interest and actuality. Tell G. J. to bring you to tea one day, quite, quite soon, will you? *I'll* tell him." And Molder murmured something fatuously conventional. G. J. showed decorously that he had caught his own name. Whereupon Lady Queenie, instead of naming a day for tea, addressed him almost bitterly:

"G. J., what's come over you? What in the name of Pan do you suppose all you males are fighting each other for?" She paused effectively. "Good god! If I began to dress like a housemaid the Germans would be in London in a month. Our job as women is quite delicate enough without you making it worse by any damned sentimental superficiality... I want you to bring Mr Molder to tea *to-morrow*, and if you can't come he must come alone..."

With a last strange look at Molder she retired into the glitter of the crowded larger room.

"She been driving any fresh men to suicide lately?" Major Craive demanded acidly under his breath.

G. J. raised his eyebrows.

Then: "That's not *you*, Frankie!" said the Major with a start of recognition towards the Staff lieutenant.

"Yes, sir," said Molder.

They shook hands. At the previous Christmas they had lain out together on the cliffs of the east coast in wild weather, waiting to repel a phantom army of thirty thousand Germans.

"It was the red hat put me off," the Major explained.

"Not my fault, sir," Molder smiled.

"Devilish glad to see you, my boy."

G. J. murmured to Molder:

"You don't want to go and have tea with her, do you?"

And Molder answered, with the somewhat fatuous, self-conscious grin that no amount of intelligence can keep out of the face of a good-looking fellow who knows that he has made an impression:

"Well, I don't know – "

G. J. raised his eyebrows again, but with indulgence, and winked at Craive.

The Major shut his lips tight, then stood with his mouth open for a second or two in the attitude of a man suddenly receiving the onset of a great and original idea.

"She's right, hang it all!" he exclaimed. "She's right! Of course she is! Why, what's all this" – he waved an arm at the whole scene – "what's all this but sex? Look at 'em! And look at their portraits! You aren't going to tell me! What's the good of pretending? Hang it all, when my own aunt comes down to breakfast in a low-cut blouse that would have given her fits even in the evening ten years ago!… And jolly fine too. I'm all for it. The more of it the merrier – that's what I say. And don't any of you highbrows go trying to alter it. If you do I retire, and you can defend your own bally Front."

"Craive," said G. J. affectionately, "until you and Queen came along Molder and I really thought we were at a picture exhibition, and we still think so, don't we, Molder?" The Lieutenant nodded. "Now, as you're here, just let me show you one or two things."

"Oh!" breathed the Major, "have pity. It's not any canvas woman that I want – By Jove!" He caught sight of an invention of Félicien Rops, a pig on the end of a string, leading, or being driven by, a woman who wore nothing but stockings, boots and a hat. "What do you call that?"

"My dear fellow, that's one of the most famous etchings in the world."

"Is it?" the Major said. "Well, I'm not surprised. There's more in this business than I imagined." He set himself to examine all the exhibits by Rops, and when he had finished he turned to G. J.

"Listen here, G. J. We're going to make a night of it. I've decided on that."

"Sorry, dear heart," said G. J. "I'm engaged with Molder to-night. We shall have some private chamber-music at my rooms – just for ourselves. You ought to come. Much better for your health."

"What time will the din be over?"

"About eleven."

"Now I say again – listen here. Let's talk business. I'll come to your chamber-music. I've been before, and survived, and I'll come again. But afterwards you'll come with me to the Guinea-Fowl."

"But, my dear chap, I can't throw Molder out into Vigo Street at eleven o'clock," G. J. protested, startled by the blunt mention of the notorious night-club in the young man's presence.

"Naturally you can't. He'll come along with us. Frankie and I have nearly fallen into the North Sea or German Ocean together, haven't we, Frankie? It'll be my show. And I'll turn up with the stuff – one, two or three pretty ladies according as your worship wishes."

G. J. was now more than startled; he was shocked; he felt his cheeks reddening. It was the presence of Molder that confused him. Never had he talked to Molder on any subjects but the arts, and if they had once or twice lighted on the topic of women it was only in connection with the arts. He was really

126

interested in and admired Molder's unusual aesthetic intelligence, and he had done what he could to foster it, and he immensely appreciated Molder's youthful esteem for himself. Moreover, he was easily old enough to be Molder's father. It seemed to him that though two generations might properly mingle in anything else, they ought not to mingle in licence. Craive's crudity was extraordinary.

"See here!" Craive went on, serious and determined. "You know the sort of thing I've come from. I got four days unexpected. I had to run down to my uncle's. The old things would have died if I hadn't. To-morrow I go back. This is my last night. I haven't had a scratch up to now. But my turn's coming, you bet. Next week I may be in heaven or hell or anywhere, or blind for life or without my legs or any damn thing you please. But I'm going to have to-night, and you're going to join in."

G. J. saw the look of simple, half-worshipful appeal that sometimes came into Craive's rather ingenuous face. He well knew that look, and it always touched him. He remembered certain descriptive letters which he had received from Craive at the Front, – they corresponded faithfully. He could not have explained the intimacy of his relations with Craive. They had begun at a club, over cards. The two had little in common – Craive was a stockbroker when world-wars did not happen to be in progress – but G. J. greatly liked him because, with all his crudity, he was such a decent, natural fellow, so kind-hearted, so fresh and unassuming. And Craive on his part had developed an admiration for G. J. which G. J. was quite at a loss to account for. The one clue to the origin of the mysterious attachment between them had been a naive phrase which he had once overheard Craive utter to a mutual acquaintance: "Old G. J.'s so subtle, isn't he?"

G. J. said to himself, reconsidering the proposal:

"And why on earth not?"

And then aloud, soothingly, to Craive:

"All right! All right!"

The Major brightened and said to Molder:

"You'll come, of course?"

"Oh, rather!" answered Molder, quite simply.

And G. J., again to himself, said:

"I am a simpleton."

The Major's pleading, and the spectacle of the two officers with their precarious hold on life, humiliated G. J. as well as touched him. And, if only in order to avoid the momentary humiliation, he would have been well content to be able to roll back his existence and to have had a military training and to be with them in the sacred and proud uniform.

"Now listen here!" said the Major. "About the aforesaid pretty ladies – "

There they stood together in the corner, hiding several of Rops's eccentricities, ostensibly discussing art, charity, world-politics, the strategy of war, the casualty lists.

23

THE CALL

Christine found the night at the Guniea-foul rather dull. The supper-room, garish and tawdry in its decorations, was functioning as usual. The round tables and the square tables, the tables large and the tables small, were well occupied with mixed parties and couples. Each table had its own yellow illumination, and the upper portion of the room, with a certain empty space in the centre of it, was bafflingly shadowed. Between two high, straight falling curtains could be seen a section of the ball-room, very bright against the curtains, with the figures of dancers whose bodies seemed to be glued to each other, pale to black or pale to khaki, passing slowly and rhythmically across. The rag-time music, over a sort of ground-bass of syncopated tom-tom, surged through the curtains like a tide of the sea of Aphrodite, and bathed everyone at the supper-tables in a mysterious aphrodisiacal fluid. The waiters alone were insensible to its influence. They moved to and fro with the impassivity and disdain of eunuchs separated for ever from the world's temptations. Loud laughs or shrill little shrieks exploded at intervals from the sinister melancholy of the interior.

On Christine's left, at a round table in a corner, sat G. J.; on her right, the handsome boy Molder. On Molder's right, Miss Aida Altown spread her amplitude, and on G. J.'s left was a young girl known to the company as Alice. Major Craive, the host, the splendid quality of whose hospitality was proved by the flowers, the fruit, the bottles, the cigar-boxes and the cigarette-boxes on the table, sat between Alice and Aida Altown.

The three women on principle despised and scorned each other with false warm smiles and sudden outbursts of compliment. Christine knew that the other two detested her as being "one of those French girls" who, under the protection of Free Trade, came to London and, by their lack of scruple and decency, took the bread out of the mouths of the nice, modest, respectable, English girls. She on her side disdained both of them, not merely because they were courtesans (which somehow Christine considered she really was not), but also for their characteristic insipidity, lackadaisicalness and ignorance of the technique of the profession. They expected to be paid for doing nothing.

Aida Altown she knew by sight as belonging to a great rival Promenade. Aida had reached the purgatory of obesity which Christine always feared. Despite the largeness of her mass, she was a very beautiful woman in the English manner, blonde, soft, idle, without a trace of temperament, and incomparably dull and stupid. But she was ageing; she had been favourably known in the West End continuously (save for a brief escapade in New York) for perhaps a quarter of a century. She was at the period when such as she realise with flaccid alarm that they have no future, and when they are ready to risk grave imprudences for youths who feel flattered by their extreme maturity. Christine gazed calmly at her, supercilious and secure in the immense advantage of at least fifteen years to the good.

And if she shrugged her shoulders at Aida for being too old, Christine did the same at Alice for being too young. Alice was truly a girl – probably not more than seventeen. Her pert, pretty, infantile face was an outrage against the code. She was a mere amateur, with everything to learn, absurdly presuming upon the very quality which would vanish first. And she was a fool. She obviously had no sense, not even the beginnings of sense. She was wearing an impudently expensive frock which must have cost quite five times as much as Christine's own, though the latter in the opinion of the wearer was by far the more authentically *chic*. And she talked proudly at large about her losses on the turf and of the swindles practised upon her. Christine admitted that the girl could make plenty of money, and would continue to make money for a long, long time, bar accidents, but her final conclusion about Alice was: "She will end on straw."

The supper was over. The conversation had never been vivacious, and now it was half-drowned in champagne. The girls had wanted to hear about the war, but the Major, who had arrived in a rather dogmatic mood, put an absolute ban on shop. Alice had then kept the talk, such as it was, upon her favourite topic – revues. She was an encyclopaedia of knowledge concerning revues past, present, and to come. She had once indeed figured for a few grand weeks in a revue chorus, thereby acquiring unique status in her world. The topic palled upon both Aida and Christine. And Christine had said to herself: "They are aware of nothing, those two," for Aida and Alice had proved to be equally and utterly ignorant of the superlative social event of the afternoon, the private view at the Reynolds Galleries – at which indeed Christine had not assisted, but of which she had learnt all the intimate details from G. J. What, Christine demanded, *could* be done with such a pair of ninnies?

She might have been excused for abandoning all attempt to behave as a woman of the world should at a supper party. Nevertheless, she continued good-naturedly and conscientiously in the performance of her duty to charm, to divert, and to enliven. After all, the ladies were there to captivate the males, and if Aida and Alice dishonestly flouted obligations, Christine would not. She would, at any rate, show them how to behave.

131

She especially attended to G. J., who having drunk little, was taciturn and preoccupied in his amiabilities. She divined that something was the matter, but she could not divine that his thoughts were saddened by the recollection at the Guinea-Fowl of the lovely music which he had heard earlier in his drawing-room and by the memory of the Major's letters and of what the Major had said at the Reynolds Galleries about the past and the possibilities of the future. The Major was very benevolently intoxicated, and at short intervals he raised his glass to G. J., who did not once fail to respond with an affectionate smile which Christine had never before seen on G. J.'s face.

Suddenly Alice, who had been lounging semi-somnolent with an extinct cigarette in her jewelled fingers, sat up and said in the uncertain voice of an inexperienced girl who has ceased to count the number of glasses emptied:

"Shall I recite? I've been trained, you know."

And, not waiting for an answer, she stood and recited, with a surprisingly correct and sure pronunciation of difficult words to show that she had, in fact, received some training:

> Helen, thy beauty is to me
> Like those Nicean barks of yore,
> That gently o'er a perfumed sea
> The weary, wayworn wanderer bore
> To his own native shore.
> On desperate seas long wont to roam,
> Thy hyacinth hair, thy classic face,
> Thy naiad airs have brought me home
> To the glory that was Greece,
> To the grandeur that was Rome.
> Lo! In your brilliant window niche,
> How statue-like I see thee stand,
> The agate lamp within thy hand!
> Ah, Psyche from the regions which

Are Holy Land!

The uncomprehended marvellous poem, having startled the whole room, ceased, and the rag-time resumed its sway. A drunken "Bravo!" came from one table, a cheer from another. Young Alice nodded an acknowledgment and sank loosely into her chair, exhausted by her last effort against the spell of champagne and liqueurs. And the naive, big Major, bewitched by the child, subsided into soft contact with her, and they almost tearfully embraced. A waiter sedately replaced a glass which Alice's drooping, negligent hand had over-turned, and wiped the cloth. G. J. was silent. The whole table was silent.

"*Est-ce de la grande poésie?*" asked Christine of G. J., who did not reply. Christine, though she condemned Alice as now disgusting, had been taken aback and, in spite of herself, much impressed by the surprising display of elocution.

"*Oui*," said Molder, in his clipped, self-conscious Oxford French.

Two couples from other tables were dancing in the middle of the room.

Molder demanded, leaning towards her:

"I say, do you dance?"

"But certainly," said Christine. "I learnt at the convent." And she spoke of her convent education, a triumphant subject with her, though she had actually spent less than a year in the convent.

After a few moments they both rose, and Christine, bending over G. J., whispered lovingly in his ear:

"Dear, thou wilt not be jealous if I dance one turn with thy young friend?"

She was addressing the wrong person. Already throughout the supper Aida, ignoring the fact that the whole structure of civilised society is based on the rule that at a meal a man must talk first to the lady on his right and then to the lady on his left and so on infinitely, had secretly taken exception to the periodic intercourse – and particularly the intercourse in French – between Christine and Molder, who was officially "hers". That these two should go off and dance together was the supreme insult to her. By ill-chance she had not sufficient physical command of herself.

Christine felt that Molder would have danced better two hours earlier; but still he danced beautifully. Their bodies fitted like two parts of a jigsaw puzzle that have discovered each other. She realised that G. J. was middle-aged, and regret tinctured the ecstasy of the dance. Then suddenly she heard a loud, imploring cry in her ear:

"Christine!"

She looked round, pale, still dancing, but only by inertia.

Nobody was near her. The four people at the Major's table gave no sign of agitation or even of interest. The Major still had Alice more or less in his arms.

"What was that?" she asked wildly.

"What was what?" said Molder, at a loss to understand her extraordinary demeanour.

And she heard the cry again, and then again:

"Christine! Christine!"

She recognised the voice. It was the voice of the officer whom she had taken to Victoria Station one Sunday night months and months ago.

"Excuse me!" she said, slipping from Molder's hold, and she hurried out of the room to the ladies' cloakroom, got her wraps, and ran past the watchful guardian, through the dark, dubious portico of the club into the street. The thing was done in a moment, and why she did it she could not tell. She knew simply that she must do it, and that she was under the dominion of those unseen powers in whom she had always believed. She forgot the Guinea-Fowl as completely as though it had been a pre-natal phenomenon with her.

24

THE SOLDIER

But outside she lost faith. Half s dozen motor-cars were slumbering in a row near the door of the Guinea-Fowl, and they all stirred monstrously yet scarcely perceptibly at the sight of the woman's figure, solitary, fragile and pale in the darkness. They seemed for an instant to lust for her; and then, recognising that she was not their prey, to sink back into the torpor of their inexhaustible patience. The sight of them was prejudicial to the dominion of the unseen powers. Christine admitted to herself that she had drunk a lot, that she was demented, that her only proper course was to return dutifully to the supper-party. She wondered what, if she did not so return, she could possibly say to justify herself to G. J.

Nevertheless she went on down the street, hurrying, automatic, and reached the main thoroughfare. It was dark with the new protective darkness. The central hooded lamps showed like poor candles, making a series of rings of feeble illumination on the vast invisible floor of the road. Nobody was afoot; not a soul. The last of the motor-buses that went about killing and maiming people in the new protective darkness had long since reached its yard. The seductive dim violet bulbs were all extinguished on the entrances of the theatres, and, save for a thread of light at some lofty window here and there, the curving façades of the street were as undecipherable as the heavens above or as the asphalte beneath.

Then Christine's ear detected a faint roar. It grew louder; it became terrific; and a long succession of huge loaded army waggons with peering head-lamps thundered past at full speed, one close behind the next, shaking the very avenue. The slightest misjudgment by the leading waggon in the confusion of light and darkness – and the whole convoy would have pitched itself together in a mass of iron, flesh, blood and ordnance; but the convoy went ruthlessly and safely forward till its final red tail-lamp swung round a corner and vanished. The avenue ceased to shake. The thunder died away, and there was silence again. Whence and why the convoy came, and at whose dread omnipotent command? Whither it was bound? What it carried? No answer in the darkness to these enigmas!… And Christine was afraid of England. She remembered people in Ostend saying that England would never go to war. She, too, had said it, bitterly. And now she was in the midst of the unmeasured city which had darkened itself for war, and she was afraid of an unloosed might…

What madness was she doing? She did not even know the man's name. She knew only that he was "Edgar W." She would have liked to be his *marraine*, according to the French custom, but he had never written to her. He was still in her debt for the hotel bill and the taxi fare. He had not even kissed her at the station. She tried to fancy that she heard his voice calling "Christine" with frantic supplication in her ears, but she could not. She turned into another side street, and saw a lighted doorway. Two soldiers were standing in the veiled radiance. She could just read the lower half of the painted notice: "All service men welcome. Beds. Meals. Writing and reading rooms. Always open." She passed on. One of the soldiers, a non-commissioned officer of mature years, solemnly winked at her, without moving an unnecessary muscle. She looked modestly down.

Twenty yards further on she described near a lamp-post a tall soldier whose somewhat bent body seemed to be clustered over with pots, pans, tins, bags, valises, satchels and weapons, like the figure of some military Father Christmas on his surreptitious rounds. She knew that he must be a poor benighted fellow just back from the trenches. He was staring up at the place where the street-sign ought to have been. He glanced at her, and said, in a fatigued, gloomy, aristocratic voice:

"Pardon me, Madam. Is this Denman Street? I want to find the Denman Hostel."

Christine looked into his face. A sacred dew suffused her from head to foot. She trembled with an intimidated joy. She felt the mystic influences of all the unseen powers. She knew herself with holy dread to be the chosen of the very clement Virgin, and the channel of a miraculous intervention. It was the most marvellous, sweetest thing that had ever happened. It was humanly incredible, but it had happened.

"Is it you?" she murmured in a soft, breaking voice.

The man stooped and examined her face.

She said, while he gazed at her: "Edgar!... See – the wrist watch," and held up her arm, from which the wide sleeve of her mantle slipped away.

And the man said: "Is it you?"

She said: "Come with me. I will look after you."

The man answered glumly:

"I have no money – at least not enough for you. And I owe you a lot of money already. You are an angel. I'm ashamed."

"What do you mean?" Christine protested. "Do you forget that you gave me a five-pound note? It was more than enough to pay the hotel... As for the rest, let us not speak of it. Come with me."

"Did I?" muttered the man.

She could feel the very clement Virgin smiling approval of her fib; it was exactly such a fib as the Virgin herself would have told in a quandary of charity. And when a taxi came round the corner, she knew that the Virgin disguised as a taxi-driver was steering it, and she hailed it with a firm and yet loving gesture.

The taxi stopped. She opened the door, and in her sombre mantle and bright trailing frock and glinting, pale shoes she got in, and the military Father Christmas with much difficulty and jingling and clinking insinuated himself after her into the vehicle, and banged to the door. And at the same moment one of the soldiers from the Hostel ran up:

"Here, mate!... What do you want to take his money from him for, you damned w – ?"

But the taxi drove off. Christine had not understood. And had she understood, she would not have cared. She had a divine mission; she was in bliss.

"You did not seem surprised to meet me," she said, taking Edgar's rough hand.

"No."

"Had you called out my name – 'Christine'?"

"No."

"You are sure?"

"Yes."

"Perhaps you were thinking of me? I was thinking of you."

"Perhaps. I don't know. But I'm never surprised."

"You must be very tired?"

"Yes."

"But why are you like that? All these things? You are not an officer now."

"No. I had to resign my commission – just after I saw you." He paused, and added drily: "Whisky." His deep rich voice filled the taxi with the resigned philosophy of fatalism.

"And then?"

"Of course I joined up again at once," he said casually. "I soon got out to the Front. Now I'm on leave. That's mere luck."

She burst into tears. She was so touched by his curt story, and by the grotesquerie of his appearance in the faint light from the exterior lamp which lit the dial of the taximeter, that she lost control of herself. And the man gave a sob, or possibly it was only a gulp to hide a sob. And she leaned against him in her thin garments. And he clinked and jingled, and his breath smelt of beer.

25

THE RING

The flat was in darkness, except for the little lamp by the bedside. The soldier lay asleep in his flannel shirt in the wide bed, and Christine lay awake next him. His clothes were heaped on a chair. His eighty pounds' weight of kit were deposited in a corner of the drawing-room. On the table in the drawing-room were the remains of a meal. Christine was thinking, carelessly and without apprehension, of what she should say to G. J. She would tell him that she had suddenly felt unwell. No! That would be silly. She would tell him that he really had not the right to ask her to meet such women as Aida and Alice. Had he no respect for her? Or she would tell him that Aida had obviously meant to attack her, and that the dance with Lieutenant Molder was simply a device to enable her to get away quietly and avoid all scandal in a resort where scandal was intensely deprecated. She could tell him fifty things, and he would have to accept whatever she chose to tell him. She was mystically happy in the incomparable marvel of the miracle, and in her care of the dull, unresponding man. Her heart yearned thankfully, devotedly, passionately to the Virgin of the VII Dolours.

In the profound nocturnal silence broken only by the man's slow, regular breathing, she heard a sudden ring. It was the

140

front-door bell ringing in the kitchen. The bell rang again and again obstinately. G. J.'s party was over, then, and he had arrived to make inquiries. She smiled, and did not move. After a few moments she could hear Marthe stirring. She sprang up, and then, cunningly considerate, slipped from under the bedclothes as noiselessly and as smoothly as a snake, so that the man should not be disturbed. The two women met in the little hall, Christine in the immodesty of a lacy and diaphanous garment, and Marthe in a coarse cotton nightgown covered with a shawl. The bell rang once more, loudly, close to their ears.

"Are you mad?" Christine whispered with fierceness. "Go back to bed. Let him ring."

26

THE RETURN

It was afternoon in April, 1916. G. J. rang the right bell at the entrance of the London home of the Lechfords. Lechford House, designed about 1840 by an Englishman of genius who in this rare instance had found a patron with the wit to let him alone, was one of the finest examples of domestic architecture in the West End. Inspired by the formidable palaces of Rome and Florence, the artist had conceived a building in the style of the Italian renaissance, but modified, softened, chastened, civilised, to express the bland and yet haughty sobriety of the English climate and the English peerage. People without an eye for the perfect would have correctly described it as a large plain house in grey stone, of three storeys, with a width of four windows on either side of its black front door, a jutting cornice, and rather elaborate chimneys. It was, however, a masterpiece for the connoisseur, and foreign architects sometimes came with cards of admission to pry into it professionally. The blinds of its principal windows were down – not because of the war; they were often down, for at least four other houses disputed with Lechford House the honour of sheltering the Marquis and his wife and their sole surviving child. Above the roof a wire platform for the catching of bombs had given the mansion a somewhat ridiculous appearance, but otherwise Lechford

House managed to look as though it had never heard of the European War.

One half of the black entrance swung open, and a middle-aged gentleman dressed like Lord Lechford's stockbroker, but who was in reality his butler, said in answer to G. J.'s enquiry:

"Lady Queenie is not at home, sir."

"But it is five o'clock," protested G. J., suddenly sick of Queen's impudent unreliability. "And I have an appointment with her at five."

The butler's face relaxed ever so little from its occupational inhumanity of a suet pudding; the spirit of compassion seemed to inform it for an instant.

"Her ladyship went out about a quarter of an hour ago, sir."

"When d'you think she'll be back?"

The suet pudding was restored.

"That I could not say, sir."

"Damn the girl!" said G. J. to himself; and aloud: "Please tell her ladyship that I've called."

"Mr Hoape, is it not, sir?"

"It is."

By the force of his raisin eyes the butler held G. J. as he turned to descend the steps.

"There's nobody at home, sir, except Mrs Carlos Smith. Mrs Carlos Smith is in Lady Queenie's apartments."

"Mrs Carlos Smith!" exclaimed G. J., who had not seen Concepcion for some seventeen months; nor heard from her for nearly as long, nor heard of her since the previous year.

"Yes, sir."

"Ask her if she can see me, will you?" said G. J. impetuously, after a slight pause.

He stepped on to the tessellated pavement of the outer hall. On the raised tessellated pavement of the inner hall stood two meditative youngish footmen, possibly musing upon the problems of the intensification of the Military Service Act which were then exciting journalists and statesmen. Beyond was the renowned staircase, which, rising with insubstantial grace, lost itself in silvery altitude like the way to heaven. Presently G. J. was mounting the staircase and passing statues by Canova and Thorwaldsen, and portraits of which the heads had been painted by Lawrence and the hands and draperies by Lawrence's hireling, and huger canvasses on which the heads and breasts had been painted by Rubens and everything else by Rubens's regiment of hirelings. The guiding footman preceded him through a great chamber which he recognised as the drawing-room in its winding sheet, and then up a small and insignificant staircase; and G. J. was on ground strange to him, for never till then had he been higher than the first-floor in Lechford House.

Lady Queenie's apartments did violence to G. J.'s sensibilities as an upholder of traditionalism in all the arts, of the theory that every sound movement in any art must derive from its predecessor. Some months earlier he had met for a few minutes the creative leader of the newest development in internal decoration, and he vividly remembered a saying of the grey-haired, slouch-hatted man: "At the present day the only people in the world with really vital preceptions about decoration are African niggers, and the only inspiring productions are the coloured cotton stuffs designed for the African native market." The remark had amused and stimulated him, but he had never troubled to go in search of examples of the inspiring influence of African taste on London domesticity. He now saw perhaps the supreme instance lodged in Lechford House, like a new and truculent state within a great Empire.

Lady Queenie had imposed terms on her family, and under threats of rupture, of separation, of scandal, Lady Queenie's exotic nest had come into existence in the very fortress of unchangeable British convention. The phenomenon was a war phenomenon due to the war, begotten by the war; for Lady Queenie had said that if she was to do war-work without disaster to her sanity she must have the right environment. Thus the putting together of Lady Queenie's nest had proceeded concurrently with the building of national projectile factories and of square miles of offices for the girl clerks of ministries and departments of government.

The footman left G. J. alone in a room designated the boudoir. G. J. resented the boudoir, because it was like nothing that he had ever witnessed. The walls were irregularly covered with rhombuses, rhomboids, lozenges, diamonds, triangles, and parallelograms; the carpet was treated likewise, and also the upholstery and the cushions. The colourings of the scene in their excessive brightness, crudity and variety surpassed G. J.'s conception of the possible. He had learned the value of colour before Queen was born, and in the Albany had translated principle into practice. But the hues of the boudoir made the gaudiest effects of Regency furniture appear sombre. The place resembled a gigantic and glittering kaleidoscope deranged and arrested.

G. J.'s glance ran round the room like a hunted animal seeking escape, and found no escape. He was as disturbed as he might have been disturbed by drinking a liqueur on the top of a cocktail. Nevertheless he had to admit that some of the contrasts of pure colour were rather beautiful, even impressive; and he hated to admit it. He was aware of a terrible apprehension that he would never be the same man again, and that henceforth his own abode would be eternally stricken for him with the curse of insipidity. Regaining somewhat his nerve, he looked for pictures. There were no pictures. But every piece of furniture was painted with primitive sketches of human figures, or of flowers, or of vessels, or of animals. On the front of the mantelpiece were perversely but brilliantly depicted, with a high degree of finish, two nude, crouching women who gazed longingly at each other across the impassable semicircular abyss of the fireplace; and just above their heads, on a scroll, ran these words:

"The ways of God are strange."

145

He heard movements and a slight cough in the next room, the door leading to which was ajar. Concepcion's cough; he thought he recognised it. Five minutes ago he had had no notion of seeing her; now he was about to see her. And he felt excited and troubled, as much by the sudden violence of life as by the mere prospect of the meeting.

After her husband's death Concepcion had soon withdrawn from London. A large engineering firm on the Clyde, one of the heads of which happened to be constitutionally a pioneer, was establishing a canteen for its workmen, and Concepcion, the tentacles of whose influence would stretch to any length, had decided that she ought to take up canteen work, and in particular the canteen work of just that firm. But first of all, to strengthen her prestige and acquire new prestige, she had gone to the United States, with a powerful introduction to Sears, Roebuck and Company of Chicago, in order to study industrial canteenism in its most advanced and intricate manifestations. Portraits of Concepcion in splendid furs on the deck of the steamer in the act of preparing to study industrial canteenism in its most advanced and intricate manifestations had appeared in the illustrated weeklies. The luxurious trip had cost several hundreds of pounds, but it was war expenditure, and, moreover, Concepcion had come into considerable sums of money through her deceased husband. Her return to Britain had never been published. Advertisements of Concepcion ceased. Only a few friends knew that she was in the most active retirement on the Clyde. G. J. had written to her twice but had obtained no replies. One fact he knew, that she had not had a child. Lady Queenie had not mentioned her; it was understood that the inseparables had quarrelled in the heroic manner and separated for ever.

She entered the boudoir slowly. G. J. grew self-conscious, as it were because she was still the martyr of destiny and he was not. She wore a lavender-tinted gown of Queen's; he knew it was Queen's because he had seen precisely such a gown on

Queen, and there could not possibly be another gown precisely like that very challenging gown. It suited Queen, but it did not suit Concepcion. She looked older; she was thirty-two, and might have been taken for thirty-five. She was very pale, with immense fatigued eyes; but her ridiculous nose had preserved all its originality. And she had the same slightly masculine air – perhaps somewhat intensified – with an added dignity. And G. J. thought: "She is as mysterious and unfathomable as I am myself." And he was impressed and perturbed.

With a faint, sardonic smile, glancing at him as a physical equal from her unusual height (she was as tall as Lady Queenie), she said abruptly and casually:

"Am I changed?"

"No," he replied as abruptly and casually, clasping almost inimically her ringed hand – she was wearing Queenie's rings. "But you're tired. The journey, I suppose."

"It's not that. We sat up till five o'clock this morning, talking."

"Who?"

"Queen and I."

"What did you do that for?"

"Well, you see, we'd had the devil's own row – " She stopped, leaving his imagination to complete the picture of the meeting and the night talk.

He smiled awkwardly – tried to be paternal, and failed.

"What about?"

"She never wanted me to leave London. I came back last night with only a handbag just as she was going out to dinner. She didn't go out to dinner. Queen is a white woman. Nobody knows how white Queen is. I didn't know myself until last night."

There was a pause. G. J. said:

"I had an appointment here with the white woman, on business."

"Yes, I know," said Concepcion negligently. "She'll be home soon."

Something infinitesimally malicious in the voice and gaze sent the singular idea shooting through his mind that Queen had gone out on purpose so that Concepcion might have him alone for a while. And he was wary of both of them, as he might have been of two pagan goddesses whom he, a poor defiant mortal, suspected of having laid an eye on him for their own ends.

"*You*'ve changed, anyhow," said Concepcion.

"Older?"

"No. Harder."

He was startled, not displeased.

"How – harder?"

"More sure of yourself," said Concepcion, with a trace of the old harsh egotism in her tone. "It appears you're a perfect tyrant on the Lechford Committee now you're vice-chairman, and all the more footling members dread the days when you're in the chair. It appears also that you've really overthrown two chairmen, and yet won't take the situation yourself."

He was still more startled, but now positively flattered by the world's estimate of his activities and individuality. He saw himself in a new light.

"This what you were talking about until five a.m.?"

The butler entered.

"Shall I serve tea, Madam?"

Concepcion looked at the man scornfully:

"Yes."

One of the minor stalwarts entered and arranged a table, and the other followed with a glittering, steaming tray in his hands, while the butler hovered like a winged hippopotamus over the operation. Concepcion half sat down by the table, and then, altering her mind, dropped on to a vast chaise-longue, as wide as a bed, and covered with as many cushions as would have stocked a cushion shop, which occupied the principal place in front of the hearth. The hem of her rich gown just touched the floor. G. J. could see that she was wearing the transparent deep-purple stockings that Queen wore with the transparent lavender gown. Her right shoulder rose high from the mass of the body, and her head was sunk between two cushions. Her voice came smothered from the cushions:

"Damn it! G. J. Don't look at me like that."

He was standing near the mantelpiece.

"Why?" he exclaimed. "What's the matter, Con?"

There was no answer. He lit a cigarette. The ebullient kettle kept lifting its lid in growing impatience. But Concepcion seemed to have forgotten the tea. G. J. had a thought, distinct like a bubble on a sea of thoughts, that if the tea was already made, as no doubt it was, it would soon be stewed. Concepcion said:

"The matter is that I'm a ruined woman, and Queen can't understand."

And in the bewildering voluptuous brightness and luxury of the room G. J. had the sensation of being a poor, baffled ghost groping in the night of existence. Concepcion's left arm slipped over the edge of the day-bed and hung limp and pale, the curved fingers touching the carpet.

27

THE CLYDE

She was sitting up on the Chaise-longue and had poured out
the tea – he had pushed the tea-table towards the chaise-longue
– and she was talking in an ordinary tone just as though she had
not immodestly bared her spirit to him and as though she knew
not that he realised she had done so. She was talking at length,
as one who in the past had been well accustomed to giving
monologues and to holding drawing-rooms in subjection while
she chattered, and to making drawing-rooms feel glad that they
had consented to subjection. She was saying:
"You've no idea what the valley of the Clyde is now. You
can't have. It's filled with girls, and they come into it every
morning by train to huge stations specially built for them, and
they make the most ghastly things for killing other girls' lovers
all day, and they go back by train at night. Only some of them
work all night. I had to leave my own works to organise the
canteen of a new filling factory. Five thousand girls in that
factory. It's frightfully dangerous. They have to wear special
clothing. They have to take off every stitch from their bodies in
one room, and run in their innocence and nothing else to
another room where the special clothing is. That's the only way
to prevent the whole place being blown up one beautiful day.
But five thousand of them! You can't imagine it. You'd like to,

G. J., but you can't. However, I didn't stay there very long. I wanted to go back to my own place. I was adored at my own place. Of course the men adored me. They used to fight about me sometimes. Terrific men. Nothing ever made me happier than that, or so happy. But the girls were more interesting. Two thousand of them there. You'd never guess it, because they were hidden in thickets of machinery. But see them rush out endlessly to the canteen for tea! All sorts. Lots of devils and cats. Some lovely creatures, heavenly creatures, as fine as a queen. They adored me too. They didn't at first, some of them. But they soon tumbled to it that I was the modern woman, and that they'd never seen me before, and it was a great discovery. Absurdly easy to raise yourself to be the idol of a crowd that fancies itself canny! Incredibly easy! I used to take their part against the works-manager as often as I could; he was a fiend; he hated me; but then I was a fiend, too, and I hated him more. I used often to come on at six in the morning, when they did, and 'sign on'. It isn't really signing on now at all; there's a clock dial and a whole machine for catching you out. They loved to see me doing that. And I worked the lathes sometimes, just for a bit, just to show that I wasn't ashamed to work. Etc... All that sentimental twaddle. It pleased them. And if any really vigorous-minded girl had dared to say it was sentimental twaddle, there would have been a crucifixion or something of the sort in the cloakrooms. The mob's always the same. But what pleased them far more than anything was me knowing them by their Christian names. Not all, of course; still, hundreds of them. Marvellous feats of memorising I did! I used to go about muttering under my breath: 'Winnie, wart on left hand, Winnie, wart on left hand, wart on left hand, Winnie.' You see? And I've sworn at them – not often; it wouldn't do, naturally. But there was scarcely a woman there that I couldn't simply blast in two seconds if I felt like it. On the other hand, I assure you I could be very tender. I was surprised how tender I could be, now and then, in my little office. They'd tell me anything – sounds sentimental, but they would – and some of them had no more notion that there's such a thing on earth as propriety than a monkey has. I thought I knew everything before I went to the Clyde valley. Well, I didn't." Concepcion looked at G. J. "You know you're very innocent, G. J., compared to me."

"I should hope so!" said G. J., impenetrably.

"What do you think of it all?" she demanded in a fresh tone, leaning a little towards him.

He replied: "I'm impressed."

He was, in fact, very profoundly impressed; but he had to illustrate the hardness in himself which she had revealed to him. (He wondered whether the members of the Lechford Committee really did credit him with having dethroned a couple of chairmen. The idea was new to his modesty. Perhaps he had been under-estimating his own weight on the committee. No doubt he had.) All constraint was now dissipated between Concepcion and himself. They were behaving to each other as though their intimacy had never been interrupted for a single week. She amazed him, sitting there in the purple stockings and the affronting gown, and he admired. Her material achievement alone was prodigious. He pictured her as she rose in the winter dark and in the summer dawn to go to the works and wrestle with so much incalculable human nature and so many complex questions of organisation, day after day, week after week, month after month, for nearly eighteen months. She had kept it up; that was the point. She had shown what she was made of, and what she was made of was unquestionably marvellous.

He would have liked to know about various things to which she had made no reference. Did she live in a frowsy lodging-house near the great works? What kind of food did she get? What did she do with her evenings and her Sundays? Was she bored? Was she miserable or exultant? Had she acquaintances, external interests; or did she immerse herself completely, inclusively, in the huge, smoking, whirring, foul, perilous hell which she had described? The contemplation of the horror of the hell gave him – and her, too, he thought – a curious feeling which was not un-pleasurable. It had savour. He would not, however, inquire from her concerning details. He preferred, on reflection, to keep the details mysterious, as mysterious as her individuality and as the impression of her worn eyes. The setting of mystery in his mind suited her.

He said: "But of course your relations with those girls were artificial, after all."

"No, they weren't. I tell you the girls were perfectly open; there wasn't the slightest artificiality."

"Yes, but were you open, to them? Did you ever tell them anything about yourself, for instance?"

"Oh, no!"

"Did they ever ask you to?"

"No! They wouldn't have thought of doing so."

"That's what I call artificiality. By the way, how have you been ruined? Who ruined you? Was it the hated works-manager?" There had been no change in his tone; he spoke with the utmost detachment.

"I was coming to that," answered Concepcion, apparently with a detachment equal to his. "Last week but one in one of the shops there was a girl standing in front of a machine, with her back to it. About twenty-two – you must see her in your mind – about twenty-two, nice chestnut hair. Cap over it, of course – that's the rule. Khaki overalls and trousers. Rather high-heeled patent-leather boots – they fancy themselves, thank God! – and a bit of lace showing out of the khaki at the neck. Red cheeks; she was fairly new to the works. Do you see her? She meant to be one of the devils. Earning two pounds a week nearly, and eagerly spending it all. Fully awake to all the possibilities of her body. I was in the shop. I said something to her, and she didn't hear at first – the noise of some of the shops is shattering. I went close to her and repeated it. She laughed out of mere vivacity, and threw back her head as people do when they laugh. The machine behind her must have caught some hair that wasn't under her cap. All her hair was dragged from under the cap, and in no time all her hair was torn out and the whole of her scalp ripped clean off. In a second or two I got her on to a trolley – I did it – and threw an overall over her and ran her to the dressing-station, close to the main office entrance. There was a car there. One of the directors was just driving off. I stopped him. It wasn't a case for our dressing-station. In three minutes I had her at the hospital – three minutes. The car was soaked in blood. But she didn't lose consciousness, that child didn't. She's dead now. She's buried. Her body that she meant to use so profusely for her own delights is squeezed up in the little black box in the dark and the silence, down below where the spring can't get at it... I had no sleep for two nights. On the second day a doctor at the hospital said that I must take at least three months' holiday. He said I'd had a nervous breakdown. I didn't know I had, and I don't know now. I said I wouldn't take any holiday, and that nothing would induce me to."

"Why, Con?"

"Because I'd sworn, absolutely sworn to myself, to stick that job till the war was over. You understand, I'd sworn it. Well, they wouldn't let me on to the works. And yesterday one of the directors brought me up to town himself. He was very kind, in his Clyde way. Now you understand what I mean when I say I'm ruined. I'm ruined with myself, you see. I didn't stick it. I couldn't. But there were twenty or thirty girls who saw the accident. They're sticking it."

"Yes," he said in a voice soft and moved, "I understand." And while he spoke thus aloud, though his emotion was genuine, and his desire to comfort and sustain her genuine, and his admiration for her genuine, he thought to himself: "How theatrically she told it! Every effect was studied, nearly every word. Well, she can't help it. But does she imagine I can't see that all the casualness was deliberately part of the effect?"

She lit a cigarette and leaned her half-draped elbows on the tea-table, and curved her ringed fingers, which had withstood time and fatigue much better than her face; and then she reclined again on the chaise-longue, on her back, and sent up smoke perpendicularly, and through the smoke seemed to be trying to decipher the enigmas of the ceiling. G. J. rose and stood over her in silence. At last she went on:

"The work those girls do is excruciating, hellish, and they don't realise it. That's the worst of it. They'll never be the same again. They're ruining their health, and, what's more important, their looks. You can see them changing under your eyes. Ours was the best factory on the Clyde, and the conditions were unspeakable, in spite of canteens, and rest-rooms, and libraries, and sanitation, and all this damned 'welfare'. Fancy a girl chained up for twelve hours every day to a thundering, whizzing, iron machine that never gets tired. The machine's just as fresh at six o'clock at night as it was at six o'clock in the morning, and just as anxious to maim her if she doesn't look out for herself – more anxious. The whole thing's still going on; they're at it now, this very minute. You're interested in a factory, aren't you, G. J.?"

"Yes," he answered gently, but looked with seemingly callous firmness down at her.

"The Reveille Company, or some such name."

"Yes."

"Making tons of money, I hear."

"Yes."

"You're a profiteer, G. J."

"I'm not. Long since I decided I must give away all my extra profits."

"Ever go and look at your factory?"

"No."

"Any nice young girls working there?"

"I don't know."

"If there are, are they decently treated?"

"Don't know that, either."

"Why don't you go and see?"

155

"It's no business of mine."

"Yes, it is. Aren't you making yourself glorious as a philanthropist out of the thing?"

"I tell you it's no business of mine," he insisted evenly. "I couldn't do anything if I went. I've no status."

"Rotten system."

"Possibly. But systems can't be altered like that. Systems alter themselves, and they aren't in a hurry about it. This system isn't new, though it's new to you."

"You people in London don't know what work is."

"And what about your Clyde strikes?" G. J. retorted.

"Well, all that's settled now," said Concepcion rather uneasily, like a champion who foresees a fight but lacks confidence.

"Yes, but – " G. J. suddenly altered his tone to the persuasive: "You must know all about those strikes. What was the real cause? We don't understand them here."

"If you really want to know – nerves," she said earnestly and triumphantly.

"Nerves?"

"Overwork. No rest. No change. Everlasting punishment. The one incomprehensible thing to me is that the whole of Glasgow didn't go on strike and stay out for ever."

"There's just as much overwork in London as there is on the Clyde."

"There's a lot more talking – Parliament, Cabinet, Committees. You should hear what they say about it in Glasgow."

"Con," he said kindly, "you don't suspect it, but you're childish. It's the job of one part of London to talk. If that part of London didn't talk your tribes on the Clyde couldn't work, because they wouldn't know what to do, nor how to do it. Talking has to come before working, and let me tell you it's more difficult, and it's more killing, because it's more responsible. Excuse this common sense made easy for beginners, but you brought it on yourself."

She frowned. "And what do you do? Do you talk or work?"
She smiled.

"I'll tell you this!" said he, smiling candidly and benevolently.
'It took me a dickens of a time really to *put* myself into anything
that meant steady effort. I'd lost the habit. Natural enough, and
I'm not going into sackcloth about it. However, I'm improving.
I'm going to take on the secretaryship of the Lechford
Committee. Some of 'em mayn't want me, but they'll have to
have me. And when they've got me they'll have to look out. All
of them, including Queen and her mother."

"Will it take the whole of your time?"

"Yes. I'm doing three days a week now."

"I suppose you think you've beaten me."

"Con, I do ask you not to be a child."

"But I am a child. Why don't you humour me? You know I've
had a nervous breakdown. You used to humour me."

He shook his head.

"Humouring you won't do *your* nervous breakdown any
good. It might some women's – but not yours."

"You shall humour me!" she cried. "I haven't told you half my
ruin. Do you know I meant to love Carly all my life. I felt sure
I should. Well, I can't! It's gone, all that feeling – already! In less
than two years! And now I'm only sorry for him and sorry for
myself. Isn't it horrible? Isn't it horrible?"

"Try not to think," he murmured.

She sat up impetuously.

"Don't talk such damned nonsense! 'Try not to think'! Why,
my frightful unhappiness is the one thing that keeps me alive."

"Yes," G. J. yielded. "It was nonsense."

She sank back. He saw moisture in her eyes and felt it in his
own.

28

SALOME

Lday Queenie arrived in haste, as though relentless time had pursued her up the stairs.

"Why, you're in the dark here!" she exclaimed impatiently, and impatiently switched on several lights. "Sorry I'm late, G. J.," she said perfunctorily, without taking any trouble to put conviction into her voice. "How have you two been getting on?"

She looked at Concepcion and G. J. in a peculiar way, inquisitorial and implicatory.

Then, towards the door:

"Come in, come in, Dialin."

A young soldier with the stripe of a lance-corporal entered, slightly nervous and slightly defiant.

"And you, Miss I-forget-your-name."

A young woman entered; she had very red lips and very high heels, and was both more nervous and more defiant than the young soldier.

"This is Mr Dialin, you know, Con, second ballet-master at the Ottoman. I met him by sheer marvellous chance. He's only got ten minutes; he hasn't really got that; but he's going to see me do my Salome dance."

Lady Queenie made no attempt to introduce Miss I-forget-your-name, who of her own accord took a chair with a curious, dashed effrontery. It appeared that she was attached to Mr Dialin. Lady Queenie cast off rapidly gloves, hat and coat, and then, having rushed to the bell and rung it fiercely several times, came back to the chaise-longue and gazed at it and at the surrounding floor.

"Would you mind, Con?"

Concepcion rose. Lady Queenie, rushing off again, pushed several more switches, and from a thick cluster of bulbs in front of a large mirror at the end of the room there fell dazzling sheets of light. A footman presented himself.

"Push the day-bed right away towards the window," she commanded.

The footman inclined and obeyed, and the lance-corporal superiorly helped him. Then the footman was told to energise the gramophone, which in its specially designed case stood in a corner. The footman seemed to be on intimate terms with the gramophone. Meanwhile Lady Queenie, with a safety-pin, was fastening the back hem of her short skirt to the front between the knees. Still bending, she took her shoes off. Her scent impregnated the room.

"You see, it will be barefoot," she explained to Mr Dialin.

The walls of London were already billed with an early announcement of the marvels of the Pageant of Terpsichore, which was to occur at the Albert Hall, under the superintendence of the greatest modern English painters, in aid of a fund for soldiers disabled by deafness. The performers were all ladies of the upper world, ladies bearing names for the most part as familiar as the names of streets – and not a stage-star among them. Amateurism was to be absolutely untainted by professionalism in the prodigious affair; therefore the prices of tickets ruled high, and queens had conferred their patronage.

Lady Queenie removed several bracelets and a necklace, and, seizing a plate, deposited it on the carpet.

"That piece of bread-and-butter," she said, "is the head of my beloved John."

The clever footman started the gramophone, and Lady Queenie began to dance. The lance-corporal walked round her, surveying her at all angles, watching her like a tiger, imitating movements, suggesting movements, sketching emotions with his arm, raising himself at intervals on the toes of his thick boots. After a few moments Concepcion glanced at G. J., conveying to him a passionate, adoring admiration of Queen's talent.

G. J., startled by her brightened eyes so suddenly full of temperament, nodded to please her. But the fact was that he saw naught to admire in the beautiful and brazen amateur's performance. He wondered that she could not have discovered something more original than to follow the footsteps of Maud Allan in a scene which years ago had become stale. He wondered that, at any rate, Concepcion should not perceive the poor, pretentious quality of the girlish exhibition. And as he looked at the mincing Dialin he pictured the lance-corporal helping to serve a gun. And as he looked at the youthful, lithe Queenie posturing in the shower-bath of rays amid the blazing chromatic fantasy of the room, and his nostrils twitched to her pungent perfume, he pictured the reverberating shell-factory on the Clyde where girls had their scalps torn off by unappeasable machinery, and the filling-factory where five thousand girls stripped themselves naked in order to lessen the danger of being blown to bits... After a climax of capering Queen fell full length on her stomach upon the carpet, her soft chin accurately adjusted to the edge of the plate. The music ceased. The gramophone gnashed on the disc until the footman lifted its fang.

Miss I-forget-your-name raised both her feet from the floor, stuck her legs out in a straight, slanting line, and condescendingly clapped. Then, seeing that Queen was worrying the piece of bread-and-butter with her teeth, she exclaimed in agitation:

"Ow my!"

Mr Dialin assisted the breathless Queen to rise, and they went off into a corner and he talked to her in low tones. Soon he looked at his wrist-watch and caught the summoning eye of Miss I-forget-your-name.

"But it's pretty all right, isn't it?" said Queen.

"Oh, yes! Oh, yes!" he soothed her with an expert's casualness. "Naturally, you want to work it up. You fell beautifully. Now you go and see Crevelli – he's the man."

"I shall get him to come here. What's his address?"

"I don't know. He's just moved. But you'll see it in the April number of *The Dancing Times*."

As the footman was about to escort Mr Dialin and his urgent lady downstairs Queen ordered:

"Bring me up a whisky-and-soda."

"It's splendid, Queen," said Concepcion enthusiastically when the two were alone with G. J.

"I'm so glad you think so, darling. How are you, darling?" She kissed the older woman affectionately, fondly, on the lips, and then gave G. J. a challenging glance.

"Oh!" she exclaimed, and called out very loud: "Robin! I want you at once."

The secretarial Miss Robinson, carrying a note-book, appeared like magic from the inner room.

"Get me the April number of *The Dancing News*."

"*Times*," G. J. corrected.

"Well, *Times*. It's all the same. And write to Mr Opson and say that we really must have proper dressing-room accommodation. It's most important."

"Yes, your ladyship. Your ladyship has the sub-committee as to entrance arrangements for the public at half-past six."

"I shan't go. Telephone to them. I've got quite enough to do without that. I'm utterly exhausted. Don't forget about *The Dancing Times* and to write to Mr Opson."

"Yes, your ladyship."

"G. J.," said Queen after Robin had gone, "you are a pig if you don't go on that subcommittee as to entrance arrangements. You know what the Albert Hall is. They'll make a horrible mess of it, and it's just the sort of thing you can do better than anybody."

"Yes. But a pig I am," answered G. J. firmly. Then he added: "I'll tell you how you might have avoided all these complications."

"How?"

"By having no pageant and simply going round collecting subscriptions. Nobody would have refused you. And there'd have been no expenses to come off the total."

Lady Queenie put her lips together.

"Has he been behaving in this style to you, Con?"

"A little – now and then," said Concepcion.

Later, when the chaise-longue and Queen's shoes had been replaced, and the tea-things and the head of John the Baptist taken away, and all the lights extinguished save one over the mantelpiece, and Lady Queenie had nearly finished the whisky-and-soda, and nothing remained of the rehearsal except the safety-pin between Lady Queenie's knees, G. J. was still waiting for her to bethink herself of the Hospitals subject upon which he had called by special request and appointment to see her. He took oath not to mention it first. Shortly afterwards, stiff in his resolution, he departed.

In three minutes he was in the smoking-room of his club, warming himself at a fine, old, huge, wasteful grate, in which burned such a coal fire as could not have been seen in France, Italy, Germany, Austria, Russia, nor anywhere on the continent of Europe. The war had as yet changed nothing in the impregnable club, unless it was that ordinary matches had recently been substituted for the giant matches on which the club had hitherto prided itself. The hour lay neglected midway between tea and dinner, and there were only two other members in the vast room – solitaries, each before his own grand fire.

G. J. took up *The Times*, which his duties had prevented him from reading at large in the morning. He wandered with a sense of ease among its multifarious pages, and, in full leisure, brought his information up to date concerning the state of the war and of the country. Air-raids by Zeppelins were frequent, and some authorities talked magniloquently about the "defence of London." Hundreds of people had paid immense sums for pictures and objects of art at the Red Cross Sale at Christie's, one of the most successful social events of the year. The House of Commons was inquisitive about Mesopotamia as a whole, and one British Army was still trying to relieve another British Army besieged in Kut. German submarine successes were obviously disquieting. The supply of beer was reduced. There were to be forty principal aristocratic dancers in the Pageant of Terpsichore. The Chancellor of the Exchequer had budgeted for five hundred millions, and was very proud. The best people were at once proud and scared of the new income tax at 5s. in the £. They expressed the fear that such a tax would kill income or send it to America. The theatrical profession was quite sure that the amusements tax would involve utter ruin for the theatrical profession, and the match trade was quite sure that the match tax would put an end to matches, and some unnamed modest individuals had apparently decided that the travel tax must and forthwith would be dropped. The story of the evacuation of Gallipoli had grown old and tedious. Cranks were still vainly trying to prove to the blunt John Bullishness of the Prime Minister that the Daylight Saving Bill was not a piece of mere freak legislation. The whole of the West End and all the inhabitants of country houses in Britain had discovered a new deity in Australia and spent all their spare time and lungs in asserting that all other deities were false and futile; his earthly name was Hughes. Jan Smuts was fighting in the primeval forests of East Africa. The Germans were discussing their war aims; and on the Verdun front they had reached Mort Homme in the usual way, that was, according to the London Press, by sacrificing more men than any place could possibly be worth; still, they had reached Mort Homme. And though our losses and the French losses were everywhere – one might assert, so to speak – negligible, nevertheless the steadfast band of thinkers and fact-facers who held a monopoly of true patriotism were extremely anxious to extend the Military Service Act, so as to rope into the Army every fit male in the island except themselves.

The pages of *The Times* grew semi-transparent, and G. J. descried Concepcion moving mysteriously in a mist behind them. Only then did he begin effectively to realise her experiences and her achievement and her ordeal on the distant, romantic Clyde. He said to himself: "I could never have stood what she has stood." She was a terrific woman; but because she was such a mixture of the mad-heroic and the silly-foolish, he rather condescended to her. She lacked what he was sure he possessed, and what he prized beyond everything – poise. And had she truly had a nervous breakdown, or was that fancy? Did she truly despair of herself as a ruined woman, doubly ruined, or was she acting a part, as much in order to impress herself as in order to impress others? He thought the country and particularly its Press, was somewhat like Concepcion as a complex. He condescended to Queenie also, not bitterly, but with sardonic pity. There she was, unalterable by any war, instinctively and ruthlessly working out her soul and her destiny. The country was somewhat like Queenie too. But, of course, comparison between Queenie and Concepcion was absurd. He had had to defend himself to Concepcion. And had he not defended himself?

True, he had begun perhaps too slowly to work for the war; however, he had begun. What else could he have done beyond what he had done? Become a special constable? Grotesque. He simply could not see himself as a special constable, and if the country could not employ him more usefully than in standing on guard over an electricity works or a railway bridge in the middle of the night, the country deserved to lose his services. Become a volunteer? Even more grotesque. Was he, a man turned fifty, to dress up and fall flat on the ground at the word of some fantastic jackanapes, or stare into vacancy while some inspecting general examined his person as though it were a tailor's mannikin? He had tried several times to get into a Government department which would utilise his brains, but without success. And the club hummed with the unimaginable stories related by disappointed and dignified middle-aged men whose too eager patriotism had been rendered ridiculous by the vicious foolery of Government departments. No! He had some work to do and he was doing it. People were looking to him for decision, for sagacity, for initiative; he supplied these things. His work might grow even beyond his expectations; but if it did not he should not worry. He felt that, unfatigued, he could and would contribute to the mass of the national resolution in the latter and more racking half of the war.

Morally, he was profiting by the war. Nay, more, in a deep sense he was enjoying it. The immensity of it, the terror of it, the idiocy of it, the splendour of it, its unique grandeur as an illustration of human nature, thrilled the spectator in him. He had little fear for the result. The nations had measured themselves; the factors of the equation were known. Britain conceivably might not win, but she could never lose. And he did not accept the singular theory that unless she won this war another war would necessarily follow. He had, in spite of all, a pretty good opinion of mankind, and would not exaggerate its capacity for lunatic madness. The worst was over when Paris was definitely saved. Suffering would sink and die like a fire. Privations were paid for day by day in the cash of fortitude. Taxes would always be met. A whole generation, including himself, would rapidly vanish and the next would stand in its place. And at worst, the path of evolution was unchangeably appointed. A harsh, callous philosophy. Perhaps.

What impressed him, and possibly intimidated him beyond anything else whatever, was the onset of the next generation. He thought of Queenie, of Mr Dialin, of Miss I-forget-your-name, of Lieutenant Molder. How unconsciously sure of themselves and arrogant in their years! How strong! How unapprehensive! (And yet he had just been taking credit for his own freedom from apprehensiveness!) They were young – and he was so no longer. Pooh! (A brave "pooh"!) He was wiser than they. He had acquired the supreme and subtly enjoyable faculty, which they had yet painfully to acquire, of nice, sure, discriminating, all-weighing judgment... Concepcion had divested herself of youth. And Christine, since he knew her, had never had any youthfulness save the physical. There were only these two.

Said a voice behind him:

"You dining here to-night?"

"I am."

"Shall we crack a bottle together?" (It was astonishing and deplorable how clichés survived in the best clubs!)

"By all means."

The voice spoke lower:

"That Bollinger's all gone at last."

"You were fearing the worst the last time I saw you," said G. J.

"Auction afterwards?" the voice suggested.

"Afraid I can't," said G. J. after a moment's hesitation. "I shall have to leave early."

29

THE STREETS

After dinner G. J. walked a little eastwards from the club, and, entering Leicester Square from the south, crossed it, and then turned westwards again on the left side of the road leading to Piccadilly Circus. It was about the time when Christine usually went from her flat to her Promenade. Without admitting a definite resolve to see Christine that evening he had said to himself that he would rather like to see her, or that he wouldn't mind seeing her, and that he might, if the mood took him, call at Cork Street and catch her before she left. Having advanced thus far in the sketch of his intentions, he had decided that it would be a pity not to take precautions to encounter her in the street, assuming that she had already started but had not reached the theatre. The chance of meeting her on her way was exceedingly small; nevertheless he would not miss it. Hence his roundabout route; and hence his selection of the chaste as against the unchaste pavement of Coventry Street. He knew very little of Christine's professional arrangements, but he did know, from occasional remarks of hers, that owing to the need for economy and the difficulty of finding taxis she now always walked to the Promenade on dry nights, and that from a motive of self-respect she always took the south side of Piccadilly and the south side of Coventry Street in order to avoid the risk of ever being mistaken for something which she was not.

It was a dry night, but very cloudy. Points of faint illumination, mysteriously travelling across the heavens and revealing the otherwise invisible cushioned surface of the clouds, alone showed that searchlights were at their work of watching over the heedless town. Entertainments had drawn in the people from the streets; motor-buses were half empty; implacable parcels-vans, with thin, exhausted boys scarcely descried on their rear perches, forced the more fragile traffic to yield place to them. Footfarers were few, except on the north side of Coventry Street, where officers, soldiers, civilians, police and courtesans marched eternally to and fro, peering at one another in the thick gloom that, except in the immediate region of a lamp, put all girls, the young and the ageing, the pretty and the ugly, the good-natured and the grasping, on a sinister enticing equality. And they were all, men and women and vehicles, phantoms flitting and murmuring and hooting in the darkness. And the violet glow-worms that hung in front of theatres and cinemas seemed to mark the entrances to unimaginable fastnesses, and the side streets seemed to lead to the precipitous edges of the universe where nothing was.

G. J. recognised Christine just beyond the knot of loiterers at the Piccadilly Tube. The improbable had happened. She was walking at what was for her a rather quick pace, purposeful and preoccupied. For an instant the recognition was not mutual; he liked the uninviting stare that she gave him as he stopped.

"It is thou?" she exclaimed, and her dimly-seen face softened suddenly into a delighted, adoring smile.

He was moved by the passion which she still had for him. He felt vaguely and yet acutely an undischarged obligation in regard to her. It was the first time he had met her in such circumstances. A constraint fell between them. In five minutes she would have been in her Promenade engaged upon her highly technical business, displaying her attractions while appearing to protect herself within a virginal timidity (for this was her natural method). In any case, even had he not set forth on purpose to find her, he could scarcely have accompanied her to the doors of the theatre and there left her to the night's routine. They both hesitated, and then, without a word, he turned aside and she followed close, acquiescent by training and by instinct. Knowing his sure instinct for what was proper, she knew at once that hazard had saved her from the night's routine, and she was full of quiet triumph. He, of course, though absolutely loyal to her, had for dignity's sake to practise the duplicity of pretending to make up his mind what he should do.

They went through the Tube station and were soon in one of the withdrawn streets between Coventry Street and Pall Mall East. The episode had somehow the air of an adventure. He looked at her; the hat was possibly rather large, but, in truth, she was the image of refinement, delicacy, virtue, virtuous surrender. He thought it was marvellous that there should exist such a woman as she. And he thought how marvellous was the protective vastness of the town, beneath whose shield he was free – free to live different lives simultaneously, to make his own laws, to maintain indefinitely exciting and delicious secrecies. Not half a mile off were Concepcion and Queen, and his amour was as safe from them as if he had hidden it in the depths of some hareemed Asiatic city.

Christine said politely:

"But I detain thee?"

"As for that," he replied, "what does that matter, after all?"

"Thou knowest," she said in a new tone, "I am all that is most worried. In this London they are never willing to leave you in peace."

"What is it, my poor child?" he asked benevolently.

"They talk of closing the Promenade," she answered.

"Never!" he murmured easily, reassuringly.

He remembered the night years earlier when, as a protest against some restrictive action of a County Council, the theatre of varieties whose Promenade rivalled throughout the whole world even the Promenade of the Folies-Bergère, shut its doors and darkened its blazing façade, and the entire West End seemed to go into a kind of shocked mourning. But the next night the theatre had reopened as usual and the Promenade had been packed. Close the Promenades! Absurd! Not the full bench of archbishops and bishops could close the Promenades! The thing was inconceivable, especially in war-time, when human nature was so human.

"But it is quite serious!" she cried. "Everyone speaks of it... What idiots! What frightful lack of imagination! And how unjust! What do they suppose we are going to do, we other women? Do they intend to put respectable women like me on to the pavement? It is a fantastic idea! Fantastic!... And the night-clubs closing too!"

"There is always the other place."

"The Ottoman? Do not speak to me of the Ottoman. Moreover, that also will be suppressed. They are all mad." She gave a great sigh. "Oh! What a fool I was to leave Paris! After all, in Paris, they know what it is, life! However, I weary thee. Let us say no more about it."

She controlled her agitation. The subject was excessively delicate, and that she should have expressed herself so violently on it showed the powerful reality of the emotion it had aroused in her. Unquestionably the decency of her livelihood was at stake. She had convinced him of the peril. But what could he say? He could not say, "Do not despair. You are indispensable; therefore you will not be dispensed with. These crises have often arisen before, and they always end in the same manner. And are there not the big hotels, the chic cinemas, certain restaurants? Not to mention the clientèle which you must have made for yourself?" Such remarks were impossible. But not more impossible than the very basis of his relations with her. He was aware again of the weight of an undischarged obligation to her. His behaviour towards her had always been perfection, and yet was she not his creditor? He had a conscience, and it was illogical and extremely inconvenient.

At that moment a young man flew along the silent, shadowed street, and as he passed them shouted somewhat hysterically the one word:

"Zepps!"

Christine clutched his arm. They stood still.

"Do not be frightened," said G. J. with perfect tranquillity.

"But I hear guns," she protested.

He, too, heard the distant sounds of guns, and it occurred to him that the sounds had begun earlier, while they were talking.

"I expect it's only anti-aircraft practice," he replied. "I seem to remember seeing a warning in the paper about there being practice one of these nights."

Christine, increasing the pressure on his arm and apparently trying to drag him away, complained:

"They ought to give warning of raids. That is elementary. This country is so bizarre."

"Oh!" said G. J., full of wisdom and standing his ground. "That would never do. Warnings would make panics, and they wouldn't help in the least. We are just as safe here as anywhere. Even supposing there is an air-raid, the chance of any particular spot being hit must be several million to one against. And I don't think for a moment there is an air-raid."

"Why?"

"Well, I don't," G. J. answered with calm superiority. The fact was that he did not know why he thought there was not an air-raid. To assume that there was not an air-raid, in the absence of proof positive of the existence of an air-raid, was with him constitutional: a state of mind precisely as illogical, biased and credulous as the alarmist mood which he disdained in others. Also he was lacking in candour, for after a few seconds the suspicion crept into his mind that there might indeed be an air-raid – and he would not utter it.

"In any case," said Christine, "they always give warning in Paris."

He thought:

"I'd better get this woman home," and said aloud: "Come along."

"But is it safe?" she asked anxiously.

He saw that she was the primeval woman, exactly like Concepcion and Queen. First she wanted to run, and then when he was ready to run she asked: "Is it safe?" And he felt very indulgent and comfortably masculine. He admitted that it would be absurd to expect the conduct of a frightened Christine to be governed by the operations of reason. He was not annoyed, because personally he simply did not care a whit whether they moved or not. While they were hesitating a group of people came round the corner. These people were talking loudly, and as they approached G. J. discerned that one of them was pointing to the sky.

"There she is! There she is!" shouted an eager voice. Seeing more human society in G. J. and Christine, the group stopped near them.

G. J. gazed in the indicated direction, and lo! there was a point of light in the sky.

And then guns suddenly began to sound much nearer.

"What did I tell you?" said another voice. "I told you they'd cleared the corner at the bottom of St. James's Street for a gun. Now they've got her going. Good for us they're shooting southwards."

Christine was shaking on G. J.'s arm.

"It's all right! It's all right!" he murmured compassionately, and she tightened her clutch on him in thanks.

He looked hard at the point of light, which might have been anything. The changing forms of thin clouds continually baffled the vision.

"By god!" shouted the first voice. "She's hit. See her stagger? She's hit. She'll blaze up in a moment. One down last week. Another this. Look at her now. She's afire."

The group gave a weak cheer.

Then the clouds cleared for an instant and revealed a crescent. G. J. said:

"That's the moon, you idiots. It's not a Zeppelin."

Even as he spoke he wondered, and regretted, that he should be calling them idiots. They were complete strangers to him. The group vanished, crestfallen, round another corner. G. J. laughed to Christine. Then the noise of guns was multiplied. That he was with Christine in the midst of an authentic air-raid could no longer be doubted. He was conscious of the wine he had drunk at the club. He had the sensation of human beings, men like himself, who ate and drank and laced their boots, being actually at that moment up there in the sky with intent to kill him and Christine. It was a marvellous sensation, terrible but exquisite. And he had the sensation of other human beings beyond the sea, giving deliberate orders in German for murder, murdering for their lives; and they, too, were like himself, and ate and drank and either laced their boots or had them laced daily. And the staggering apprehension of the miraculous lunacy of war swept through his soul.

30

THE CHILD'S ARM

"You see," He said to Christine, "It was not a Zeppelin... We shall be quite safe here."

But in that last phrase he had now confessed to her the existence of an air-raid. He knew that he was not behaving with the maximum of sagacity. There were, for example, hotels with subterranean grill-rooms close by, and there were similar refuges where danger would be less than in the street, though the street was narrow and might be compared to a trench. And yet he had said, "We shall be quite safe here." In others he would have condemned such an attitude.

Now, however, he realised that he was very like others. An inactive fatalism had seized him. He was too proud, too idle, too negligent, too curious, to do the wise thing. He and Christine were in the air-raid, and in it they should remain. He had just the senseless, monkeyish curiosity of the staring crowd so lyrically praised by the London Press. He was afraid, but his curiosity and inertia were stronger than his fear. Then came a most tremendous explosion – the loudest sound, the most formidable physical phenomenon that G. J. had ever experienced in his life. The earth under their feet trembled. Christine gave a squeal and seemed to subside to the ground, but he pulled her up again, not in calm self-possession, but by the sheer

automatism of instinct. A spasm of horrible fright shot through
him. He thought, in awe and stupefaction:

"A bomb!"

He thought about death and maiming and blood. The
relations between him and those everyday males aloft in the sky
seemed to be appallingly close. After the explosion perfect
silence – no screams, no noise of crumbling – perfect silence,
and yet the explosion seemed still to dominate the air! Ears
ached and sang. Something must be done. All theories of safety
had been smashed to atoms in the explosion. G. J. dragged
Christine along the street, he knew not why. The street was
unharmed. Not the slightest trace in it, so far as G. J. could tell
in the gloom, of destruction! But where the explosion had been,
whether east, west, south or north, he could not guess. Except
for the disturbance in his ears the explosion might have been a
hallucination.

Suddenly he saw at the end of the street a wide thoroughfare,
and he could not be sure what thoroughfare it was. Two motor-
buses passed the end of the street at mad speed; then two taxis;
then a number of people, men and women, running hard.
Useless and silly to risk the perils of that wide thoroughfare! He
turned back with Christine. He got her to run. In the thick
gloom he looked for an open door or a porch, but there was
none. The houses were like the houses of the dead. He made
more than one right angle turn. Christine gave a sign that she
could go no farther. He ceased trying to drag her. He was
recovering himself. Once more he heard the guns – childishly
feeble after the explosion of the bomb. After all, one spot was
as safe as another.

The outline of a building seemed familiar. It was an
abandoned chapel; he knew he was in St. Martin's Street. He
was about to pull Christine into the shelter of the front of the
chapel, when something happened for which he could not find
a name. True, it was an explosion. But the previous event had
been an explosion, and this one was a thousandfold more

intimidating. The earth swayed up and down. The sound alone of the immeasurable cataclysm annihilated the universe. The sound and the concussion transcended what had been conceivable. Both the sound and the concussion seemed to last for a long time. Then, like an afterthought, succeeded the awful noise of falling masses and the innumerable crystal tinkling of shattered glass. This noise ceased and began again...

G. J. was now in a strange condition of mild wonder. There was silence in the dark solitude of St. Martin's Street. Then the sound of guns supervened once more, but they were distant guns. G. J. discovered that he was not holding Christine, and also that, instead of being in the middle of the street, he was leaning against the door of a house. He called faintly, "Christine!" No reply. "In a moment," he said to himself, "I must go out and look for her. But I am not quite ready yet." He had a slight pain in his side; it was naught; it was naught, especially in comparison with the strange conviction of weakness and confusion.

He thought:

"We've not won this war yet," and he had qualms.

One poor lamp burned in the street. He started to walk slowly and uncertainly towards it. Near by he saw a hat on the ground. It was his own. He put it on. Suddenly the street lamp went out. He walked on, and stepped ankle-deep into broken glass. Then the road was clear again. He halted. Not a sign of Christine! He decided that she must have run away, and that she would run blindly and, finding herself either in Leicester Square or Lower Regent Street, would by instinct run home. At any rate, she could not be blown to atoms, for they were together at the instant of the explosion. She must exist, and she must have had the power of motion. He remembered that he had had a stick; he had it no longer. He turned back and, taking from his pocket the electric torch which had lately come into fashion, he examined the road for his stick. The sole object of interest which the torch revealed was a child's severed arm, with a fragment of brown frock on it and a tinsel ring on one of the fingers of the dirty little hand. The blood from the other end had stained the ground. G. J. abruptly switched off the torch. Nausea overcame him, and then a feeling of the most intense pity and anger overcame the nausea. (A month elapsed before he could mention his discovery of the child's arm to anyone at all.) The arm lay there as if it had been thrown there. Whence had it come? No doubt it had come from over the housetops...

He smelt gas, and then he felt cold water in his boots. Water was advancing in a flood along the street. "Broken mains, of course," he said to himself, and was rather pleased with the promptness of his explanation. At the elbow of St. Martin's Street, where a new dim vista opened up, he saw policemen, then firemen; then he heard the beat of a fire-engine, upon whose brass glinted the reflection of flames that were flickering in a gap between two buildings. A huge pile of debris encumbered the middle of the road. The vista was closed by a barricade, beyond which was a pressing crowd. "Stand clear there!" said a policeman to him roughly. "There's a wall going to fall there any minute." He walked off, hurrying with relief from the half-lit scene of busy, dim silhouettes. He could scarcely understand it; and he was incapable of replying to the policeman. He wanted to be alone and to ponder himself back into perfect composure. At the elbow again he halted afresh. And as he stood figures in couples, bearing stretchers, strode past him. The stretchers were covered with cloths that hung down. Not the faintest sound came from beneath the cloths.

After a time he went on. The other exit of St. Martin's Street was being barricaded as he reached it. A large crowd had assembled, and there was a sound of talking like steady rain. He pushed grimly through the crowd. He was set apart from the idle crowd. He would tell the crowd nothing. In a minute he was going westwards on the left side of Coventry Street again. The other side was as populous with saunterers as ever. The violet glow-worms still burned in front of the theatres and cinemas. Motor-buses swept by; taxis swept by; parcels vans swept by, hooting. A newsman was selling papers at the corner. Was he in a dream now? Or had he been in a dream in St. Martin's Street? The vast capacity of the capital for digesting experience seemed to endanger his reason. Save for the fragments of eager conversation everywhere overheard, there was not a sign of disturbance of the town's habitual life. And he was within four hundred yards of the child's arm and of the spot where the procession of stretcher-bearers had passed. One thought gradually gained ascendancy in his mind: "I am saved!" It became exultant: "I might have been blown to bits, but I am saved!" Despite the world's anguish and the besetting imminence of danger, life and the city which he inhabited had never seemed so enchanting, so lovely, as they did then. He hurried towards Cork Street, hopeful.

31

"Romance"

At two periods of the day Martha, with great effort and for professional purposes, achieved some degree of personal tidiness. The first period began at about four o'clock in the afternoon. By six o'clock or six-thirty she had slipped back into the sloven. The second period began at about ten o'clock at night. It was more brilliant while it lasted, but owing to the accentuation of Marthe's characteristics by fatigue it seldom lasted more than an hour. When Marthe opened the door to G. J. she was at her proudest, intensely conscious of being clean and neat, and unwilling to stand any nonsense from anybody. Of course she was polite to G. J. as the chief friend of the establishment and a giver of good tips, but she deprecated calls by gentlemen in the evening, for unless they were made by appointment the risk of complications at once arose.

The mention of an air-raid rendered her definitely inimical. Formerly Marthe had been more than average nervous in air-raids, but she had grown used to them and now defied them. As she kept all windows closed on principle she heard less of raids than some people. G. J. did not explain the circumstances. He simply asked if Madame had returned. No, Madame had not returned. True, Marthe had not been unaware of guns and things, but there was no need to worry; Madame must have arrived at the theatre long before the guns started. Marthe really could not be bothered with these unnecessary apprehensions. She had her duties to attend to like other folks, and they were heavy, and she washed her hands of air-raids; she accepted no responsibility for them; for her, within the flat, they did not exist, and the whole German war-machine was thereby foiled. G. J. was on the point of a full explanation, but he checked himself. A recital of the circumstances would not immediately help, and it might hinder. Concealing his astonishment at the excesses of which unimaginative stolidity is capable, even in an Italian, he turned down the stairs again.

He stopped in the middle of the stairs, because he did not know what he was going to do, and he seemed to lack force for decisions. No harm could have happened to Christine; she had run off, that was certain. And yet – had he not often heard of the impish tricks of explosions? Of one person being taken and another left? Was it not possible that Christine had been blown to the other end of the street, and was now lying there?... No! Either she was on her way home, or, automatically, she had scurried to the theatre, which was close to St. Martin's Street, and been too fearful to venture forth again. Perhaps she was looking somewhere for *him*. Yet she might be dead. In any case, what could he do? Ring up the police? It was too soon. He decided that he would wait in Cork Street for half an hour. This plan appealed to him for the mere reason that it was negative.

As he opened the front door he saw a taxi standing outside. The taxi-man had taken one of the lamps from its bracket, and was looking into the interior of the cab, which was ornate with toycurtains and artificial flowers to indicate to the world that he was an owner-driver and understood life. Hearing the noise of the door, he turned his head – he was wearing a bowler hat and a smart white muffler – and said to G. J., with self-respecting respect for a gentleman:

"This is No. 170, isn't it, sir?"

"Yes."

The taxi-man jerked his head to draw G. J.'s attention to the interior of the vehicle. Christine was half on the seat and half on the floor, unconscious, with shut eyes.

Instantly G. J. was conscious of making a complete recovery from all the effects, physical and moral, of the air-raid.

"Just help me to get her out, will you?" he said in a casual tone, "and I'll carry her upstairs. Where did you pick the lady up?"

"Strand, sir, nearly opposite Romano's."

"The dickens you did!"

"Shock from air-raid, I suppose, sir."

"Probably."

"She did seem a little upset when she hailed me, or I shouldn't have taken her. I was off home, and I only took her to oblige."

The taxi-man ran quickly round to the other side of the cab and entered it by the off-door, behind Christine. Together the men lifted her up.

"I can manage her," said G. J. calmly.

"Excuse me, sir, you'll have to get hold lower down, so as her waist'll be nearly as high as your shoulder. My brother's a fireman."

"Right," said G. J. "By the way, what's the fare?"

Holding Christine across his shoulder with the right arm, he unbuttoned his overcoat with his left hand and took out change from his trouser pocket for the driver.

"You might pull the door to after me," he said, in response to the driver's expression of thanks.

"Certainly, sir."

The door banged. He was alone with Christine on the long, dark, inclement stairs. He felt the contours of her body through her clothes. She was limp, helpless. She was a featherweight. She was nothing at all; inexpressibly girlish, pathetic, dear. Never had G. J. felt as he felt then. He mounted the stairs rather quickly, with firm, disdaining steps, and, despite his being a little out of breath, he had a tremendous triumph over the stolidity of Marthe when she answered his ring. Marthe screamed, and in the scream readjusted her views concerning air-raids.

"It's queer this swoon lasting such a long time!" he reflected, when Christine had been deposited on the sofa in the sitting-room, and the common remedies and tricks tried without result, and Marthe had gone into the kitchen to make hot water hotter.

He had established absolute empire over Marthe. He had insisted on Marthe not being silly; and yet, though he had already been silly himself in his absurd speculations as to the possibility of Christine's death, he was now in danger of being silly again. Did ordinary swoons ever continue as this one was continuing? Would Christine ever come out of it? He stood with his back to the fireplace, and her head and shoulders were right under him, so that he looked almost perpendicularly down upon them. Her face was as pale as ivory; every drop of blood seemed to have left it; the same with her neck and bosom; her limbs had dropped anyhow, in disarray; a fur jacket was untidily cast over her black muslin dress. But her waved hair, fresh from the weekly visit of the professional coiffeur, remained in the most perfect order.

G. J. looked round the room. It was getting very shabby. Its pale enamelled shabbiness and the tawdry ugliness of nearly every object in it had never repelled and saddened him as they did then. The sole agreeable item was a large photograph of the mistress in a rich silver frame which he had given her. She would not let him buy knicknacks or draperies for her drawing-room; she preferred other presents. And now that she lay in the room, but with no power to animate it, he knew what the room really looked like; it looked like a dentist's waiting-room, except that no dentist would expose copies of *La Vie Parisienne* to the view of clients. It had no more individuality than a dentist's waiting-room. Indeed it was a dentist's waiting-room. He remembered that he had had similar ideas about the room at the beginning of his acquaintance with Christine; but he had partially forgotten them, and moreover, they had not by any means been so clear and desolating as in that moment.

He looked from the photograph to her face. The face was like the photograph, but in the swoon its wistfulness became unbearable. And it was so young. What was she? Twenty-seven? She could not be twenty-eight. No age! A girl! And talk about experience! She had had scarcely any experience, save one kind of experience. The monotony and narrowness of her life was terrifying to him. He had fifty interests, but she had only one. All her days were alike. She had no change and no holiday; no past and no future; no family; no intimate friends – unless Marthe was an intimate friend; no horizons, no prospects. She witnessed life in London through the distorting, mystifying veil of a foreign language imperfectly understood. She was the most solitary girl in London, or she would have been were there not a hundred thousand or so others in nearly the same case... Stay! Once she had delicately allowed him to divine that she had been to Bournemouth with a gentleman for a week-end. He could recall nothing else. Nightly, or almost nightly, she listened to the same insufferably tedious jokes in the same insufferably tedious revue. But the authorities were soon going to deprive her of the opportunity of doing that. And then she would cease to receive even the education that revues can furnish, and in her mind no images would survive but images connected with the material arts of love. For, after all, what had they truly in common, he and she, but a periodical transient excitation?

When next he looked at her, her eyes were wide open and a flush was coming, as imperceptibly as the dawn, into her cheeks. He took her hands again and rubbed them. Marthe returned, and Christine drank. She gazed, in weak silence, first at Marthe and then at G. J. After a few moments no one spoke. Marthe took off Christine's boots, and rubbed her stockinged feet, and then kissed them violently.

"Madame should go to bed."

"I am better."

Marthe left the room, seeming resentful.

"What has passed?" Christine murmured, without smiling.

"A faint in the taxi, my poor child. That was all," said G. J. calmly.

"But how is it that I find myself here?"

"I carried thee upstairs in my arms."

"Thou?"

"Why not?" He spoke lightly, with careful negligence. "It appears that thou wast in the Strand."

"Was I? I lost thee. Something tore thee from me. I ran. I ran till I could not run. I was sure that never more should I see thee alive. Oh! My Gilbert, what terrible moments! What a catastrophe! Never shall I forget those moments!"

G. J. said, with bland supremacy:

"But it is necessary that thou shouldst forget them. Master thyself. Thou knowst now what it is – an air-raid. It was an ordinary air-raid. There have been many like it. There will be many more. For once we were in the middle of a raid – by chance. But we are safe – that is enough."

"But the deaths?"

He shook his head.

"But there must have been many deaths!"

"I do not know. There will have been deaths. There usually are." He shrugged his shoulders.

Christine sat up and gave a little screech.

"Ah!" She burst out, her features suddenly transformed by enraged protest. "Why wilt thou act thy cold man?"

He was amazed at the sudden nervous strength she showed.

"But, my little one – "

She cried:

"Why wilt thou act thy cold man? I shall become mad in this sacred England. I shall become totally mad. You are all the same, all, all, men and women. You are marvels – let it be so! – but you are not human. Do you then wish to be taken for telegraph-poles? Always you are pretending something. Pretending that you have no sentiments. And you are soaked in sentimentality. But no! You will not show it! You will not applaud your soldiers in the streets. You will not salute your flag. You will not salute even a corpse. You have only one phrase: 'It is nothing'. If you win a battle, 'It is nothing' If you lose one, 'It is nothing'. If you are nearly killed in an air-raid, 'It is nothing'. And if you were killed outright and could yet speak, you would say, with your eternal sneer, 'It is nothing'. You other men, you make love with the air of turning on a tap. As for your women, god knows – ! But I have a horror of Englishwomen. Prudes but wantons. Can I not guess? Always hypocrites. Always holding themselves in. My god, that pinched smile! And your women of the world especially. Have they a natural gesture? Yet does not everyone know that they are rotten with vice and perversity? And your actresses!... And they talk of us! Ah, well! For me, I can say that I earn my living honestly, every sou of it. For all that I receive, I give. And they would throw me on to the pavement to starve, me whose function in society – "

She collapsed in sobs, and with averted face held out her arms in appeal. G. J., at once admiring and stricken with compassion, bent and clasped her neck, and kissed her, and kept his mouth on hers. Her tears dropped freely on his cheeks. Her sobs shook both of them. Gradually the sobs decreased in violence and frequency. In an infant's broken voice she murmured into his mouth:

"My wolf! Is it true – that thou didst carry me here in thy arms? I am so proud."

He was not in the slightest degree irritated or grieved by her tirade. But the childlike changeableness and facility of her emotions touched him. He savoured her youth, and himself felt curiously young. It was the fact that within the last year he had grown younger.

He thought of great intellectuals, artists, men of action, princes, kings – historical figures – in whom courtesans had inspired immortal passion. He thought of the illustrious courtesans who had made themselves heroic in legend, women whose loves were countless and often venal, and yet whose renown had come down to posterity as gloriously as that of supreme poets. He thought of lifelong passionate attachments, which to the world were inexplicable, and which the world never tired of leniently discussing. He overheard people saying: "Yes. Picked her up somewhere, in a Promenade. She worships him, and he adores her. Don't know where he hides her. You see them about together sometimes – at concerts, for instance. Mysterious-looking creature she is. Plays the part very well, too. Strange affair. But, of course, there's no accounting for these things."

The role attracted him. And there could be no doubt that she did worship him utterly. He did not analyse his feeling for her – perhaps could not. She satisfied something in him that was profound. She never offended his sensibilities, nor wearied him. Her manners were excellent, her gestures full of grace and modesty, her temperament extreme. A unique combination! And if the tie between them was not real and secure, why should he have yearned for her company that night after the scenes with Concepcion and Queen. Those women challenged him, discomposed him, fretted him, fought him, left his nerves raw. She soothed. Why should he not, in the French phrase, "put her among her own furniture?" In a proper artistic environment, an environment created by himself, of taste and moderate luxury, she would be exquisite. She would blossom. And she would blossom for him alone. She would live for his footstep on her threshold; and when he was not there she would dream amid cushions like a cat. In the right environment she would become another being, that was to say, the same being, but orchidised. And when he was old, when he was sixty-five, she would still be young, still be under forty and seductive. And the publishing of his last will and testament, under which she inherited all, would render her famous throughout all the West

End, and the word "romance" would spring to every lip. He searched in his mind for the location of suitable flats.

"Is it true that thou didst carry me in thine arms?" repeated Christine.

He murmured into her mouth:

"Is it true? Can she doubt? The proof, then."

And he picked her up as though she had been a doll, and carried her into the bedroom. As she lay on the bed, she raised her arm and looked at the broken wrist-watch and sighed.

"My mascot. It is not a *blague*, my mascot."

Shortly afterwards she began to cry again, at first gently; then sobs supervened.

"She must sleep," he said firmly.

She shook her head.

"I cannot. I have been too upset. It is impossible that I should sleep."

"She must."

"Go and buy me a drug."

"If I go and buy her a drug, will she undress and get into bed while I am away?"

She nodded.

Calling Marthe, and taking the latch-key of the street-door, he went to his chemist's in Dover Street and bought some potassium bromide and sal volatile. When he came back Marthe whispered to him:

"She sleeps. She has told me everything as I undressed her. The poor child!"

32

MRS BRAIDING

G. J. went home at once, partly so that Christine should not be disturbed, partly because he desired solitude in order to examine and compose his mind. Mrs Braiding had left an agreeable modest fire – fit for cold April – in the drawing-room. He had just sat down in front of it and was tranquillising himself in the familiar harmonious beauty of the apartment (which, however, did seem rather insipid after the decorative excesses of Queen's room), when he heard footsteps on the little stairway from the upper floor. Mrs Braiding entered the drawing-room.

This was a Mrs Braiding very different from the Mrs Braiding of 1914, a shameless creature of more rounded contours than of old, and not quite so spick and span as of old. She was carrying in her arms that which before the war she could not have conceived herself as carrying. The being was invisible in wraps, but it was there; and she seemed to have no shame for it, seemed indeed to be proud of it and defiant about it.

Braiding's military career had been full of surprises. He had expected within a few months of joining the colours to be dashing gloriously and homicidally at panic-stricken Germans across the plains of Flanders, to be, in fact, saving the Empire at the muzzle of rifle and the point of bayonet. In truth, he found that for interminable, innumerable weeks his job was to save the

Empire by cleaning harness on the East Coast of England – for under advice he had transferred to the artillery. Later, when his true qualifications were discovered, he had to save the Empire by polishing the buttons and serving the morning tea and buying the cigarettes of a major who in 1914 had been a lawyer by profession and a soldier only for fun. The major talked too much, and to the wrong people. He became lyric concerning the talents of Braiding to a dandiacal Divisional General at Colchester, and soon, by the actuating of mysterious forces and the filling up of many Army forms, Braiding was removed to Colchester, and had to save the Empire by valeting the Divisional General. Foiled in one direction, Braiding advanced in another. By tradition, when a valet marries a lady's maid, the effect on the birth-rate is naught. And it is certain that but for the war Braiding would not have permitted himself to act as he did. The Empire, however, needed citizens. The first rumour that Braiding had done what in him lay to meet the need spread through the kitchens of the Albany like a new gospel, incredible and stupefying – but which imposed itself. The Albany was never the same again.

All the kitchens were agreed that Mr Hoape would soon be stranded. The spectacle of Mrs Braiding as she slipped out of a morning past the porter's lodge mesmerised beholders. At last, when things had reached the limit, Mrs Braiding slipped out and did not come back. Meanwhile a much younger sister of hers had been introduced into the flat. But when Mrs Braiding went the virgin went also. The flat was more or less closed, and Mr Hoape had slept at his club for weeks. At length the flat was reopened, but whereas three had left it, four returned.

That a bachelor of Mr Hoape's fastidiousness should tolerate in his home a woman with a tiny baby was remarkable; it was as astounding perhaps as any phenomenon of the war, and a sublime proof that Mr Hoape realised that the Empire was fighting for its life. It arose from the fact that both G. J. and Braiding were men of considerable sagacity. Braiding had issued an order, after seeing G. J., that his wife should not leave G. J.'s service. And Mrs Braiding, too, had her sense of duty. She was very proud of G. J.'s war-work, and would have thought it disloyal to leave him in the lurch, and so possibly prejudice the war-work – especially as she was convinced that he would never get anybody else comparable to herself.

At first she had been a little apologetic and diffident about her offspring. But soon the man-child had established an important position in the flat, and though he was generally invisible, his individuality pervaded the whole place. G. J. had easily got accustomed to the new inhabitant. He tolerated and then liked the babe. He had never nursed it – for such an act would have been excessive – but he had once stuck his finger in its mouth, and he had given it a perambulator that folded up. He did venture secretly to hope that Braiding would not imagine it to be his duty to provide further for the needs of the Empire.

That Mrs Braiding had grown rather shameless in motherhood was shown by her quite casual demeanour as she now came into the drawing-room with the baby, for this was the first time she had ever come into the drawing-room with the baby, knowing her august master to be there.

"Mrs Braiding," said G. J. "That child ought to be asleep."

"He is asleep, sir," said the woman, glancing into the mysteries of the immortal package, "but Maria hasn't been able to get back yet because of the raid, and I didn't want to leave him upstairs alone with the cat. He slept all through the raid."

"It seems some of you have made the cellar quite comfortable."

"Oh, yes, sir. Particularly now with the oilstove and the carpet. Perhaps one night you'll come down, sir."

"I may have to. I shouldn't have been much surprised to find some damage here to-night. They've been very close, you know… Near Leicester Square." He could not be troubled to say more than that.

"Have they really, sir? It's just like them," said Mrs Braiding. And she then continued in exactly the same tone: "Lady Queenie Paulle has just been telephoning from Lechford House, sir." She still – despite her marvellous experiences – impishly loved to make extraordinary announcements as if they were nothing at all. And she felt an uplifted satisfaction in having talked to Lady Queenie Paulle herself on the telephone.

"What does *she* want?" G. J. asked impatiently, and not at all in a voice proper for the mention of a Lady Queenie to a Mrs Braiding. He was annoyed; he resented any disturbance of the repose which he so acutely needed.

Mrs Braiding showed that she was a little shocked. The old harassed look of bearing up against complex anxieties came into her face.

"Her ladyship wished to speak to you, sir, on a matter of importance. I didn't know *where* you were, sir."

That last phrase was always used by Mrs Braiding when she wished to imply that she could guess where G. J. had been. He did not suppose that she was acquainted with the circumstances of his amour, but he had a suspicion amounting to conviction that she had conjectured it, as men of science from certain derangements in their calculations will conjecture the existence of a star that no telescope has revealed.

"Well, better leave Lady Queenie alone for to-night."

"I promised her ladyship that I would ring her up again in any case in a quarter of an hour. That was approximately ten minutes ago."

He could not say:

"Be hanged to your promises!"

Reluctantly he went to the telephone himself, and learnt from Lady Queenie, who always knew everything, that the raiders were expected to return in about half an hour, and that she and Concepcion desired his presence at Lechford House. He replied coldly that he was too tired to come, and was indeed practically in bed. "But you must come. Don't you understand we want you?" said Lady Queenie autocratically, adding: "And don't forget that business about the hospitals. We didn't attend to it this afternoon, you know." He said to himself: "And whose fault was that?" and went off angrily, wondering what mysterious power of convention it was that compelled him to respond to the whim of a girl whom he scarcely even respected.

33

THE ROOF

The main door of Lechford House was ajar, and at the sound of G. J.'s footsteps on the marble of the porch it opened. Robin, the secretary, stood at the threshold. Evidently she had been set to wait for him.

"The men-servants are all in the cellars," said she perkily.

G. J. retorted with sardonic bitterness:

"And quite right, too. I'm glad someone's got some sense left."

Yet he did not really admire the men-servants for being in the cellars. Somehow it seemed mean of them not to be ready to take any risks, however unnecessary.

Robin, hiding her surprise and confusion in a nervous snigger, banged the heavy door, and led him through the halls and up the staircases. As she went forward she turned on electric lamps here and there in advance, turning them off by the alternative switches after she had passed them, so that in the vast, shadowed, echoing interior the two appeared to be preceded by light and pursued by a tide of darkness. She was mincingly feminine, and very conscious of the fact that G. J. was a fine gentleman. In the afternoon, and again to-night – at first, he had taken her for a mere girl; but as she halted under a lamp to hold a door for him at the entrance to the upper stairs, he perceived that it must have been a long time since she was a girl. Often had he warned himself that the fashion of short skirts and revealed stockings gave a deceiving youthfulness to the middle-aged, and yet nearly every day he had to learn the lesson afresh.

He was just expecting to be shown into the boudoir when Robin stopped at a very small door.

"Her ladyship and Mrs Carlos Smith are out on the roof. This is the ladder," she said, and illuminated the ladder.

G. J. had no choice but to mount. Luckily he had kept his hat. He put it on. As he climbed he felt a slight recurrence of the pain in his side which he had noticed in St. Martin's Street. The roof was a very strange, tempestuous place, and insecure. He had an impression similar to that of being at sea, for the wind, which he had scarcely observed in the street, made melancholy noises in the new protective wire-netting that stretched over his head. This bomb-catching contrivance, fastened on thick iron stanchions, formed a sort of second roof, and was a very solid and elaborate affair which must have cost much money. The upstreaming light from the ladder-shaft was suddenly extinguished. He could see nobody, and the loneliness was uncomfortable.

Somehow, when Robin had announced that the ladies were on the roof he had imagined the roof as a large, flat expanse. It was nothing of the kind. So far as he could distinguish in the deep gloom it had leaden pathways, but on either hand it sloped sharply up or sharply down. He might have fallen sheer into a chasm, or stumbled against the leaden side of a slant. He descried a lofty construction of carved masonry with an iron ladder clamped into it, far transcending the net. Not immediately did he comprehend that it was merely one of the famous Lechford chimney-stacks looming gigantic in the night. He walked cautiously onward and came to a precipice and drew back, startled, and took another pathway at right angles to the first one. Presently the protective netting stopped, and he was exposed to heaven; he had reached the roof of the servants' quarters towards the back of the house.

He stood still and gazed, accustoming himself to the night. The moon was concealed, but there were patches of dim stars. He could make out, across the empty Green Park, the huge silhouette of Buckingham Palace, and beyond that the tower of Westminster Cathedral. To his left he could see part of a courtyard or small square, with a foreshortened black figure, no doubt a policeman, carrying a flash-lamp. The tree-lined Mall seemed to be utterly deserted. But Piccadilly showed a line of faint stationary lights and still fainter moving lights. A mild hum and the sounds of motor-horns and cab-whistles came from Piccadilly, where people were abroad in ignorance that the raid was not really over. All the heavens were continually restless with long, shifting rays from the anti-aircraft stations, but the rays served only to prove the power of darkness.

Then he heard quick, smooth footsteps. Two figures, one behind the other, approached him, almost running, eagerly, girlishly, with little cries. The first was Queen, who wore a white skirt and a very close-fitting black jersey. Concepcion also wore a white skirt and a very close-fitting black jersey, but with a long mantle hung loosely from the shoulders. Both were bareheaded.

"Isn't it splendid, G. J.?" Queen burst out enthusiastically. Again G. J. had the sensation of being at sea – perhaps on the deck of a yacht. He felt that rain ought to have been beating on the face of the excited and careless girl. Before answering, he turned up the collar of his overcoat. Then he said:

"Won't you catch a chill?"

"I'm never cold," said Queen. It was true. "I shall always come up here for raids in future."

"You seem to be enjoying it."

"I love it. I love it. I only thought of it to-night. It's the next best thing to being a man and being at the Front. It *is* being at the Front."

Her face was little more than a pale, featureless oval to him in the gloom, but he could divine from the vibrations of her voice that she was as ecstatic as a young maid at her first dance.

"And what about that business interview that you've just asked for on the 'phone?" G. J. acidly demanded.

"Oh, we'll come to that later. We wanted a man here – not to save us, only to save us from ourselves – and you were the best we could think of, wasn't he, Con? But you've not heard about my next bazaar, G. J., have you?"

"I thought it was a Pageant."

"I mean after that. A bazaar. I don't know yet what it will be for, but I've got lots of the most topping ideas for it. For instance, I'm going to have a First-Aid Station."

"What for? Air-raid casualties?"

Queen scorned his obtuseness, pouring out a cataract of swift sentences.

"No. First-Aid to lovely complexions. Help for Distressed Beauties. I shall get Roger Fry to design the Station and the costumes of my attendants. It will be marvellous, and I tell you there'll always be a queue waiting for admittance. I shall have all the latest dodges in the sublime and fatal art of make-up, and if any of the Bond Street gang refuse to help me I'll damn well ruin them. But they won't refuse because they know what I'll do. Gontran is coming in with his new steaming process for waving. Con, you must try that. It's a miracle. Waving's no good for my style of coiffure, but it would suit you. You always wouldn't wave, but you've got to now, my seraph. The electric heater works in sections. No danger. No inconvenience to the poor old scalp. The waves will last for six months or more. It has to be seen to be believed, and even then you can't believe it. Its only fault is that it's too natural to be natural. But who wants to be natural? This modern craze for naturalness seems to me to be rather unwholesome, not to say perverted. What?"

She seized G. J.'s arm convulsively.

Concepcion had said nothing. G. J. sought her eyes in the darkness, but did not find them.

"So much for the bazaar!" he said.

Queen suddenly cried aloud:

"What is it, Robin? Has Captain Brickly telephoned?"

"Yes, my lady," came a voice faintly across the gloom from the region of the ladder-shaft.

"They're coming! They'll be here directly!" exclaimed Queen, loosing G. J. and clapping her hands.

G. J. thought of Robin affixed to the telephone, and some scarlet-shouldered officer at the War Office quitting duty for the telephone, in order to keep the capricious girl informed of military movements simply because she had taken the trouble to be her father's daughter, and in so doing had acquired the right to treat the imperial machine as one of her nursery toys. And he became unreasonably annoyed.

"I suppose you were cowering in your Club during the first Act?" she said, with vivacity.

"Yes," G. J. briefly answered. Once more he was aware of a strong instinctive disinclination to relate what had happened to him. He was too proud to explain, and perhaps too tired.

"You ought to have been up here. They dropped two bombs close to the National Gallery; pity they couldn't have destroyed a Landseer or two while they were so near! There were either seven or eight killed and eighteen wounded, so far as is known. But there were probably more. There was quite a fire, too, but that was soon got under. We saw it all except the explosion of the bombs. We weren't looking in the right place – no luck! However, we saw the Zepp. What a shame the moon's disappeared again! Listen! Listen!... Can't you hear the engines?"

G. J. shrugged his shoulders. Nothing could be heard above the faint hum of Piccadilly. The wind seemed to have diminished to a chill, fitful zephyr.

Concepcion had sat down on a coping.

"Look!" she exclaimed in a startled whisper, and sprang erect.

To the south, down among the trees, a red light flashed and was gone. The faint, irregular hum of Piccadilly persisted for a couple of seconds, and then was drowned in the loud report, which seemed to linger and wander in the great open spaces. G. J.'s flesh crept. He comprehended the mad ecstasy of Queen, and because he comprehended it his anger against her increased.

"Can you see the Zepp?" murmured Queen, as it were ferociously. "It must be within range, or they wouldn't have fired. Look along the lines of the searchlights. One of them, at any rate, must have got on to it. We saw it before. Can't you see it? I can hear the engines, I think."

Another flash was followed by another resounding report. More guns spoke in the distance. Then a glare arose on the southern horizon.

"Incendiary bomb!" muttered Queen. She stood stock-still, with her mouth open, entranced.

The Zeppelin or the Zeppelins remained invisible and inaudible. Yet they must be aloft there, somewhere amid the criss-cross of the unresting searchlights. G. J. waited, powerfully impressed, incapable of any direct action, gazing blankly now at the women and now at the huge undecipherable heaven and earth, and receiving the chill zephyr on his face. The nearmost gun had ceased to fire. Occasionally there was perfect silence – for no faintest hum came from Piccadilly, and nothing seemed to move there. The further guns recommenced, and then the group heard a new sound, rather like the sound of a worn-out taxi accelerating before changing gear. It grew gradually louder. It grew very loud. It seemed to be ripping the envelope of the air. It seemed as if it would last for ever – till it finished with a gigantic and intimidating *plop* quite near the front of Lechford House. Queen said:

"Shrapnel – and a big lump!"

G. J. could see the quick heave of her bosom imprisoned in the black. She was breathing through her nostrils.

"Come downstairs into the house," he said sharply – more than sharply, brutally. "Where in the name of God is the sense of stopping up here? Are you both mad?"

Queen laughed lightly.

"Oh, G. J.! How funny you are! I'm really surprised you haven't left London for good before now. By rights you ought to belong to the Hook-it Brigade. Do you know what they do? They take a ticket to any station north or west, and when they get out of the train they run to the nearest house and interview the tenant. Has he any accommodation to let? Will he take them in as boarders? Will he take them as paying guests? Will he let the house furnished? Will he let it unfurnished? Will he allow them to camp out in the stables? Will he sell the blooming house? So there isn't a house to be had on the North Western nearer than Leighton Buzzard."

"Are you going? Because I am," said G. J. Concepcion murmured:

"Don't go."

"I shall go – and so will you, both of you."

"G. J.," Queen mocked him, "you're in a funk."

"I've got courage enough to go, anyhow," said he. "And that's more than you have."

"You're losing your temper."

As a fact he was. He grabbed at Queen, but she easily escaped him. He saw the whiteness of her skirt in the distance of the roof, dimly rising. She was climbing the ladder up the side of the chimney. She stood on the top of the chimney, and laughed again. A gun sounded.

G. J. said no more. Using his flash-lamp he found his way to the ladder-shaft and descended. He was in the warm and sheltered interior of the house; he was in another and a saner world. Robin was at the foot of the ladder; she blinked under his lamp.

"I've had enough of that," he said, and followed her to the illuminated boudoir, where after a certain hesitation she left him. Alone in the boudoir he felt himself to be a very shamed and futile person, and he was still extremely angry. The next moment Concepcion entered the boudoir.

"Ah!" he murmured, curiously appeased.

"You're quite right," said Concepcion simply.

He said:

"Can you give me any reason, Con, why we should make a present of ourselves to the Hun?"

Concepcion repeated:

"You're quite right."

"Is she coming?"

Concepcion made a negative sign. "She doesn't know what fear is, Queen doesn't."

"She doesn't know what sense is. She ought to be whipped, and if I got hold of her I'd whip her."

"She'd like nothing better," said Concepcion.

G. J. removed his overcoat and sat down.

34

IN THE BOUDOIR

"We aren't so desperately safe even here," said G. J., firmly pursuing the moral triumph which Concepcion's very surprising and comforting descent from the roof had given him.

"Don't go to extremes," she answered.

"No, I won't." He thought of the valetry in the cellars, and the impossible humiliation of joining them; and added: "I merely state." Then, after a moment of silence: "By the way, was it only *her* idea that I should come along, or did the command come from both of you?" The suspicion of some dark, feminine conspiracy revisited him.

"It was Queen's idea."

"Oh! Well, I don't quite understand the psychology of it."

"Surely that's plain."

"It isn't in the least plain."

Concepcion loosed and dropped her cloak, and, not even glancing at G. J., went to the fire and teased it with the poker. Bending down, with one hand on the graphic and didactic mantelpiece, and staring into the fire, she said quietly:

"Queen's in love with you, of course."

The words were a genuine shock to his sarcastic and rather embittered and bullying mood. Was he to believe them? The vibrant, uttering voice was convincing enough. Was he to show

201

the conventional incredulity proper to such an occasion? Or
was he to be natural, brutally natural? He was drawn first to one
course and then to the other, and finally spoke at random, by
instinct:

"What have I been doing to deserve this?"

Concepcion replied, still looking into the fire:

"As far as I can gather it must be your masterful ways at the
Hospital Committee that have impressed her, and especially
your unheard-of tyrannical methods with her august mother."

"I see... Thanks!"

It had not occurred to him that he had treated the
Marchioness tyrannically; he treated her like anybody else; he
now perceived that this was to treat her tyrannically. His
imagination leapt forward as he gazed round the weird and
exciting room which Queen had brought into existence for the
illustration of herself, and as he pictured the slim, pale figure
outside clinging in the night to the vast chimney, and as he
listened to the faint intermittent thud of far-off guns. He had a
spasm of delicious temptation. He was tempted by Queen's
connections and her prospective wealth. If anybody was to
possess millions after the war, Queen would one day possess
millions. Her family and her innumerable powerful relatives
would be compelled to accept him without the slightest reserve,
for Queen issued edicts; and through all those big people he
would acquire immense prestige and influence, which he could
use greatly. Ambition flared up in him – ambition to impress
himself on his era. And he reflected with satisfaction on the
strangeness of the fact that such an opportunity should have
come to him, the son of a lawyer, solely by virtue of his own
individuality. He thought of Christine, and poor little Christine
was shrunk to nothing at all; she was scarcely even an object of
compassion; she was a prostitute.

But far more than by Queen's connections and prospective
wealth he was tempted by her youth and beauty; he saw her
beautiful and girlish, and he was sexually tempted. Most of all

he was tempted by the desire to master her. He saw again the foolish, elegant, brilliant thing on the chimney pretending to defy him and mock at him. And he heard himself commanding sharply: "Come down. Come down and acknowledge your ruler. Come down and be whipped." (For had he not been told that she would like nothing better?) And he heard the West End of London and all the country-houses saying, "She obeys *him* like a slave." He conceived a new and dazzling environment for himself; and it was undeniable that he needed something of the kind, for he was growing lonely; before the war he had lived intensely in his younger friends, but the war had taken nearly all of them away from him, many of them for ever.

Then he said in a voice almost resentfully satiric, and wondered why such a tone should come from his lips:

"Another of her caprices, no doubt."

"What do you mean – another of her caprices?" said Concepcion, straightening herself and leaning against the mantelpiece.

He had noticed, only a moment earlier, on the mantelpiece, a large photograph of the handsome Molder, with some writing under it.

"Well, what about that, for example?"

He pointed. Concepcion glanced at him for the first time, and her eyes followed the direction of his finger.

"That! I don't know anything about it."

"Do you mean to say that while you were gossiping till five o'clock this morning, you two, she didn't mention it?"

"She didn't."

G. J. went right on, murmuring:

"Wants to do something unusual. Wants to astonish the town."

"No! No!"

"Then you seriously tell me she's fallen in love with me, Con?"

"I haven't the slightest doubt of it."

"Did she say so?"

There was a sound outside the door. They both started like plotters in danger, and tried to look as if they had been discussing the weather or the war. But no interruption occurred.

"Well, she did. I know I shall be thought mischievous. If she had the faintest notion I'd breathed the least hint to you, she'd quarrel with me eternally – of course. I couldn't bear another quarrel. If it had been anybody else but you I wouldn't have said a word. But you're different from anybody else. And I couldn't help it. You don't know what Queen is. Queen's a white woman."

"So you said this afternoon."

"And so she is. She has the most curious and interesting brain, and she's as straight as a man."

"I've never noticed it."

"But I know. I know. And she's an exquisite companion."

"And so on and so on. And I expect the scheme is that I am to make love to her and be worried out of my life, and then propose to her and she'll accept me." The word "scheme" brought up again his suspicion of a conspiracy. Evidently there was no conspiracy, but there was a plot – of one... A nervous breakdown? Was Concepcion merely under an illusion that she had had a nervous breakdown, or had she in truth had one, and was this singular interview a result of it?

Concepcion continued with surprising calm magnanimity:

"I know her mind is strange, but it's lovely. No one but me has ever seen into it. She's following her instinct, unconsciously – as we all do, you know. And her instinct's right, in spite of everything. Her instinct's telling her just now that she needs a master. And that's exactly what she does need. We must remember she's very young – "

"Yes," G. J. interrupted, bursting out with a kind of savagery that he could not explain. "Yes. She's young, and she finds even my age spicy. There'd be something quite amusingly piquant for her in marrying a man nearly thirty years her senior."

Concepcion advanced towards him. There she stood in front of him, quite close to his chair, gazing down at him in her tight black jersey and short white skirt; she was wearing black stockings now. Her serious face was perfectly unruffled. And in her worn face was all her experience; all the nights and days on the Clyde were in her face; the scalping of the young Glasgow girl was in her face, and the failure to endure either in work or in love. There was complete silence within and without – not the echo of an echo of a gun. G. J. felt as though he were at bay.

She said:

"People like you and Queen don't want to bother about age. Neither of you has any age. And I'm not imploring you to have her. I'm only telling you that she's there for you if you want her. But doesn't she attract you? Isn't she positively irresistible?" She added with poignancy: "I know if I were a man I should find her irresistible."

"Just so."

A look of sacrifice came into Concepcion's eyes as she finished:

"I'd do anything, anything, to make Queen happy."

"Yes, you would," retorted G. J. icily, carried away by a ruthless and inexorable impulse. "You'd do anything to make her happy even for three months. Yes, to make her happy for three weeks you'd be ready to ruin my whole life. I know you and Queen." And the mild image of Christine formed in his mind, soothingly, infinitely desirable. What balm, after the nerve-racking contact of these incalculable creatures!

Concepcion retired with a gesture of the arm and sat down by the fire.

"You're terrible, G. J.," she said wistfully. "Queen wouldn't be thrown away on you, but you'd be thrown away on her. I admit it. I didn't think you had it in you. I never saw a man develop as you have. Marriage isn't for you. You ought to roam in the primeval forest, and take and kill."

205

"Not a bit," said G. J., appeased once more. "Not a bit... But the new relations of the sexes aren't in my line."

"*New?* My poor boy, are you so ingenuous after all? There's nothing very new in the relations of the sexes that I know of. They're much what they were in the Garden of Eden."

"What do you know of the Garden of Eden?"

"I get my information from Milton," she replied cheerfully, as though much relieved.

"Have you read *Paradise Lost*, then, Con?"

"I read it all through in my lodgings. And it's really rather good. In fact, the remarks of Raphael to Adam in the eighth book – I think it is – are still just about the last word on the relations of the sexes:

"Oft-times nothing profits more
Than self-esteem, grounded on just and right
Well-managed; of that skill the more thou know'st,
The more she will acknowledge thee her head
And to realities yield all her shows."

G. J., marvelling, exclaimed with sudden enthusiasm:

"By Jove! You're an astounding woman, Con. You do me good!"

There was a fresh noise beyond the door, and the door opened and Robin rushed in, blanched and hysterical, and with her seemed to rush in terror.

"Oh! Madame!" she cried. "As there was no more firing I went on to the roof, and her ladyship – " She covered her face and sobbed.

G. J. jumped up.

"Go and see," said Concepcion in a blank voice, not moving. "I can't... It's the message straight from Potsdam that's arrived."

35

QUEEN DEAD

G. J. emerged form the crowded and malodorous Coroner's Court with a deep sense of the rigour and the thoroughness of British justice, and especially of its stolidity.

There had been four inquests, all upon the bodies of air-raid victims: a road-man, his wife, an orphan baby – all belonging to the thick central mass of the proletariat, for a West End slum had received a bomb full in the face – and Lady Queenie Paulle. The policemen were stolid; the reporters were stolid; the proletariat was stolid; the majority of the witnesses were stolid, and in particular the representatives of various philanthropic agencies who gave the most minute evidence about the habits and circumstances of the slum; and the jurymen were very stolid, and never more so than when, with stubby fingers holding ancient pens, they had to sign quantities of blue forms under the strict guidance of a bareheaded policeman.

The world of Queenie's acquaintances made a strange, vivid contrast to this grey, grim, blockish world; and the two worlds regarded each other with the wonder and the suspicious resentment of foreigners. Queen's world came expecting to behave as at a cause célèbre of, for example, divorce. Its representatives were quite ready to tolerate unpleasing contacts and long stretches of tedium in return for some glimpse of the squalid and the privilege of being able to say that they had been present at the inquest. But most of them had arrived rather late, and they had reckoned without the Coroner, and comparatively few obtained even admittance.

The Coroner had arrived on the stroke of the hour, in a silk hat and frock coat, with a black bag, and had sat down at his desk and begun to rule the proceedings with an absolutism that no High Court Judge would have attempted. He was autocrat in a small, close, sordid room; but he was autocrat. He had already shown his quality in some indirect collisions with the Marquis of Lechford. The Marquis felt that he could not stomach the exposure of his daughter's corpse in a common mortuary with other corpses of he knew not whom. Long experience of the marquisate had taught him to believe that everything could be arranged. He found, however, that this matter could not be arranged. There was no appeal from the ukase of the Coroner. Then he wished to be excused from giving evidence, since his evidence could have no direct bearing on the death. But he was informed by a mere clerk, who had knowledge of the Coroner's ways, that if he did not attend the inquest would probably be adjourned for his attendance. The fact was, the Coroner had appreciated as well as anybody that heaven and the war had sent him a cause célèbre of the first-class. He saw himself the supreme being of a unique assize. He saw his remarks reproduced verbatim in the papers, for, though localities might not be mentioned, there was no censor's ban upon the *obiter dicta* of coroners. His idiosyncrasy was that he hid all his enjoyment in his own breast. Even had he had the use of a bench, instead of a mere chair, he would never have allowed titled ladies in mirific black hats to share it with him. He was an icy radical, sincere, competent, conscientious and vain. He would be no respecter of persons, but he was a disrespecter of persons above a certain social rank. He said, "Open that window." And that window was opened, regardless of the identity of the person who might be sitting under it. He said:

"This court is unhealthily full. Admit no more." And no more could be admitted, though the entire peerage waited without.

The Marquis had considered that the inquest on his daughter might be taken first. The other three cases were taken first, and, even taken concurrently, they occupied an immense period of time. All the bodies were, of course, "viewed" together, and the absence of the jury seemed to the Marquis interminable; he thought the despicable tradesmen were gloating unduly over the damaged face of his daughter. The Coroner had been marvellously courteous to the procession of humble witnesses. He could not have been more courteous to the exalted; and he was not. In the sight of the Coroner all men were equal.

G. J. encountered him first. "I did my best to persuade her ladyship to come down," said G. J. very formally. "I am quite sure you did," said the Coroner with the dryest politeness. "And you failed." The policeman had related events from the moment when G. J. had fetched him in from the street. The policeman could remember everything, what everybody had said, the positions of all objects, the characteristics and extent of the wire-netting, the exact posture of the deceased girl, the exact minute of his visit. He and the Coroner played to each other like well-rehearesd actors. Mrs Carlos Smith's ordeal was very brief, and the Coroner dismissed her with an expression of sympathy that seemed to issue from his mouth like carved granite. With the doctor alone the Coroner had become human; the Coroner also was a doctor. The doctor had talked about a relatively slight extravasation of blood, and said that death had been instantaneous. Said the Coroner: "The body was found on the wire-netting; it had fallen from the chimney. In your opinion, was the fall a contributory cause of death?" The doctor said, No. "In your opinion death was due to an extremely small piece of shrapnel which struck the deceased's head slightly above the left ear, entering the brain?" The doctor said, Yes.

The Marquis of Lechford had to answer questions as to his parental relations with his daughter. How long had he been away in the country? How long had the deceased been living in Lechford House practically alone? How old was his daughter? Had he given any order to the effect that nobody was to be on the roof of his house during an air-raid? Had he given any orders at all as to conduct during an air-raid? The Coroner sympathised deeply with his lordship's position, and felt sure that his lordship understood that; but his lordship would also understand that the policy of heads of households in regard to air-raids had more than a domestic interest – it had, one might say, a national interest; and the force of prominent example was one of the forces upon which the Government counted, and had the right to count, for help in the regulation of public conduct in these great crises of the most gigantic war that the world had ever seen. "Now, as to the wire-netting," had said the Coroner, leaving the subject of the force of example. He had a perfect plan of the wire-netting in his mind. He understood that the chimney-stack rose higher than the wire-netting, and that the wire-netting went round the chimney-stack at a distance of a foot or more, leaving room so that a person might climb up the perpendicular ladder. If a person fell from the top of the chimney-stack it was a chance whether that person fell on the wire-netting, or through the space between the wire-netting and the chimney on to the roof itself. The jury doubtless understood. (The jury, however, at that instant had been engaged in examining the bit of shrapnel which had been extracted from the brain of the only daughter of a Marquis.) The Coroner understood that the wire-netting did not extend over the whole of the house. "It extends over all the main part of the house," his lordship had replied. "But not over the back part of the house?" His lordship agreed. "The servants' quarters, probably?" His lordship nodded. The Coroner had said: "The wire-netting does not extend over the servants' quarters," in a very even voice. A faint hiss in court had been extinguished by the sharp glare of the Coroner's eyes. His lordship, a thin, antique figure, in a long cloak that none but himself would have ventured to wear, had stepped down, helpless.

There had been much signing of depositions. The Coroner had spoken of The Hague Convention, mentioning one article by its number. The jury as to the first three cases – in which the victims had been killed by bombs – had returned a verdict of wilful murder against the Kaiser. The Coroner, suppressing the applause, had agreed heartily with the verdict. He told the jury that the fourth case was different, and the jury returned a verdict of death from shrapnel. They gave their sympathy to all the relatives, and added a rider about the inadvisability of running unnecessary risks, and the Coroner, once more agreeing heartily, had thereon made an effective little speech to a hushed, assenting audience.

There were several motor-cars outside. G. J. signalled across the street to the taxi-man who telephoned every morning to him for orders. He had never owned a motor-car, and, because he had no ambition to drive himself, had never felt the desire to own one. The taxi-man experienced some delay in starting his engine. G. J. lit a cigarette. Concepcion came out, alone. He had expected her to be with the Marquis, with whom she had arrived. She was dressed in mourning. Only on that day, and once before – on the day of her husband's funeral – had he seen her in mourning. She looked now like the widow she was. Nevertheless, he had not quite accustomed himself to the sight of her in mourning.

"I wonder whether I can get a taxi?" she asked.

"You can have mine," said he. "Where do you want to go?"

She named a disconcerting address near Shepherd's Market.

At that moment a Pressman with a camera came boldly up and snapped her. The man had the brazen demeanour of a racecourse tout. But Concepcion seemed not to mind at all, and G. J. remembered that she was deeply inured to publicity. Her portrait had already appeared in the picture papers along with that of Queen, but the papers had deemed it necessary to remind a forgetful public that Mrs Carlos Smith was the same lady as the super-celebrated Concepcion Iquist. The taxi-man hesitated for an instant on hearing the address, but only for an instant. He had earned the esteem and regular patronage of G. J. by a curious hazard. One night G. J. had hailed him, and the man had said in a flash, without waiting for the fare to speak, "The Albany, isn't it, sir? I drove you home about two months ago." Thenceforward he had been for G. J. the perfect taxi-man.

In the taxi Concepcion said not a word, and G. J. did not disturb her. Beneath his superficial melancholy he was sustained by the mere joy of being alive. The common phenomena of the streets were beautiful to him. Concepcion's calm and grieved vitality seemed mysteriously exquisite. He had had similar sensations while walking along Coventry Street after his escape from the explosion of the bomb. Fatigue and annoyance and sorrow had extinguished them for a time, but now that the episode of Queen's tragedy was closed they were born anew. Queen, the pathetic victim of the indiscipline of her own impulses, was gone. But he had escaped. He lived. And life was an affair miraculous and lovely.

"I think I've been here before," said he, when they got out of the taxi in a short, untidy, indeterminate street that was a cul-de-sac. The prospect ended in a garage, near which two women chauffeurs were discussing a topic that interested them. A hurdy-gurdy was playing close by, and a few ragged children stared at the hurdy-gurdy, on the end of which a baby was cradled. The fact that the street was midway between Curzon Street and Piccadilly, and almost within sight of the monumental new mansion of an American duchess, explained the existence of the building in front of which the taxi had stopped. The entrance to the flats was mean and soiled. It repelled, but Concepcion unapologetically led G. J. up a flight of four stone steps and round a curve into a little corridor. She halted at a door on the ground floor.

"Yes," said G. J. with admirable calm, "I do believe you've got the very flat I once looked at with a friend of mine. If I remember it didn't fill the bill because the tenant wouldn't sublet it unfurnished. When did you get hold of this?"

"Yesterday afternoon," Concepcion answered. "Quick work. But these feats can be accomplished. I've only taken it for a month. Hotels seem to be all full. I couldn't open my own place at a moment's notice, and I didn't mean to stay on at Lechford House, even if they'd asked me to."

G. J.'s notion of the vastness and safety of London had received a shock. He was now a very busy man, and would quite sincerely have told anybody who questioned him on the point that he hadn't a moment to call his own. Nevertheless, on the previous morning he had spent a considerable time in searching for a nest in which to hide his Christine and create romance; and he had come to this very flat. More, there had been two flats to let in the block. He had declined them – the better one because of the furniture, the worse because it was impossibly small, and both because of the propinquity of the garage. But supposing that he had taken one and Concepcion the other! He recoiled at the thought...

Concepcion's new home, if not impossibly small, was small, and the immensity and abundance of the furniture made it seem smaller than it actually was. Each little room had the air of having been furnished out of a huge and expensive secondhand emporium. No single style prevailed. There were big carved and inlaid antique cabinets and chests, big hanging crystal candelabra, and big pictures (some of them apparently family portraits, the rest eighteenth-century flower-pieces) in big gilt frames, with a multiplicity of occasional tables and bric-à-brac. Gilt predominated. The ornate cornices were gilded. Human beings had to move about like dwarfs on the tiny free spaces of carpet between frowning cabinetry. The taste and the aim of the author of this home defied deduction. In the first room a charwoman was cleaning. Concepcion greeted her like a sister. In the next room, whose window gave on to a blank wall, tea was laid for one in front of a gas-fire. Concepcion reached down a cup and saucer from a glazed cupboard and put a match to the spirit-lamp under the kettle.

"Let me see, the bedroom's up here, isn't it?" said G. J., pointing along a passage that was like a tunnel.

Concepcion, yielding to his curiosity, turned on lights everywhere and preceded him. The passage, hung with massive canvases, had scarcely more than width enough for G. J.'s shoulders. The tiny bedroom was muslined in every conceivable manner. It had a colossal bed, surpassing even Christine's. A muslined maid was bending over some drapery-shop boxes on the floor and removing garments therefrom. Concepcion greeted her like a sister. "Don't let me disturb you, Emily," she said, and to G. J., "Emily was poor Queenie's maid, and she has come to me for a little while." G. J. amicably nodded. Tears came suddenly into the maid's eyes. G. J. looked away and saw the bathroom, which, also well muslined, was completely open to the bedroom.

"Whose *is* this marvellous home?" he added when they had gone back to the drawing-room.

"I think the original tenant is the wife of somebody who's interned."

"How simple the explanation is!" said G. J. "But I should never have guessed it."

They started the tea in a strange silence. After a minute or two G. J. said:

"I mustn't stay long."

"Neither must I." Concepcion smiled.

"Got to go out?"

"Yes."

There was another silence. Then Concepcion said:

"I'm going to Sarah Churcher's. And as I know she has her Pageant Committee at five-thirty, I'd better not arrive later than five, had I?"

"What is there between you and Lady Churcher?"

"Well, I'm going to offer to take Queen's place on the organising Committee."

"Con!" he exclaimed impulsively, "you aren't?"

In an instant the atmosphere of the little airless, electric-lit, gas-fumed apartment was charged with a fluid that no physical chemistry could have traced. Concepcion said midly:

"I am. I owe it to Queen's memory to take her place if I can. Of course I'm no dancer, but in other things I expect I can make myself useful."

G. J. replied with equal mildness:

"You aren't going to mix yourself up with that crowd again – after all you've been through! The Pageant business isn't good enough for you, Con, and you know it. You know it's odious."

She murmured:

"I feel it's my duty. I feel I owe it to Queen. It's a sort of religion with me, I expect. Each person has his own religion, and I doubt if one's more dogmatic than another."

He was grieved; he had a sense almost of outrage. He hated to picture Concepcion subduing herself to the horrible environment of the Pageant enterprise. But he said nothing more. The silence resumed. They might have conversed, with care, about the inquest, or about the funeral, which was to take place at the Castle, in Cheshire. Silence, however, suited them best.

"Also I thought you needed repose," said G. J. when Concepcion broke the melancholy enchantment by rising to look for cigarettes.

"I must be allowed to work," she answered after a pause, putting a cigarette between her teeth. "I must have something to do – unless, of course, you want me to go to the bad altogether."

It was a remarkable saying, but it seemed to admit that he was legitimately entitled to his critical interest in her.

"If I'd known that," he said, suddenly inspired, "I should have asked you to take on something for *me*." He waited; she made no response, and he continued: "I'm secretary of my small affair since yesterday. The paid secretary, a nice enough little thing, has just run off to the Women's Auxiliary Corps in France and left me utterly in the lurch. Just like domestic servants, these earnest girl-clerks are, when it comes to the point! No imagination. Wanted to wear khaki, and no doubt thought she was doing a splendid thing. Never occurred to her the mess I should be in. I'd have asked you to step into the breach. You'd have been frightfully useful."

"But I'm no girl-clerk," Concepcion gently and carelessly protested.

"Well, she wasn't either. I shouldn't have wanted you to be a typist. We have a typist. As a matter of fact, her job needed a bit more brains than she'd got. However – "

Another silence. G. J. rose to depart. Concepcion did not stir. She said softly:

"I don't think anybody realises what Queen's death is to me. Not even you." On her face was the look of sacrifice which G. J. had seen there as they talked together in Queen's boudoir during the raid.

He thought, amazed:

"And they'd only had about twenty-four hours together, and part of that must have been spent in making up their quarrel!"

Then aloud:

"I quite agree. People can't realise what they haven't had to go through. I've understood that ever since I read in the paper the day before yesterday that 'two bombs fell close together and one immediately after the other' in a certain quarter of the West End. That was all the paper said about those two bombs."

"Why! What do you mean?"

"And I understood it when poor old Queen gave me some similar information on the roof."

"What *do* you mean?"

"I was between those two bombs when they fell. One of 'em blew me against a house. I've been to look at the place since. And I'm dashed if I myself could realise then what I'd been through."

She gave a little cry. Her face pleased him.

"And you weren't hurt?"

"I had a pain in my side, but it's gone," he said laconically.

"And you never said anything to us! Why not?"

"Well – there were so many other things..."

"G. J., you're astounding!"

"No, I'm not. I'm just myself."

"And hasn't it upset your nerves?"

"Not as far as I can judge. Of course one never knows, but I think not. What do you think?"

She offered no response. At length she spoke with queer emotion:

"You remember that night I said it was a message direct from Potsdam? Well, naturally it wasn't. But do you know the thought that tortures me? Supposing the shrapnel that killed Queen was out of a shell made at my place in Glasgow!... It might have been... Supposing it was!"

"Con," he said firmly, "I simply won't listen to that kind of talk. There's no excuse for it. Shall I tell you what, more than anything else, has made me respect you since Queen was killed? Ninety-nine women out of a hundred would have managed to remind me, quite illogically and quite inexcusably, that I was saying hard things about poor old Queen at the very moment when she was lying dead on the roof. You didn't. You knew I was very sorry about Queen, but you knew that my feelings as to her death had nothing whatever to do with what I happened to be saying when she was killed. You knew the difference between sentiment and sentimentality. For God's sake, don't start wondering where the shell was made."

She looked up at him, saying nothing, and he savoured the intelligence of her weary, fine, alert, comprehending face. He did not pretend to himself to be able to fathom the enigmas of that long glance. He had again the feeling of the splendour of what it was to be alive, to have survived. Just as he was leaving she said casually:

"Very well. I'll do what you want."

"What I want?"

"I won't go to Sarah Churcher's."

"You mean you'll come as assistant secretary?"

She nodded. "Only I don't need to be paid."

And he, too, fell into a casual tone:

"That's excellent."

Thus, by this nonchalance, they conspired to hide from themselves the seriousness of that which had passed between them. The grotesque, pretentious little apartment was mysteriously humanised; it was no longer the reception-room of a furnished flat by chance hired for a month; they had lived in it.

She finished, eagerly smiling:

"I can practise my religion just as much with you as with Sarah Churcher, can't I? Queen was on your committee, too. Yes, I shan't be deserting her."

The remark disquieted his triumph. That aspect of the matter had not occurred to him.

36

COLLAPSE

Late that same afternoon G. J., in the absence of the chairman, presided as honorary secretary over a meeting of the executive committee of the Lechford hospitals. In the course of the war the committee had changed its habitation more than once. The hotel which had at first given it a home had long ago been commandeered by the Government for a new Government department, and its hundreds of chambers were now full of the clicking of typewriters and the dictation of officially phrased correspondence, and the conferences which precede decisions, and the untamed footsteps of messenger-flappers, and the making of tea, and chatter about cinemas, blouses and headaches. Afterwards the committee had been the guest of a bank and of a trust company, and had for a period even paid rent to a common landlord. But its object was always to escape the formality of rent-paying, and it was now lodged in an untenanted mansion belonging to a viscount in a great Belgravian square. Its sign was spread high across the façade; its posters were in the windows; and on the door was a notice such as in 1914 nobody had ever expected to see in that quadrangle of guarded sacred castles: "Turn the handle and walk in."

The mansion, though much later in date, was built precisely on the lines of a typical Bloomsbury boarding-house. It had the same basement, the same general disposition of rooms, the same abundance of stairs and paucity of baths, the same chilly draughts and primeval devices for heating, and the same superb disregard for the convenience of servants. The patrons of domestic architecture had permitted architects to learn nothing in seventy years except that chimney-flues must be constructed so that they could be cleaned without exposing sooty infants to the danger of suffocation or incineration.

The committee sat on the first floor in the back drawing-room, whose furniture consisted of a deal table, windsor chairs, a row of hat-pegs, a wooden box containing coal, half a poker, two unshaded lights; the walls, from which all the paper had been torn off, were decorated with lists of sub-committees, posters, and rows of figures scrawled here and there in pencil. The room was divided from the main drawing-room by the usual folding-doors. The smaller apartment had been chosen in the winter because it was somewhat easier to keep warm than the other one. In the main drawing-room the honorary secretary camped himself at a desk near the fireplace.

When the clock struck, G. J., one of whose monastic weaknesses was a ritualistic regard for punctuality, was in his place at the head of the table, and the table well filled with members, for the honorary secretary's harmless foible was known and admitted. The table and the chairs, the scraping of the chair-legs on the bare floor, the agenda papers and the ornamentation thereof by absent-minded pens, were the same as in the committee's youth. But the personnel of the committee had greatly changed, and it was enlarged – as its scope had been enlarged. The two Lechford hospitals behind the French lines were now only a part of the committee's responsibilities. It had a special hospital in Paris, two convalescent homes in England, and an important medical unit somewhere in Italy. Finance was becoming its chief anxiety, for the reason that, though soldiers had not abandoned in disgust the practice of being wounded, philanthropists were unquestionably showing signs of fatigue. It had collected money by postal appeals, by advertisements, by selling flags, by competing with drapers' shops, by intimidation, by ruse and guile, and by all the other recognised methods. Of late it had depended largely upon the very wealthy, and, to a less extent, upon G. J., who having gradually constituted the committee his hobby, had contributed some thousands of pounds from his share of the magic profits of the Reveille Company. Everybody was aware of the immense importance of G. J.'s help. G. J. never showed it in his demeanour, but the others continually showed it in theirs. He had acquired authority. He had also acquired the sure manner of one accustomed to preside.

"Before we begin on the agenda," he said – and as he spoke a late member crept apologetically in and tiptoed to the heavily charged hat-pegs – "I would like to mention about Miss Trewas. Some of you know that through an admirable but somewhat disordered sense of patriotism she has left us at a moment's notice. I am glad to say that my friend Mrs Carlos Smith, who, I may tell you, has had a very considerable experience of organisation, has very kindly agreed, subject of course to the approval of the committee, to step temporarily into the breach. She will be an honorary worker, like all of us here, and I am sure that the committee will feel as grateful to her as I do."

As there had been smiles at the turn of his phrase about Miss Trewas, so now there were fervent, almost emotional, "Hear-hears."

"Mrs Smith, will you please read the minutes of the last meeting."

Concepcion was sitting at his left hand. He kept thinking, "I'm one of those who get things done." Two hours ago, and the idea of enlisting her had not even occurred to him, and already he had taken her out of her burrow, brought her to the offices, coached her in the preliminaries of her allotted task, and introduced several important members of the committee to her! It was an achievement.

Never had the minutes been listened to with such attention as they obtained that day. Concepcion was apparently not in the least nervous, and she read very well – far better than the deserter Miss Trewas, who could not open her mouth without bridling. Concepcion held the room. Those who had not seen before the celebrated Concepcion Iquist now saw her and sated their eyes upon her. She had been less a woman than a legend. The romance of South America enveloped her, and the romance of her famous and notorious uncle, of her triumph over the West End, her startling marriage and swift widowing, her journey to America and her complete disappearance, her attachment to Lady Queenie, and now her dramatic reappearance.

And the sharp condiment to all this was the general knowledge of the bachelor G. J.'s long intimacy with her, and of their having both been at Lechford House on the night of the raid, and both been at the inquest on the body of Lady Queenie Paulle on that very day. But nobody could have guessed from their placid and self-possessed demeanour that either of them had just emerged from a series of ordeals. They won a deep and full respect. Still, some people ventured to have their own ideas; and an ingenuous few were surprised to find that the legend was only a woman after all, and a rather worn woman, not indeed very recognisable from her innumerable portraits. Nevertheless the respect for the pair was even increased when G. J. broached the first item on the agenda – a resolution of respectful sympathy with the Marquis and Marchioness of Lechford in their bereavement, of profound appreciation of the services of Lady Queenie on the committee, and of an intention to send by the chairman to the funeral a wreath to be subscribed for by the members. G. J. proposed the resolution himself, and it was seconded by a lady and supported by a gentleman whose speeches gave no hint that Lady Queenie had again and again by her caprices nearly driven the entire committee into a lunatic asylum and had caused several individual resignations.

G. J. put the resolution without a tremor; it was impressively carried; and Concepcion wrote down the terms of it quite calmly in her secretarial notes. The performance of the pair was marvellous, and worthy of the English race.

Then arrived Sir Stephen Bradern. Sir Stephen was chairman of the French Hospitals Management Sub-committee.

G. J. said:

"Sir Stephen, you are just too late for the resolution as to Lady Queenie Paulle."

"I deeply apologise, Mr Chairman," replied the aged but active Sir Stephen, nervously stroking his rather long beard. "I hope, however, that I may be allowed to associate myself very closely with the resolution." After a suitable pause and general silence he went on: "I've been detained by that Nurse Smaith that my sub-committee's been having trouble with. You'll find, when you come to them, that she's on my sub-committee's minutes. I've just had an interview with her, and she says she wants to see the executive. I don't know what you think, Mr Chairman – " He stopped.

G. J. smiled.

"I should have her brought in," said the lady who had previously spoken. "If I might suggest," she added.

A boy scout, who seemed to have long ago grown out of his uniform, entered with a note for somebody. He was told to bring in Nurse Smaith.

She proved to be a rather short and rather podgy woman, with a reddish, not rosy, complexion, and red hair. The ugly red-bordered cape of the British Red Cross did not suit her better than it suited any other wearer. She was in full, strict, starched uniform, and prominently wore medals on her plenteous breast. She looked as though, if she had a sister, that sister might be employed in a large draper's shop at Brixton or Islington. In saying "Gid ahfternoon" she revealed the purity of a cockney accent undefiled by Continental experiences. She sat down in a manner sternly defensive. She was nervous and abashed, but evidently dangerous. She belonged to the type which is courageous in spite of fear. She had resolved to interview the committee, and though the ordeal frightened her, she desperately and triumphantly welcomed it.

"Now, Nurse Smaith," said G. J. diplomatically. "We are always very glad to see our nurses, even when our time is limited. Will you kindly tell the committee as briefly as possible just what your claim is?"

And the nurse replied, with medals shaking:

"I'm claiming, as I've said before, two weeks' salary in loo of notice, and my fare home from France; twenty-five francs salary and ninety-five francs expenses. And I sy nothing of excess luggage."

"But you didn't *come* home."

"I have come home, though."

One of those members whose destiny it is always to put a committee in the wrong remarked:

"But surely, Nurse, you left our employ nearly a year ago. Why didn't you claim before?"

"I've been at you for two months at least, and I was ill for six months in Turin; they had to put me off the train there," said Nurse Smaith, getting self-confidence.

"As I understand," said G. J. "You left us in order to join a Serbian unit of another society, and you only returned to England in February."

"I didn't leave you, sir. That is, I mean, I left you, but I was told to go."

"Who told you to go?"

"Matron."

Sir Stephen benevolently put in:

"But the matron had always informed us that it was you who said you wouldn't stay another minute. We have it in the correspondence."

"That's what *she* says. But I sy different. And I can prove it."

Said G. J.:

"There must be some misunderstanding. We have every confidence in the matron, and she's still with us."

"Then I'm sorry for you."

He turned warily to another aspect of the subject.

"Do I gather that you went straight from Paris to Serbia?"

"Yes. The unit was passing through, and I joined it."

"But how did you obtain your passport? You had no certificate from us?"

Nurse Smaith tossed her perilous red hair.

"Oh! No difficulty about that. I am not *without* friends, as you may say." Some of the committee looked up suspiciously, aware that the matron had in her report hinted at mysterious relations between Nurse Smaith and certain authorities. "The doctor in charge of the Serbian unit was only too glad to have me. Of course, if you're going to believe everything matron says – " Her tone was becoming coarser, but the committee could neither turn her out nor cure her natural coarseness, nor indicate to her that she was not using the demeanour of committee-rooms. She was firmly lodged among them, and she went from bad to worse. "Of course, if you're going to swallow everything matron says – ! It isn't as if I was the only one."

"May I ask if you are at present employed?"

"I don't *quite* see what that's got to do with it," said Nurse Smaith, still gaining ground.

"Certainly not. Nothing. Nothing at all. I was only hoping that these visits here are not inconvenient to you."

"Well, as it seems so important, I *my* sy I'm going out to Salonika next week, and that's why I want this business settled." She stopped, and as the committee remained diffidently and apprehensively silent, she went on: "It isn't as if I was the only one. Why! When we were in the retreat of the Serbian Army owver the mahntains I came across by chance, if you call it chance, another nurse that knew all about *her* – been under her in Bristol for a year."

A young member, pricking up, asked:

"Were you in the Serbian retreat, Nurse?"

"If I hadn't been I shouldn't be here now," said Nurse Smaith, entirely recovered from her stage-fright and entirely pleased to be there then. "I lost all I had at Ypek. All I took was my medals, and them I did take. There were fifty of us, British, French and Russians. We had nearly three weeks in the mahntains. We slept rough all together in one room, when there was a room, and when there wasn't we slept in stables. We had nothing but black bread, and that froze in the haversacks, and if we took our boots off we had to thaw them the next morning before we could put them on. If we hadn't had three saucepans we should have died. When we went dahn the hills two of us had to hold every horse by his head and tail to keep them from falling. However, nearly all the horses died, and then we took the packs off them and tried to drag the packs along by hand; but we soon stopped that. All the bridle-paths were littered with dead horses and oxen. And when we came up with the Serbian Army we saw soldiers just drop down and die in the snow. I read in the paper there were no children in the retreat, but I saw lots of children, strapped to their mother's backs. Yes; and they fell down together and froze to death. Then we got to Scutari, and glad I was."

She glanced round defiantly, but not otherwise moved, at the committee, the hitherto invisible gods of hospitals and medical units. The nipping wind of reality had blown into the back drawingroom. The committee was daunted. But some of its members, less daunted than the rest, had the presence of mind to wonder why it seemed strange and strangely chilling that a rather coarse, stout woman with a cockney accent and little social refinement should have passed through, and emerged so successfully from, the unimaginable retreat. If Nurse Smaith had been beautiful and slim and of elegant manners they could not have controlled their chivalrous enthusiasm.

"Very interesting," said someone.

Glancing at G. J., Nurse Smaith proceeded:

"You sy I didn't come home. But the money for my journey was due to me. That's what I sy. Twenty-five francs for two weeks' wages and ninety-five francs journey money."

"As regards the journey money," observed Sir Stephen blandly, "we've never paid so much, if my recollection serves me. And of course we have to remember that we're dealing with public funds."

Nurse Smaith sprang up, looking fixedly at Concepcion. Concepcion had thrown herself back in her chair, and her face was so drawn that it was no more the same face.

"Even if it is public funds," Concepcion shrieked, "can't you give ninety-five francs in memory of those three saucepans?" Then she relapsed on to the table, her head in her hands, and sobbed violently, very violently. The sobs rose and fell in the scale, and the whole body quaked.

G. J. jumped to his feet. Half the shocked and alarmed committee was on its feet. Nurse Smaith had run round to Concepcion and had seized her with a persuasive, soothing gesture. Concepcion quite submissively allowed herself to be led out of the room by Nurse Smaith and Sir Stephen. Her sobs weakened, and when the door was closed could no longer be heard. A lady member had followed the three. The committee was positively staggered by the unprecedented affair. G. J., very pale, said:

"Mrs Smith is in competent hands. We can't do anything. I think we had better sit down." He was obeyed.

A second doctor on the committee remarked with a curious slight smile:

"I said to myself when I first saw her this afternoon that Mrs Smith had some of the symptoms of a nervous breakdown."

"Yes," G. J. concurred. "I very much regret that I allowed Mrs Smith to come. But she was determined to work, and she seemed perfectly calm and collected. I very much regret it."

Then, to hide his constraint, he pulled towards him the sheet of paper on which Concepcion had been making notes, and, remembering that a list of members present had always to be kept, he began to write down names. He was extremely angry with himself. He had tried Concepcion too high. He ought to have known that all women were the same. He had behaved like an impulsive fool. He had been ridiculous before the committee. What should have been a triumph was a disaster. The committee would bind their two names together. And at the conclusion of the meeting news of the affairs would radiate from the committee's offices in every direction throughout London. And he had been unfair to Concepcion. Their relations would be endlessly complicated by the episode. He foresaw trying scenes, in which she would make all the excuses, between her and himself.

"Perhaps it would be simpler if we decided to admit Nurse Smaith's claim," said a timid voice from the other end of the table.

G. J. murmured coldly, gazing at the agenda paper and yet dominating his committee:

"The question will come up on the minutes of the Hospitals Management Sub-committee. We had better deal with it then. The next business on the agenda is the letter from the Paris Service de Santé."

He was thinking: "How is she now? Ought I to go out and see?" And the majority of the committee was vaguely thinking, not without a certain pleasurable malice: "These Society women! They're all queer!"

37

THE INVISIBLE POWERS

Several times already the rumour had spread in the Promenade that the Promenade would be closed on a certain date, and the Promenade had not been closed. But to-night it was stated that the Promenade would be closed at the end of the week, and everybody concerned knew that the prophecy would come true. No official notice was issued, no person who repeated the tale could give a reliable authority for it; nevertheless, for some mysterious reason it convinced. The rival Promenade had already passed away. The high invisible powers who ruled the world of pleasure were moving at the behest of powers still higher than themselves; and the cloak-room attendants, in their frivolous tiny aprons, shared murmuringly behind plush portières in the woe of the ladies with large hats.

The revue being a failure, the auditorium was more than half empty. In the Promenade to each man there were at least five pretty ladies, and the ladies looked gloomily across many rows of vacant seats at the bright proscenium where jocularities of an exacerbating tedium were being enacted. Not that the jocularities were inane beyond the usual, but failure made them seem so. None had the slightest idea why the revue had failed; for precisely similar revues, concocted according to the same recipe and full of the same jocularities executed by the same players at the same salaries, had crowded the theatre for many months together. It was an incomprehensible universe.

Christine suddenly shrugged her shoulders and walked out. What use in staying to the end?

It was long after ten o'clock, and an exquisite faint light lingering in the sky still revealed the features of the people in the streets. The man who had devoted half a life to the ingenious project of lengthening the summer days by altering clocks was in his disappointed grave; but victory had come to him there, for statesmen had at last proved the possibility of that which they had always maintained to be impossible, and the wisdom of that which they had always maintained to be idiotic. The voluptuous divine melancholy of evening June descended upon the city from the sky, and even sounds were beautifully sad. The happy progress of the war could not exorcise this soft, omnipotent melancholy. Yet the progress of the war was nearly all that could be desired. Verdun was held, and if Fort Vaux had been lost there had been compensation in the fact that the enemy, through the gesture of the Crown Prince in allowing the captured commander of the fort to retain his sword, had done something to rehabilitate themselves in the esteem of mankind. Lord Kitchener was drowned, but the discovery had been announced that he was not indispensable; indeed, there were those who said that it was better thus. The Easter Rebellion was well in hand; order was understood to reign in an Ireland hidden behind the black veil of the censorship. The mighty naval battle of Jutland had quickly transformed itself from a defeat into a brilliant triumph. The disturbing prices of food were about to be reduced by means of a committee. In America the Republican forces were preparing to eject President Wilson in favour of another Hughes who could be counted upon to realise the world-destiny of the United States. An economic conference was assembling in Paris with the object of cutting Germany off from the rest of the human race after the war. And in eleven days the Russians had made prisoners of a hundred and fifty thousand Austrians, and Brusiloff had just said: "This is only the beginning." Lastly the close prospect of the resistless Allied Western offensive which would deracinate Prussian militarism was uplifting men's minds.

Christine walked nonchalantly and univitingly through the streets, quite unresponsive to the exhilaration of events.

"Marthe!" she called, when she had let herself into the flat. Contrary to orders, the little hall was in darkness. There was no answer. She lit the hall and passed into the kitchen, lighting it also. There, in the terrible and incurable squalor of Marthe's own kitchen, Marthe's apron was thrown untidily across the back of the solitary windsor chair. She knew then that Marthe had gone out, and in truth, although very annoyed, she was not altogether surprised.

Marthe had a mysterious love affair. It was astonishing, in view of the intensely aphrodisiacal atmosphere in which she lived, that Marthe did not continually have love affairs. But the day of love had seemed for Marthe to be over, and Christine found great difficulty in getting her ever to leave the flat, save on necessary household errands. On the other hand it was astonishing that any man should be attracted by the fat slattern. The moth now fluttering round her was an Italian waiter, as to whom Christine had learnt that he was being unjustly hunted by the Italian military authorities. Hence the mystery necessarily attaching to the love affair. Being French, Christine despised him. He called Marthe by her right name of "Marta," and Christine had more than once heard the pair gabbling in the kitchen in Italian. Just as though she had been a conventional *bourgeoise* Christine now accused Marthe of ingratitude because the woman was subordinating Christine's convenience to the supreme exigencies of fate. A man's freedom might be in the balance, Marthe's future might be in the balance; but supposing that Christine had come home with a gallant – and no *femme de chambre* to do service!

She walked about the flat, shut the windows, drew the blinds, removed her hat, removed her gloves, stretched them, put her things away; she gazed at the two principal rooms, at the soiled numbers of *La Vie Parisienne* and the cracked bric-à-brac in the drawing-room, at the rent in the lace bedcover, and the foul mess of toilet apparatus in the bedroom. The forlorn emptiness of the place appalled her. She had been quite fairly successful in her London career. Hundreds of men had caressed her and paid her with compliments and sweets and money. She had been really admired. The flat had had gay hours. Unmistakable aristocrats had yielded to her. And she had escaped the five scourges of her profession...

It was all over. The chapter was closed. She saw nothing in front of her but decline and ruin. She had escaped the five scourges of her profession, but part of the price of this immunity was that through keeping herself to herself she had not a friend. Despite her profession, and because of the prudence with which she exercised it, she was a solitary, a recluse.

Yes, of course she had Gilbert. She could count upon Gilbert to a certain extent, to a considerable extent; but he would not be eternal, and his fancy for her would not be eternal. Once, before Easter, she had had the idea that he meant to suggest to her an exclusive liaison. Foolish! Nothing, less than nothing, had come of it. He would not be such an imbecile as to suggest such a thing to her. Miracles did not happen, at any rate not that kind of miracle.

In the midst of her desolation an old persistent dream revisited her: the dream of a small country cottage in France, with a dog, a faithful servant, respectability, good name, works of charity, her own praying-stool in the village church. She moved to the wardrobe and unlocked one of the drawers beneath the wide doors. And rummaging under the linen and under the photographs under the linen she drew forth a package and spread its contents on the table in the drawing-room. Her securities, her bonds of the City of Paris, ever increasing! Gilbert had tried to induce her to accept more attractive investments. But she would not. Never! These were her consols, part of her religion. Bonds of the City of Paris had fallen in value, but not in her dogmatic esteem. The passionate little miser that was in her surveyed them with pleasure, even with assurance; but they were still far too few to stand for the realisation of her dream. And she might have to sell some of them soon in order to live. She replaced them carefully in the drawer with dejection unabated.

When she glanced at the table again she saw an envelope. Inexplicably she had not noticed it before. She seized it in hope – and recognised in the address the curious hand of her landlord. It contained a week's notice to quit. The tenancy of the flat was weekly. This was the last blow. All the invisible powers of London were conspiring together to shatter the profession. What in the name of the Holy Virgin had come over the astounding, incomprehensible city? Then there was a ring at the bell. Marthe? No, Marthe would never ring; she had a key and she would creep in. A lover? A rich, spendthrift, kind lover? Hope flickered anew in her desolated heart.

It was the other pretty lady – a newcomer – who lived in the house: a rather stylish woman of about thirty-five, unusually fair, with regular features and a very dignified carriage, indeed not unimposing. They had met once, at the foot of the stairs. Christine was not sure of her name. She proclaimed herself to be Russian, but Christine doubted the assertion. Her French had no trace of a foreign accent; and in view of the achievements of the Russian Army ladies were finding it advantageous to be of Russian blood. Still she had a fine cosmopolitan air to which Christine could not pretend. They engaged each other in glances.

"I hope I do not disturb you, madame."

"Not at all, madame. I am obliged to open the door myself because my servant is out."

"I thought I heard you come in, and so – "

"No," interrupted Christine, determined not to admit the defeat of having returned from the Promenade alone. "I have not been out. Probably it was my servant you heard."

"Ah!... Without doubt."

"Will you give yourself the trouble to enter, madame?"

"Ah!" exclaimed the Russian, in the sitting-room. "You will excuse me, madame, but what a beautiful photograph!"

"You are too amiable, madame. A friend had it done for me."

They sat down.

"You are deliciously installed here," said the Russian perfunctorily, looking round. "Now, madame, I have been here only three weeks. And to-night I receive a notice to quit. Shall I be indiscreet if I ask if you have received a similar notice?"

"This very evening," said Christine, in secret still more disconcerted by this further proof of a general plot against human nature. She was about to add: "I found it here on my return home," but, remembering her fib, managed to stop in time.

"Well, madame, I know little of London. Without doubt you know London to the bottom. Is it serious, this notice?"

"I think so."

"Quite serious?"

Christine said:

"You see, there is a crisis. It is the war that in London has led to the discovery that men have desires. Of course, it will pass, but – "

"Oh, of course... But it is grotesque, this crisis."

"It is perfectly grotesque," Christine agreed.

"You do not by hazard know where one can find flats to let? I hear speak of Bloomsbury and of Long Acre. But it seems to me that those quarters – "

"I am in London since now more than eighteen months," said Christine. "And as for all those things I know little. I have lived here in this flat all the time, and I go out so rarely – "

The Russian put in with eagerness:

"Oh, I also! I go out, so to speak, not at all."

"I thought I had seen you once in the Promenade at the – "

"Yes, it is true," interrupted the Russian quickly. "I went from curiosity, for distraction. You see, since the war I have lived in Dublin. I had there a friend, very highly placed in the administration. He married. One lived terrible hours during the revolt. I decided to come to London, especially as – However, I do not wish to fatigue you with all that."

Christine said nothing. The Irish Rebellion did not interest her. She was in no mood for talking about the Irish Rebellion. She had convinced herself that all Sinn Feiners were in German pay, and naught else mattered. Never, she thought, had the British Government carried ingenuousness further than in this affair! Given a free hand, Christine with her strong, direct common sense would have settled the Irish question in forty-eight hours.

The Russian, after a little pause, continued:

"I merely wished to ask you whether the notice to quit was serious – not a trick for raising the rent."

Christine shook her head to the last clause.

"And then, if the notice was quite serious, whether you knew of any flats – not too dear… Not that I mind a good rent if one receives the value of it, and is left tranquil."

The conversation might at this point have taken a more useful turn if Christine had not felt bound to hold herself up against the other's high tone of indifference to expenditure. The Russian, in demanding "tranquillity," had admitted that she regularly practised the profession – or, as English girls strangely called it, "the business" – and Christine could have followed her lead into the region of gossiping and intimate realism where detailed confidences are enlighteningly exchanged; but the tone about money was a challenge.

"I should have been enchanted to be of service to you," said Christine. "But I know nothing. I go out less and less. As for this notice, I smile at it. I have a friend upon whom I can count for everything. I have only to tell him, and he will put me among my own furniture at once. He has indeed already suggested it. So that, *je m'en fiche.*"

"I also!" said the Russian. "My new friend – he is a colonel, sent from Dublin to London – has insisted upon putting me among my own furniture. But I have refused so far – because one likes to know more of a gentleman – does not one? – before…"

"Truly!" murmured Christine.

"And there is always Paris," said the Russian.

"But I thought you were from Petrograd."

"Yes. But I know Paris well. Ah! There is only Paris! Paris is a second home to me."

"Can one get a passport easily for Paris?… I mean, supposing the air-raids grew too dangerous again."

"Why not, madame? If one has one's papers. To get a passport from Paris to London, that would be another thing, I admit… I see that you play," the Russian added, rising, with a gesture towards the piano. "I have heard you play. You play with true taste. I know, for when a girl I played much."

"You flatter me."

"Not at all. I think your friend plays too."

"Ah!" said Christine. "He!… It is an artist, that one."

They turned over the music, exchanged views about waltzes, became enthusiastic, laughed, and parted amid manifestations of good breeding and goodwill. As soon as Christine was alone, she sat down and wept. She could not longer contain her distress. Paris gleamed before her. But no! It was a false gleam. She could not make a new start in Paris during the war. The adventure would be too perilous; the adventure might end in a licensed house. And yet in London – what was there in London but, ultimately, the pavement? And the pavement meant complications with the police, with prowlers, with other women; it meant all the scourges of the profession, including probably alcoholism. It meant prostitution, to which she had never sunk!

She wished she had been killed outright in the air-raid. She had an idea of going to the Oratory the next morning, and perhaps choosing a new Virgin and soliciting favour of the image thereof. She sobbed, and, sobbing, suddenly jumped up and ran to the telephone. And even as she gave Gilbert's number, she broke it in the middle with a sob. After all, there was Gilbert.

38

THE VICTORY

"Get back into bed," said G. J., having silently opened the window in the sitting-room.

He spoke with courteous persuasion, but his peculiar intense politeness and restraint somewhat dismayed Christine. By experience she knew that they were a sure symptom of annoyance. She often, though not on this occasion, wished that he would yield to anger and make a scene; but he never did, and she would hate him for not doing so. The fact was that under the agreement which ruled their relations, she had no right to telephone to him, save in grave and instant emergency, and even then it was her duty to say first, when she got the communication: "Mr Pringle wants to speak to Mr Hoape." She had omitted, in her disquiet, to fulfil this formality. Recognising his voice, she had begun passionately, without preliminary: "Oh! Beloved, thou canst not imagine what has happened to me – " etc. Still he had come. He had cut her short, but he had left whatever he was doing and had, amazingly, walked over at once. And in the meantime she had hurriedly undressed and put on a new peignoir and slipped into bed. Of course she had had to open the door herself.

She obeyed his command like an intelligent little mouse, and he sat down on the edge of the bed. He might inspire foreboding, alarm, even terror. But he was in the flat. He was the saviour, man, in the flat. And his coming was in the nature of a miracle. He might have been out; he might have been entertaining; he might have been engaged; he might well have said that he could not come until the next day. Never before had she made such a request, and he had acceded to it immediately! Her mood was one of frightened triumph. He was being most damnably himself; his demeanour was as faultless as his dress. She could not even complain that he had forgotten to kiss her. He said nothing about her transgression of the rule as to telephoning. He was waiting, with his exasperating sense of justice and self-control, until she had acquainted him with her case. Instead of referring coldly and disapprovingly to the matter of the telephone, he said in a judicious, amicable voice:

"I doubt whether your coiffeur is all that he ought to be. I see you had your hair waved to-day."

"Yes, why?"

"You should tell the fellow to give you the new method of hair-waving, steaming with electric heaters – or else go where you can get it."

"New method?" repeated Christine the Tory doubtfully. And then with sudden sexual suspicion:

"Who told you about it?"

"Oh! I heard of it months ago," he said carelessly. "Besides, it's in the papers, in the advertisements. It lasts longer – much longer – and it's more artistic."

She felt sure that he had been discussing hair-waving with some woman. She thought of all her grievances against him. The Lechford House episode rankled in her mind. He had given her the details, but she said to herself that he had given her the details only because he had foreseen that she would hear about the case from others or read about it in the newspapers. She had not been able to stomach that he should be at Lechford House alone late at night with two women of the class she hated and feared – and the very night of her dreadful experience with him in the bomb-explosion! No explanations could make that seem proper or fair. Naturally she had never disclosed her feelings. Further, the frequenting of such a house as Lechford House was more proof of his social importance, and incidentally of his riches. The spectacle of his flat showed her long ago that previously she had been underestimating his situation in the world. The revelations as to Lechford House had seemed to show her that she was still underestimating it. She resented his modesty. She was inclined to attribute his modesty to a desire to pay her as little as he reasonably could. However, she could not in sincerity do so. He treated her handsomely, considering her pretensions, but considering his position – he had no pretensions – not handsomely. She had had an irrational idea that, having permitted her to see the splendour of his flat, he ought to have increased her emoluments – that, indeed, she should be paid not according to her original environment, but according to his. She also resented that he had never again asked her to his flat. Her behaviour on that sole visit had apparently decided him not to invite her any more. She resented his perfectly hidden resentment.

What disturbed her more than anything else was a notion in her mind, possibly a wrong notion, that she cared for him less madly than of old. She had always said to herself, and more than once sadly to him, that his fancy for her would not and could not last; but that hers for him should decline puzzled her and added to her grievances against him. She looked at him from the little nest made by her head between two pillows. Did she in truth care for him less madly than of old? She wondered. She had only one gauge, the physical.

She began to talk despairingly about Marthe, whom, of course, she had had to mention at the door. He said quietly:

"But it's not because of Marthe's caprices that I'm asked to come down to-night, I suppose?"

She told him about the closing of the Promenade in a tone of absolute, resigned certainty that admitted of no facile pooh-

poohings or reassurances. And then, glancing sidelong at the night-table, where the lamp burned, she extended her half-bared arm and picked up the landlord's notice and gave it to him to read. Watching him read it she inwardly trembled, as though she had started on some perilous enterprise the end of which might be black desperation, as though she had cast off from the shore and was afloat amid the waves of a vast, swollen river – waves that often hid the distant further bank. She felt somehow that she was playing for all or nothing. And though she had had immense experience of men, though it was her special business to handle men, she felt herself to be unskilled and incompetent. The common ruses, feints, devices, guiles, chicaneries were familiar to her; she could employ them as well as any and better than most; they succeeded marvellously and absurdly – in the common embarrassments and emergencies, because they had not to stand the test of time. Their purpose was temporary, and when the purpose had been accomplished it did not matter whether they were unmasked or not, for the adversary-victim – who, in any event, was better treated than he deserved! – either had gone for ever, or would soon forget, or was too proud to murmur, or philosophically accepted a certain amount of wile as part of the price of ecstasy. But this embarrassment and this emergency were not common. They were a supreme crisis.

"The other lady has had notice too," she said, and went on: "It's the same everywhere in this quarter. I know not if it is the same in other districts, but quite probably it is... It is the end."

She saw by the lifting of his eyebrows that he was impressed, that he secretly admitted the justifiability of her summons to him. And instantly she took a reasonable, wise, calm tone.

"It is a little serious, is it not? I do not frighten myself, but it is serious. Above all, I do not wish to trouble thee. I know all thy anxieties, and I am a woman who understands. But except thee I have not a friend, as I have often told thee. In my heart there is a place only for one. I have a horror of all those women. They

241

weary me. I am not like them, as thou well knowest. Thus my existence is solitary. I have no relations. Not one. See! Go into no matter what interior, and there are photographs. But here – not one. Yes, one. My own. I am forced to regard my own portrait. What would I not give to be able to put on my chimney-piece thy portrait! But I cannot. Do not deceive thyself. I am not complaining. I comprehend perfectly. It is impossible that a woman like me should have thy photograph on her chimney-piece." She smiled, smoothing for a moment the pucker out of her brow. "And lately I see thee so little. Thou comest less frequently. And when thou comest, well – one embraces – a little music – and then *pouf!* Thou art gone. Is it not so?"

He said:

"But thou knowest the reason, I am terribly busy. I have all the preoccupations in the world. My committee – it is not all smooth, my committee. Everything and everybody depends on me. And in the committee I have enemies too. The fact is, I have become a beast of burden. I dream about it. And there are others in worse case. We shall soon be in the third year of the war. We must not forget that."

"My little rabbit," she replied very calmly and reasonably and caressingly. "Do not imagine to thyself that I blame thee. I do not blame thee. I comprehend too well all that thou dost, all that thou art worth. In every way thou art stronger than me. I am ten times nothing. I know it. I have no grievance against thee. Thou hast always given me what thou couldst, and I on my part have never demanded too much. Say, have I been excessive? At this hour I make no claim on thee. I have done all that to me was possible to make thee happy. In my soul I have always been faithful to thee. I do not praise myself for that. I did not choose it. These things are not chosen. They come to pass – that is all. And it arrived that I was bound to go mad about thee, and to remain so. What wouldst thou? Speak not of the war. Is it not because of the war that I am in exile, and that I am ruined? I have always worked honestly for my living. And there is not on earth an officer who has encountered me who can say that I have not been particularly nice to him – because he was an officer. Thou wilt excuse me if I speak of such matters. I know I am wrong. It is contrary to my habit. But what wouldst thou? I also have done what I could for the war. But it is my ruin. Oh, my Gilbert! Tell me what I must do. I ask nothing from thee but advice. It was for that that I dared to telephone thee."

G. J. answered casually:

"I see nothing to worry about. It will be necessary to take another flat. That is all."

"But I – I know nothing of London. One tells me that it is in future impossible for women who live alone – like me – to find a flat – that is to say, respectable."

"Absurd! I will find a flat. I know precisely where there is a flat."

"But will they let it to me?"

"They will let it to *me*, I suppose," said he, still casually.

A pause ensued.

She said, in a voice trembling:

"Thou art not going to say to me that thou wilt put me among my own furniture?"

"The flat is furnished. But it is the same thing."

"Do not let such a hope shine before me – me who saw before me only the pavement. Thou art not serious."

"I never was more serious. For whom dost thou take me, little foolish one?"

She cried:

"Oh, you English! You are *chic*. You make love as you go to war. Like *that!*... One word – it is decided! And there is nothing more to say! Ah! You English!"

She had almost screamed, shuddering under the shock of his decision, for which she had impossibly hoped, but whose reality overwhelmed her. He sat there in front of her, elegant, impeccably dressed, distinguished, aristocratic, rich, in the full wisdom of his years, and in the strength of his dominating will, and in the righteousness of his heart. One could absolutely trust such as him to do the right thing, and to do it generously, and to do it all the time. And she, *she* had won him. He had recognised her qualities. She had denied any claim upon him, but by his decision he had admitted a claim – a claim that no money could satisfy. After all, for eighteen months she had been more to him than any other woman. He had talked freely to her. He had concealed naught from her. He had spoken to her of his discouragements and his weaknesses. He had had no shame before her. By her acquiescences, her skill, her warmth, her adaptability, her intense womanliness, she had created between them a bond stronger than anything that could keep them apart. The bond existed. It could not during the whole future be broken save by a disloyalty. A disloyalty, she divined, would irrevocably destroy it. But she had no fear on that score, for she knew her own nature. His decision did more than fill her with a dizzy sense of relief, a mad, intolerable happiness – it re-established her self-respect. No ordinary woman, handicapped as she was, could have captured this fastidious and shy paragon... And the notion that her passion for him had dwindled was utterly ridiculous, like the notion that he would tire of her. She was saved. She burst into wild tears.

"Ah! Pardon me!" she sobbed. "I am quite calm, really. But since the air-raid, thou knowest, I have not been quite the same... Thou! Thou art different. Nothing could disturb thy calm. Ah! If thou wert a general at the front! What sang-froid! What presence of mind! But I – "

He bent towards her, and she suddenly sprang up and seized him round the neck, and ate his lips, and while she strangled and consumed him she kept muttering to him:

"Hope not that I shall thank thee. I cannot. I cannot! The words with which I could thank thee do not exist. But I am thine, thine! All of me is thine. Humiliate me! Demand of me impossible things! I am thy slave, thy creature! Ah! Let me kiss thy beautiful grey hairs. I love thy hair. And thy ears…"

The thought of her insatiable temperament flashed through her as she held him, and of his northern sobriety, and of the profound, unchangeable difference between these two. She would discipline her temperament; she would subjugate it. Women were capable of miracles – and women alone. And she was capable of miracles.

A strange, muffled noise came to them across the darkness of the sitting-room, and G. J. raised his head slightly to listen.

"Repose! Repose thyself in the arms of thy little mother," she breathed softly. "It is nothing. It is but the wind blowing the blind against the curtains."

And later, when she had distilled the magic of the hour and was tranquillised, she said:

"And where is it, this flat?"

39

IDYLL

Christine said to Marie, Otherwise la Mère Gaston, the new servant in the new flat, who was holding in her hand a telegram addressed to "Hoape, Albany":

"Give it to me. I will put it in front of the clock on the mantelpiece."

And she lodged it among the gilt cupids that supported the clock on the fringed mantelpiece in the drawing-room. She did so with a little gesture of childlike glee expressing her satisfaction in the flat as a whole.

The flat was dark; she did not object, loving artificial light. The rooms were all very small; she loved cosiness. There was a garage close by, which might have disturbed her nights; but it did not. The bathroom was open to the bedroom; no arrangement could be better. G. J. in enumerating the disadvantages of the flat had said also that it was too much and too heavily furnished. Not at all. She adored the cumbrous and rich furniture; she did not want in her flat the empty spaces of a ballroom; she wanted to feel that she was within an interior – inside something. She gloried in the flat. She preferred it even to her memory of G. J.'s flat in the Albany. Its golden ornateness flattered her. The glittering cornices, and the big carved frames of the pictures of impossible flowers and of ladies and gentlemen in historic coiffures and costumes, appeared marvellous to her. She had never seen, and certainly had never hoped to inhabit, anything like it. But then Gilbert was always better than his word.

He had been quite frank, telling her that he knew of the existence of the flat simply because it had been occupied for a brief time by the Mrs Carlos Smith of whom she had heard and read, and who had had to leave it on account of health. (She did not remind him that once at the beginning of the war when she had noticed the name and portrait of Mrs Carlos Smith in the paper, he, sitting by her side, had concealed from her that he knew Mrs Carlos Smith. Judiciously, she had never made the slightest reference to that episode.) Though she detested the unknown Mrs Carlos Smith, she admired and envied her for a great illustrious personage, and was secretly very proud of succeeding Mrs Carlos Smith in the tenancy. And when Gilbert told her that he had had his eye on the flat for her before Mrs Carlos Smith took it, and had hesitated on account of its drawbacks, she was even more proud. And reassured also. For this detail was a proof that Gilbert had really had the intention to put her "among her own furniture" long before the night of the supreme appeal to him... Only he was always so cautious.

And Gilbert was the discoverer of la mère Gaston, too, and as frank about her as about the flat. La mère Gaston was the widow of a French soldier, domiciled in London previous to the war, who had died of wounds in one of the Lechford hospitals; and it was through the Lechford Committee that Gilbert had come across her. A few weeks earlier than the beginning of the formal liaison Mrs Braiding had fallen ill for a space, and Madame Gaston had been summoned as char-woman to aid Mrs Braiding's young sister in the Albany flat. With excellent judgment Gilbert had chosen her to succeed Marthe, whom he himself had reproachfully dismissed from Cork Street.

He was amazingly clever, was Gilbert, for he had so arranged things that Christine had been able to cut off her Cork Street career as with a knife. She had departed from Cork Street with two trunks and a few cardboard boxes – her stove was abandoned to the landlord – and vanished into London and left no trace. Except Gilbert, nobody who knew her in Cork Street was aware of her new address, and nobody who knew her in Mayfair knew that she had come from Cork Street. Her ancient acquaintances in Cork Street would ring the bell there in vain.

Madame Gaston was a neat, plump woman of perhaps forty, not looking her years. She had a comprehending eye. After three words from Gilbert she had mastered the situation, and as she perfectly realised where her interest lay she could be relied upon for discretion. In all delicate matters only her eye talked. She was a Protestant, and went to the French church in Soho Square, which she called the "Temple". Christine and she had had but one Sunday together – and Christine had gone with her to the Temple! The fact was that Christine had decided to be a Protestant. She needed a religion, and Catholicism had an inconvenience – confession. She had regularised her position, so much so that by comparison with the past she was now perfectly respectable. Yet if she had been candid in the confessional the priest would still have convicted her of mortal sin; which would have been very unfair; and she could not, in view of her respectability, have remained a Catholic without confessing, however infrequently. Madame Gaston, as soon as she was sure of her convert, referred to Catholicism as "idolatry".

"Put your apron on, Marie," said Christine. "Monsieur will be here directly."

"Ah, yes, madame!"

"Have you opened the kitchen-window to take away the smell of cooking?"

"Yes, madame."

"Am I all right, Marie?"

Madame Gaston surveyed her mistress, who turned round.

"Yes, madame. I think that monsieur will much like that negligeé." She departed to don the apron.

Between these two it was continually "monsieur," "monsieur". He was seldom there, but he was always there, always being consulted, placated, invoked, revered, propitiated, magnified. He was the giver of all good, and there was no other Allah, and he had two prophets.

Christine sang, she twittered, she pirouetted, out of sheer youthful joy. She had forgotten care and forgotten promiscuity; good fortune had washed her pure. She looked at herself in the massive bevelled mirror, and saw that she was fresh and young and lithe and graceful. And she felt triumphant. Gilbert had expressed the fear that she might get lonely and bored. He had even said that occasionally he might bring along a man, and that perhaps the man would have a very nice woman friend. She had not very heartily responded. She was markedly sympathetic towards Englishmen, but towards English women – no! And especially she did not want to know any English women in the same situation as herself. Lonely? Impossible! Bored? Impossible! She had an establishment. She had a civil list. Her days passed like an Arabian dream. She never had an unfilled moment, and when each day was over she always remembered little things which she had meant to do and had not found time to do.

She was superb sleeper, and arose at noon. Three o'clock usually struck before her day had fairly begun – unless, of course, she happened to be very busy, in which case she would be ready for contact with the world at the lunch-hour. Her main occupation was to charm, allure, and gratify a man; for that she lived. Her distractions were music, the reading of novels, *Le Journal*, and *Les Grandes Modes*. And for the war she knitted. In her new situation it was essential that she should do something for the war. Therefore she knitted, being a good knitter, and her knitting generally lay about.

She popped into the dining-room to see if the table was well set for dinner. It was, but in order to show that Marie did not know everything, she rearranged somewhat the flowers in the central bowl. Then she returned to the drawing-room, and sat down at the piano and waited. The instant of arrival approached. Gilbert's punctuality was absolute, always had been; sometimes it alarmed her. She could not have to wait more than a minute or two, according to the inexactitude of her clock... The bell rang, and simultaneously she began to play a five-finger exercise. Often in the old life she had executed upon him this innocent subterfuge, to make him think she practised the piano to a greater extent than she actually did, that indeed she was always practising. It never occurred to her that he was not deceived.

Hear Marie fly to the front door! See Christine's face, see her body, as in her pale, bright gown she peeps round the half-open door of the drawing-room! She lives, then. Her eyes sparkle for the giver of all good, for the adored, and her brow is puckered for him, and the jewels on her hand burn for him, and every pleat of her garments visible and invisible is pleated for him. She is a child. She has snatched up a chocolate, and put it between her teeth, and so she offers the half of it to him, smiling, silent. She is a child, but she is also a woman intensely skilled in her art...

"Monster!" she said. "Come this way." And she led him down the tunnel to the bedroom. There, in a corner of the bathroom, stood an antique closed toilet-stand, such as was used by men in the days before splashing and sousing were invented. She had removed it from the drawing-room.

"Open it," she commanded.

He obeyed. Its little compartments, which had been empty, were filled with a man's toilet instruments – brushes, file, scissors, shaving-soap (his own brand), a safety-razor, &c. The set was complete. She had known exactly the requirements.

"It is a little present from thy woman," she said. "In future thou wilt have no excuse – Sit down. Marie!"

"Madame?"

"Take off the boots of Monsieur."

Marie knelt.

Christine found the new slippers.

"And now this!" she said, after he had washed and used the new brushes, producing a black house-jacket with velvet collar and cuffs.

"How tired thou must be after thy day!" she murmured, patting him with tiny pats.

"Thou knowest, my little one," she said, pointing to the gas-stove in the bedroom fireplace. "For the other rooms a gas-stove – I am indifferent. But the bedroom is something else. The bedroom is sacred. I could not tolerate a gas-stove in the bedroom. A coal fire is necessary to me. You do not think so?"

"Yes," he said. "You are quite right. It shall be seen to."

"Can I give the order? Thou permittest me to give the order?"

"Certainly."

In the drawing-room she cushioned him well in the best easy-chair, and, sitting down on a pouf near him, began to knit like an industrious wife who understands the seriousness of war. Nothing escaped the attention of that man. He espied the telegram.

"What's that?"

"Ah!" she cried, springing up and giving it to him. "Stupid that I am! I forgot."

He looked at the address.

"How did this come here?" he asked mildly.

"Marie brought it – from the Albany."

"Oh!"

He opened the telegram and read it, having dropped the envelope into the silk-lined, gilded waste-paper basket by the fender.

"It is nothing serious?" she questioned.

"No. Business."

He might have shown it to her – he had shown her telegrams before – but he stuck it into his pocket. Then, without a word to Christine, he rang the bell, and Marie appeared.

"Marie! The telegram – why did you bring it here?"

"Monsieur, it was like this. I went to monsieur's flat to fetch two aprons that I had left there. The telegram was on the console in the ante-chamber. Knowing that monsieur was to come direct here, I brought it."

"Does Mrs Braiding know you brought it?"

"Ah! As for Mrs Braiding, monsieur – " Marie stopped, disclaiming any responsibility for Mrs Braiding, of whom she was somewhat jealous. "I thought to do well."

"I am sure of it. But surely you can see you have been indiscreet. Don't do it again."

"No, monsieur. I ask pardon of monsieur."

Immediately afterwards he said to Christine in a gay, careless tone:

"And this gas-stove here? Is it all right? Have we tried it? Let us try it."

"The weather is warm, dearest."

"But just to try it. I always like to satisfy myself – in time."

"Fusser!" she exclaimed, and ignited the stove.

He gazed at it absently, then picked up a cigarette and, taking the telegram from his pocket, folded it into a spill and with it lit the cigarette.

"Yes," he said meditatively. "It seems not a bad stove." And he held the spill till it had burnt to his finger-ends. Then he extinguished the stove.

She said to herself:

"He has burned the telegram on purpose. But how cleverly he did it! Ah! That man! There is none but him!"

She was disquieted about the telegram. She feared it. Her superstitiousness was awakened. She thought of her apostasy from Catholicism to Protestantism. She thought of a Holy Virgin angered. And throughout the evening and throughout the night, amid her smiles and teasings and coaxings and caresses and ecstasies and all her accomplished, voluptuous girlishness, the image of a resentful Holy Virgin flitted before her. Why should he burn a business telegram? Also, was he not at intervals a little absentminded?

40

THE WINDOW

G. J. sat on the oilcloth-covered seat of the large overhanging open bay-window. Below him was the river, tributary of the Severn; in front the Old Bridge, with an ancient street rising beyond, and above that the silhouette of the roofs of Wrikton surmounted by the spire of its vast church. To the left was the weir, and the cliffs were there also, and the last tints of the sunset.

Somebody came into the coffee-room. G. J. looked round, hoping that it might, after all, be Concepcion. But it was Concepcion's maid, Emily, an imitative young woman who seemed to have caught from her former employer the quality of strange, sinister provocativeness.

She paused a moment before speaking. Her thin figure was somewhat indistinct in the twilight.

"Mrs Smith wishes me to say that she will certainly be well enough to take you to the station in the morning, sir," said she in her specious tones. "But she hopes you will be able to stay till the afternoon train."

"I shan't." He shook his head.

"Very well, sir."

And after another moment's pause Emily, apparently with a challenging reluctance, receded through the shadows of the room and vanished.

G. J. was extremely depressed and somewhat indignant. He gazed down bitterly at the water, following with his eye the incredibly long branches of the tree that from the height of the buttresses drooped perpendicularly into the water. He had had an astounding week-end; and for having responded to Concepcion's telegram, for having taken the telegram seriously, he had deserved what he got. Thus he argued.

She had met him on the hot Saturday afternoon in a Ford car. She did not look ill. She looked as if she had fairly recovered from her acute neurasthenia. She was smartly and carelessly dressed in a summer sporting costume, and had made a strong contrast to every other human being on the platform of the small provincial station. The car drove not to the famous principal hotel, but to a small hotel just beyond the bridge. She had given him tea in the coffee-room and taken him out again, on foot, showing him the town – the half-timbered houses, the immense castle, the market-hall, the spacious flat-fronted residences, the multiplicity of solicitors, banks and surveyors, the bursting provision shops with imposing fractions of animals and expensive pies, and the drapers with ladies' blouses at 2s. 4d. Then she had conducted him to an organ recital in the vast church where, amid faint gas-jets and beadles and stalls and stained glass and holiness and centuries of history and the high respectability of the town, she had whispered sibilantly, and other people had whispered, in the long intervals of the organ. She had removed him from the church before the collection for the Red Cross, and when they had eaten a sort of dinner she had borne him away to the Russian dancers in the Moot Hall.

She said she had seen the Russian dancers once already, and that they were richly worth to him a six-hours' train journey. The posters of the Russian dancers were rather daring and seductive. The Russian dancers themselves were the most desolating stage spectacle that G. J. had ever witnessed. The troupe consisted of intensely English girls of various ages, and girl-children. The costumes had obviously been fabricated by the artistes. The artistes could neither dance, pose, group, make an entrance, make an exit, nor even smile. The ballets, obviously fabricated by the same persons as the costumes, had no plot, no beginning and no end. Crude amateurishness was the characteristic of these honest and hard-working professionals, who somehow contrived to be neither men nor women – and assuredly not epicene – but who travelled from country town to country town in a glamour of posters, exciting the towns, in spite of a perfect lack of sex, because they were the fabled Russian dancers. The Moot Hall was crammed with adults and their cackling offspring, who heartily applauded the show, which indeed was billed as a "return visit" due to "terrific success" on a previous occasion. "Is it not too marvellous," Concepcion had said. He had admitted that it was. But the boredom had been excruciating. In the street they had bought an evening paper of which he had never before heard the name, to learn news of the war. The war, however, seemed very far off; it had grown unreal. "We'll talk to-morrow," Concepcion had said, and gone abruptly to bed! Still, he had slept well in the soft climate, to the everlasting murmur of the weir.

Then the Sunday. She was indisposed, could not come down to breakfast, but hoped to come down to lunch, could not come down to lunch, but hoped to come down to tea, could not come down to tea – and so on to nightfall. The Sunday had been like a thousand years to him. He had learnt the town, and the suburbs of it; the grass-grown streets, the main thoroughfares, and the slums; by the afternoon he was recognising familiar faces in the town. He had twice made the classic round – along the cliffs, over the New Bridge (which was an antique), up the hill to the castle, through the market-place, down the High Street to the Old Bridge. He had explored the brain of the landlord, who could not grapple with a time-table, and who spent most of the time during closed hours in patiently bolting the front door which G. J. was continually opening. He had talked to the old customer who, whenever the house was open, sat at a table in the garden over a mug of cider. He had played through all the musical comedies, dance albums and pianoforte albums that littered the piano. He had read the same Sunday papers that he read in the Albany. And he had learnt the life-history of the sole servant, a very young agreeable woman with a wedding-ring and a baby, which baby she carried about with her when serving at table. Her husband was in France. She said that as soon as she had received his permission to do so she should leave, as she really could not get through all the work of the hotel and mind and feed a baby. She said also that she played the piano herself. And she regretted that baby and pressure of work had deprived her of a sight of the Russian dancers, because she had heard so much about them, and was sure they were beautiful. This detail touched G. J.'s heart to a mysterious and sweet and almost intolerable melancholy. He had not made the acquaintance of fellow-guests – for there were none, save Concepcion and Emily.

And in the evening as in the morning the weir placidly murmured, and the river slipped smoothly between the huge jutting buttresses of the Old Bridge; and the thought of the perpetuity of the river, in whose mirror the venerable town was a mushroom, obsessed him, mastered him, and made him as old as the river. He was wonder-struck and sorrow-struck by life, and by his own life, and by the incomprehensible and angering fantasy of Concepcion. His week-end took on the appearance of the monstrous. Then the door opened again, and Concepcion entered in a white gown, the antithesis of her sporting costume of the day before. She approached through the thickening shadows of the room, and the vague whiteness of her gown reminded him of the whiteness of the form climbing the chimney-ladder on the roof of Lechford House in the raid. Knowing her, he ought to have known that, having made him believe that she would not come down, she would certainly come down. He restrained himself, showed no untoward emotion, and said in a calm, genial voice: "Oh! I'm so glad you were well enough to come down."

She sat opposite to him in the window-seat, rather sideways, so that her skirt was pulled close round her left thigh and flowed free over the right. He could see her still plainly in the dusk.

"I've never yet apologised to you for my style of behaviour at the committee of yours," she began abruptly in a soft, kind, reasonable voice. "I know I let you down horribly. Yes, yes! I did. And I ought to apologise to you for to-day too. But I don't think I'll apologise to you for bringing you to Wrikton and this place. They're not real, you know. They're an illusion. There is no such place as Wrikton and this river and this window. There couldn't be, could there? Queen and I motored over here once from Paulle – it's not so very far – and we agreed that it didn't really exist. I never forgot it; I was determined to come here again some time, and that's why I chose this very spot when half Harley Street stood up and told me I mut go away somewhere after my cure and be by myself, far from the pernicious influence of friends. I think I gave you a very fair idea of the town yesterday. But I didn't show you the funniest thing in it – the inside of a solicitor's office. You remember the large grey stone house in Mill Street – the grass street, you know – with 'Simpover and Simpover' on the brass plate, and the strip of green felt nailed all round the front door to keep the wind out in winter. Well, it's all in the same key inside. And I don't know which is the funniest, the Russian dancers, or the green felt round the front door, or Mr Simpover, or the other Mr Simpover. I'm sure neither of those men is real, though they both somehow have children. You remember the yellow cards that you see in so many of the windows: 'A MAN has gone from this house to fight for King and Country!' – the elder Mr Simpover thinks it would be rather boastful to put the card in the window, so he keeps it on the mantelpiece in his private office. It's for his son. And yet I assure you the father isn't real. He is like the town, he simply couldn't be real."

"What have *you* been up to in the private office?" G. J. asked lightly.

"Making my will."

"What for?"

"Isn't it the proper thing to do? I've left everything to you."

"You haven't, Con!" he protested. There was absolutely no tranquillity about this woman. With her, the disconcerting unexpected happened every five minutes.

"Did you suppose I was going to send any of my possessions back to my tropical relatives in South America? I've left everything to you to do what you like with. Squander it if you like, but I expect you'll give it to war charities. Anyhow, I thought it would be safest in your hands."

He retorted in a tone quietly and sardonically challenging:

"But I was under the impression you were cured."

"Of my neurasthenia?"

"Yes."

"I believe I am. I gained thirteen pounds in the nursing home, and slept like a greengrocer. In fact, the Weir-Mitchell treatment, with modern improvements of course, enjoyed a marvellous triumph in my case. But that's not the point. G. J., I know you think I behaved very childishly yesterday, and that I deserved to be ill to-day for what I did yesterday. And I admit you're a saint for not saying so. But I wasn't really childish, and I haven't really been ill to-day. I've only been in a devil of a dilemma. I wanted to tell you something. I telgraphed for you so that I could tell you. But as soon as I saw you I was afraid to tell you. Not afraid, but I couldn't make up my mind whether I ought to tell you or not. I've lain in bed all day trying to decide the point. To-night I decided I oughtn't, and then all of a sudden, just now, I became an automaton and put on some things, and here I am telling you."

She paused. G. J. kept silence. Then she continued, in a voice in which persuasiveness was added to calm, engaging reasonableness:

"Now you must get rid of all your conventional ideas, G. J. Because you're rather conventional. You must be completely straight – I mean intellectually – otherwise I can't treat you as an intellectual equal, and I want to. You must be a realist – if any man can be." She spoke almost with tenderness.

He felt mysteriously shy, and with a brusque movement of the head shifted his glance from her to the river.

"Well?" he questioned, his gaze fixed on the water that continually slipped in large, swirling, glinting sheets under the bridge.

"I'm going to kill myself."

At first the words made no impression on him. He replied:

"You were right when you said this place was an illusion. It is."

And then he began to be afraid. Did she mean it? She was capable of anything. And he was involved in her, inescapably. Yes, he was afraid. Nevertheless, as she kept silence he went on – with bravado:

"And how do you intend to do it?"

"That will be my affair. But I venture to say that my way of doing it will make Wrikton historic," she said, curiously gentle.

"Trust you!" he exclaimed, suddenly looking at her. "Con, why *will* you always be so theatrical?"

She changed her posture for an easier one, half reclining. Her face and demeanour seemed to have the benign masculinity of a man's.

"I'm sorry," she answered. "I oughtn't to have said that. At any rate, to you. I ought to have had more respect for your feelings."

He said:

"You aren't cured. That's evident. All this is physical."

"Of course it's physical, G. J.," she agreed, with an intonation of astonishment that he should be guilty of an utterance so obvious and banal. "Did you ever know anything that wasn't? Did you ever even conceive anything that wasn't? If you can show me how to conceive spirit except in terms of matter, I'd like to listen to you."

"It's against nature – to kill yourself."

"Oh!" she murmured. "I'm quite used to that charge. You aren't by any means the first to accuse me of being against nature. But can you tell me where nature ends? That's another thing I'd like to know... My dear friend, you're being conventional, and you aren't being realistic. You must know perfectly well in your heart that there's no reason why I shouldn't kill myself if I want to. You aren't going to talk to me about the Ten Commandments, I suppose, are you? There's a risk, of course, on the other side – shore – but perhaps it's worth taking. You aren't in a position to say it isn't worth taking. And at worst the other shore must be marvellous. It may possibly be terrible, if you arrive too soon and without being asked, but it must be marvellous... Naturally, I believe in immortality. If I didn't, the thing wouldn't be worth doing. Oh! I should hate to be extinguished. But to change one existence for another, if the fancy takes you – that seems to me the greatest proof of real independence that anybody can give. It's tremendous. You're playing chess with fate and fate's winning, and you knock up the chess-board and fate has to begin all over again! Can't you see how tremendous it is – and how tempting it is? The temptation is terrific."

"I can see all that," said G. J. He was surprised by a sudden sense of esteem for the mighty volition hidden behind those calm, worn, gracious features. But Concepcion's body was younger than her face. He perceived, as it were for the first time, that Concepcion was immeasurably younger than himself; and yet she had passed far beyond him in experience. "But what's the origin of all this? What do you want to do it for? What's happened?"

"Then you believe I mean to do it?"

"Yes," he replied sincerely, and as naturally as he could.

"That's the tone I like to hear," said she, smiling. "I felt sure I could count on you not to indulge in too much nonsense. Well, I'm going to try the next avatar just to remind fate of my existence. I think fate's forgotten me, and I can stand anything but that. I've lost Carly, and I've lost Queen... Oh, G. J.! Isn't it awful to think that when I offered you Queen she'd already gone, and it was only her dead body I was offering you?... And I've lost my love. And I've failed, and I shall never be any more good here. I swore I would see a certain thing through, and I haven't seen it through, and I can't! But I've told you all this before... What's left? Even my unhappiness is leaving me. Unless I kill myself I shall cease to exist. Don't you understand? Yes, you do."

After a marked pause she added:

"And I may overtake Queen."

"There's one thing I don't understand," he said, "as we're being frank with each other. Why do you tell me? Has it occurred to you that you're really making me a party to this scheme of yours?"

He spoke with a perfectly benevolent detachment deriving from hers. And as he spoke he thought of a man whom he had once known and who had committed suicide, and of all that he had read about suicides and what he had thought of them. Suicides had been incomprehensible to him, and either despicable or pitiable. And he said to himself: "Here is one of them! (Or is it an illusion?) But she has made all my notions of suicide seem ridiculous."

She answered his spoken question with vivacity: "Why do I tell you? I don't know. That's the point I've been arguing to myself all night and all day. I'm not telling you. Something *in* me is forcing me to tell you. Perhaps it's much more important that you should comprehend me than that you should be spared the passing worry that I'm causing you by showing you the inside of my head. You're the only friend I have left. I knew you before I knew Carly. I practically committed suicide from my particular world at the beginning of the war. I was going back to my particular world – you remember, G. J., in that little furnished flat – I was going back to it, but you wouldn't let me. It was you who definitely cut me off from my past. I might have been gadding about safely with Sarah Churcher and her lot at this very hour, but you would have it otherwise, and so I finished up with neurasthenia. You commanded and I obeyed."

"Well," he said, ignoring all her utterance except the last words, "obey me again."

"What do you want me to do?" she demanded wistfully and yet defiantly. Her features were tenidng to disappear in the tide of night, but she happened to sit up and lean forward and bring them a little closer to him. "You've no right to stop me from doing what I want to do. What right have you to stop me? Besides, you can't stop me. Nothing can stop me. It is settled. Everything is arranged."

He, too, sat up and leaned forward. In a voice rendered soft by the realisation of the fact that he had indeed known her before Carlos Smith knew her and had imagined himself once to be in love with her, and of the harshness of her destiny and the fading of her glory, he said simply and yet, in spite of himself, insinuatingly:

"No! I don't claim any right to stop you. I understand better, perhaps, than you think. But let me come down again next week-end. Do let me," he insisted, still more softly.

Even while he was speaking he expected her to say, "You're only suggesting that in order to gain time."

But she said:

"How can you be sure it wouldn't be my inquest and funeral I should be 'letting' you come down to?"

He replied:

"I could trust you."

A delicate night-gust charged with the scent of some plant came in at the open window and deranged ever so slightly a glistening lock on her forehead. G. J., peering at her, saw the masculinity melt from her face. He saw the mysterious resurrection of the girl in her, and felt in himself the sudden exciting outflow from her of that temperamental fluid whose springs had been dried up since the day when she learnt of her widowhood. She flushed. He looked away into the dark water, as though he had profanely witnessed that which ought not to be witnessed. Earlier in the interview she had inspired him with shyness. He was now stirred, agitated, thrilled – overwhelmed by the effect on her of his own words and his own voice. He was afraid of his power, as a prophet might be afraid of his power. He had worked a miracle – a miracle infinitely more convincing than anything that had led up to it. The miracle had brought back the reign of reality.

"Very well," she quivered.

And there was a movement and she was gone. He glanced quickly behind him, but the room lay black... A transient pallor on the blackness, and the door banged. He sat a long time, solemn, gazing at the serrated silhouette of the town against a sky that obstinately held the wraith of daylight, and listening to the everlasting murmur of the invisible weir. Not a sound came from the town, not the least sound. When at length he stumbled out, he saw the figure of the landlord smoking the pipe of philosophy, and waiting with a landlord's fatalism for the last guest to go to bed. And they talked of the weather.

41

THE ENVOY

The next night G. J., having been hailed by an acquaintance, was talking at the top of the steps beneath the portal of a club in Piccadilly. It was after ten by the clocks, and nearly, but not quite, dark. A warm, rather heavy, evening shower had ceased. This was the beginning of the great macintosh epoch, by-product of the war, when the paucity of the means of vehicular locomotion had rendered macintoshes permissible, even for women with pretensions to smartness; and at intervals stylish girls on their way home from unaccustomed overtime, passed the doors in transparent macintoshes of pink, yellow or green, as scornful as military officers of the effeminate umbrella, whose use was being confined to club-men and old dowdies.

The acquaintance sought advice from G. J. about the shutting up of households for Belgian refugees. G. J. answered absently, not concealing that he was in a hurry. He had, in fact, been held up within three minutes of the scene of his secret idyll, and was anxious to arrive there. He had promised himself this surprise visit to Christine as some sort of recompense and narcotic for the immense disturbance of spirit which he had suffered at Wrikton.

That morning Concepcion had been invisible, but at his early breakfast he had received a note from her, a brief but masterly composition, if ever so slightly theatrical. He was conscious of tenderness for Concepcion, of sympathy with her, of a desire to help to restore her to that which by misfortune she had lost. But the first of these sentiments he resolutely put aside. He was determined to change his mood towards her for the sake of his own tranquillity; and he had convinced himself that his wise, calm, common sense was capable of saving her from any tragic and fatal folly. He had her in the hollow of his hand; but if she was expecting too much from him she would be gradually disappointed. He must have peace; he could not allow a bomb to be thrown into his habits; he was a bachelor of over fifty whose habits had the value of inestimable jewels and whose perfect independence was the most precious thing in the world. At his age he could not marry a volcano, a revolution, a new radio-active element exhibiting properties which were an enigma to social science. Concepcion would turn his existence into an endless drama of which she alone, with her deep-rooted, devilish talent for the sensational, would always choose the setting, as she had chosen the window and the weir. No; he must not mistake affectionate sympathy for tenderness, nor tolerate the sexual exploitation of his pity.

As he listened and talked to the acquaintance his inner mind shifted with relief to the vision of Christine, contented and simple and compliant in her nest – Christine, at once restful and exciting, Christine, the exquisite symbol of acquiescence and response. What a contrast to Concepcion! It had been a bold and sudden stroke to lift Christine to another plane, but a stroke well justified and entirely successful, fulfilling his dream.

At this moment he noticed a figure pass the doorway in whose shadow he was, and he exclaimed within himself incredulously:

"That is Christine!"

In the shortest possible delay he said "Goodnight" to his acquaintance, and jumped down the steps and followed eastwards the figure. He followed warily, for already the strange and distressing idea had occurred to him that he must not overtake her – if she it was. It was she. He caught sight of her again in the thick obscurity by the prison-wall of Devonshire House. He recognised the peculiar brim of the new hat and the new "military" umbrella held on the wrist by a thong.

What was she doing abroad? She could not be going to a theatre. She had not a friend in London. He was her London. And la mère Gaston was not with her. Theoretically, of course, she was free. He had laid down no law. But it had been clearly understood between them that she should never emerge at night alone. She herself had promulgated the rule, for she had a sense of propriety and a strong sense of reality. She had belonged to the class which respectable, broadminded women, when they bantered G. J., always called "the pretty ladies," and as a postulant for respectability she had for her own satisfaction to mind her p's and q's. She could not afford not to keep herself above suspicion.

She had been a courtesan. Did she look like one? As an individual figure in repose, no! None could have said that she did. He had long since learnt that to decide always correctly by appearance, and apart from environment and gesture, whether an unknown woman was or was not a wanton, presented a task beyond the powers of even the completest experience. But Christine was walking in Piccadilly at night, and he soon perceived that she was discreetly showing the demeanour of a courtesan at her profession – she who had hated and feared the pavement! He knew too well the signs – the waverings, the turns of the head, the variations in speed, the scarcely perceptible hesitations, the unmistakable air of wandering with no definite objective.

Near Dover Street he hastened through the thin, reflecting mire, amid beams of light and illuminated numbers that advanced upon him in both directions thundering or purring, and crossed Piccadilly, and hurried ahead of her, to watch her in safety from the other side of the thoroughfare. He could hardly

see her; she was only a moving shadow; but still he could see
her; and in the long stretch of gloom beneath the façade of the
Royal Academy he saw the shadow pause in front of a military
figure, which by a flank movement avoided the shadow and
went resolutely forward. He lost her in front of the Piccadilly
Hotel, and found her again at the corner of Air Street. She
swerved into Air Street and crossed Regent Street; he was
following. In Denman Street, close to Shaftesbury Avenue, she
stood still in front of another military figure – a common soldier
as it proved – who also rebuffed her. The thing was flagrant. He
halted, and deliberately let her go from his sight. She vanished
into the dark crowds of the Avenue.

In horrible humiliation, in atrocious disgust, he said to
himself:

"Never will I set eyes on her again! Never! Never!"

Why was she doing it? Not for money. She could only be
doing it from the nostalgia of adventurous debauch. She was
the slave of her temperament, as the drunkard is the slave of his
thirst. He had told her that he would be out of town for the
week end, on committee business. He had distinctly told her
that she must on no account expect him on the Monday night.
And her temperament had roused itself from the obscene
groves of her subconsciousness like a tiger and come up and
driven her forth. How easy for her to escape from la mère
Gaston if she chose! And yet – would she dare, even at the
bidding of the tiger, to introduce a stranger into the flat?
Unnecessary, he reflected. There were a hundred accommodating
dubious interiors between Shaftesbury Avenue and Leicester
Square. He understood; he neither accused nor pardoned; but
he was utterly revolted, and wounded not merely in his soul but
in the most sensitive part of his soul – his pride. He called
himself by the worst epithet of opprobrium: Simpleton! The
bold and sudden stroke had now become the fatuous caprice of
a damned fool. Had he, at his age, been capable of overlooking

the elementary axiom: once a wrong 'un, always a wrong 'un? Had he believed in reclamation? He laughed out his disgust...

No! He did not blame her. To blame her would have been ridiculous. She was only what she was, and not worth blame. She was nothing at all. How right, how cursedly right, were the respectable dames in the accent of amused indifference which they employed for their precious phrase, "the pretty ladies"! Well, he would treat her generously – but through his lawyer.

And in the desolation, the dismay, the disillusion, the nausea which ravaged him he was unwillingly conscious of fragments of thoughts that flickered like transient flames far below in the deep mines of his being... "You are an astounding woman, Con.".... "Do you want me to go to the bad altogether?".... In offering him Queen had not Concepcion made the supreme double sacrifice of attempting to bring together, at the price of her own separation from both of them, the two beings to whom she was most profoundly attached? It was a marvellous deed... Worry, volcanoes, revolutions – was he afraid of them?... Were they not the very essence of life?... A figure of nobility!... Sitting there now by the window over the river, listening to the weir... "I shall never be any more good." ...But she never had a gesture that was not superb... Was he really encrusted in habits? Really like men whom he knew and despised at his club?... She loved him... And what rich, flattering love was her love compared to – !... She was young... Tenderness... Such were the flames of dim promise that flickered immeasurably beneath the dark devastation of his mind. He ignored them, but he could not ignore them. He extinguished them, but they were continually relighted... A wedding?... What sort of a wedding?... Poor Carlos, pathetically buried under the ruthless happiness of others! What a shame!... Poor Carlos!

(Nice enough little cocotte, nothing else! But, of course, incurable!... He remembered all her crimes now. How she had been late in dressing for their first dinner. Her inexplicable vanishing from the supper-party, never explained, but easily explicable now, perhaps. And so on and so on... Simpleton! Ass!)

He had walked heedless of direction. He was near Lechford House. Many of its windows were lit. The great front doors were open. A commissionaire stood on guard in front of them. To the railings was affixed a newly-painted notice: "No person will be allowed to enter these premises without a pass. To this rule there is no exception." Lechford House had been "taken over" in its entirety by a Government department that believed in the virtue of mystery and of long hours. He looked up at the higher windows. He could not distinguish the chimney amid the newly-revealed stars. He thought of Queen, the white woman. Evidently he had never understood Queen, for if Concepcion admired her she was worth admiration. Concepcion never made a mistake in assessing fundamental character.

The complete silent absorption of Lechford House into the war-machine rather dismayed him. He had seen not a word as to the affair in the newspapers – and Lechford House was one of the final strongholds of privilege! He strolled on into the quietness of the Park – of which one of the gate-keepers said to him that it would be shutting in a few minutes.

He was in solitude, and surrounded by London. He stood still, and the vast sea of war seemed to be closing over him. The war was growing, or the sense of its measureless scope was growing. It had sprung, not out of this crime or that, but out of the secret invisible roots of humanity, and it was widening to the limits of evolution itself. It transcended judgment. It defied conclusions and rendered equally impossible both hope and despair. His pride in his country was intensified as months passed; his faith in his country was not lessened. And yet, wherein was the efficacy of grim words about British tenacity? The great new Somme offensive was not succeeding in the North. Was victory possible? Was victory deserved? In his daily labour he was brought into contact with too many instances of official selfishness, folly, ignorance, stupidity, and sloth, French as well as British, not to marvel at times that the conflict had not come to an ignominious end long ago through simple lack of imagination. He knew that he himself had often failed in devotion, in rectitude, in sheer grit.

The supreme lesson of the war was its revelation of what human nature actually was. And the solace of the lesson, the hope for triumph, lay in the fact that human nature must be substantially the same throughout the world. If we were humanly imperfect, so at least was the enemy.

Perhaps the frame of society was about to collapse. Perhaps Queen, deliberately courting destruction, and being destroyed, was the symbol of society. What matter? Perhaps civilisation, by its nobility and its elements of reason, and by the favour of destiny, would be saved from disaster after frightful danger, and Concepcion was its symbol...

All he knew was that he had a heavy day's work before him on the morrow, and in relief from pain and insoluble problems he turned to face that work, thankful; thankful that (owing originally to Queen!) he had discovered in the war a task which suited his powers, which was genuinely useful, and which would only finish with the war; thankful for the prospect of meeting Concepcion at the week-end and exploring with her the marvellous provocative potentialities that now drew them together; thankful, too, that he had a balanced and sagacious mind, and could judge justly. (Yes, he was already forgetting his bitter condemnation of himself as a simpleton!)

How in his human self-sufficiency could he be expected to know that he had judged the negligible Christine unjustly? Was he divine that he could see in the figure of the wanton who peered at soldiers in the street a self-convinced mystic envoy of the most clement Virgin, an envoy passionately repentant after apostasy, bound at all costs to respond to an imagined voice long unheard, and seeking – though in vain this second time – the

271

protégé of the Virgin so that she might once more succour and assuage his affliction?

Arnold Bennett

Clayhanger

In this, the first volume of an ambitious series intending to trace the parallel lives of a man and woman from youth to marriage and from marriage to old age, Bennett introduces the character of Edwin Clayhanger. A sober portrait of a boy growing up under a tyrannical father contrasts with young Edwin's glimpses of the mysterious and tantalizing Hilda Lessways. As the lives of these two characters unfold before us, Bennett uses autobiographical detail to beautifully depict the constraints and spiritual adventures of young life in the Potteries.

Hilda Lessways

In the second volume of the Clayhanger series, events in *Clayhanger* are retold from the perspective of Hilda Lessways, who is embarking on a relationship with Cannon, a charismatic entrepreneur, whose success has taken him from the Five Towns to Brighton. As Hilda's fascination with the young Clayhanger grows, one of Bennett's most living heroines must face up to her conflicting emotions, and the reality of her hopes and tragedies.

Arnold Bennett

These Twain

In *Clayhanger* and *Hilda Lessways*, Bennett followed the development of a relationship from two very different perspectives. He now draws these perspectives together in a gripping novel which sees the two young protagonists embarking upon married life. One might expect a fairy tale romance, but both Edwin and Hilda are extremely strong-willed, and this clash of personalities makes for a marriage that often hovers on the brink of failure.

This volume of the Clayhanger series contains some of Bennett's very finest work, depicting superb scenes from provincial life and painting a powerful picture of the conflict of wills in an inharmonious marriage.

The Roll Call

The final volume of the Clayhanger series sees Hilda's son, George Cannon (who quickly changes his name from Clayhanger), as an architect, in many ways representing the ambitions held by his stepfather Edwin Clayhanger. However, he possesses an arrogance endowed by family wealth and Bennett examines the difficulty of bringing up children without spoiling them with some aplomb. It is a riveting tale which sees George eventually in the army and a fitting finale to one of the finest series in English literature.

A Man from the North

Fleeing a drab and dead-end existence, Richard Larch moves south from Bursley to London, intent on pursuing a career as a writer. He is also looking for companionship and love, but finds his high hopes dashed when life in the capital is fraught with difficulties, and the glittering career proves to be more elusive than anticipated.

Melancholic and starkly realistic, *A Man from the North* is Arnold Bennett's first novel.

The Old Wives' Tale

Arnold Bennett's masterpiece, *The Old Wives' Tale*, chronicles the lives of sisters Constance and Sophia Baines, daughters of a Bursley draper. Constance, a conventional and sombre young woman, marries the shop's chief assistant, while the spirited and adventurous Sophia elopes to Paris with Gerald Scales, an irresistible but unprincipled cad. This is the utterly compelling story of their lives and loves, their triumphs and despair from early teens to old age, told with Arnold Bennett's characteristic insight and truthfulness.

How to Live on 24 Hours a Day

'You have to live on…twenty-four hours of daily time. Out of it you have to spin health, pleasure, money, content, respect, and the evolution of your immortal soul'.

This timeless classic is one of the first 'self-help' books ever written and was a best-seller in both England and America. It remains as useful today as when it was written, and offers fresh and practical advice on how to make the most of 'the daily miracle' of life.